"Was he blackmailing you, Moira?"

The gentle words filled Moira's heart with such longing that tears filled her eyes. If only she could tell Robert, explain things, lean on him, *trust* him. But she already knew the cost of trust—and she couldn't take the risk.

She pulled her wrist from Robert's grasp, turning away to swipe the tears from her eyes. "Don't be foolish.... I don't know anything about your precious onyx box. If I did, do you think I'd be here?"

A flicker of something crossed his face—was it disappointment?

He shrugged. "You must have thought it *might* be here, or you'd never have come."

"I don't have the faintest idea what you're talking about."

"I don't believe you ... Mrs. *MacJames*." He almost spit the name.

"You don't like it? MacJames is a time-honored name that—"

"I doubt you know your real name anymore, but I do. It's Moira MacAllister—*Hurst*."

Praise for
The Hurst Amulet Series

"Known for her quick-moving, humorous, and poignant stories, Hawkins begins the Hurst Amulet series with a keeper. Readers will be delighted by the perfect pacing, the humorous dialogue, and the sizzling sensual romance."

—*Romantic Times* (4½ stars, Top Pick)

"A lively romp, the perfect beginning to [Hawkins's] new series."

—*Booklist*

"Couldn't put it down.... Ms. Hawkins is one of the most talented historical romance writers out there."

—Romance Junkies (5 stars)

"Charming and witty."

—*Publishers Weekly*

"An adventurous romance filled with laughter, passion, and emotion... mystery, threats, and plenty of sexual tension, plus an engaging premise which will keep you thoroughly entertained during each highly captivating scene.... *One Night in Scotland* holds your attention from beginning to end...."

—Single Titles

"With its creative writing, interesting characters, and well-crafted situations and dialogue, *One Night in Scotland* is an excellent read. Be assured it lives up to all the virtues one has learned to expect from this talented writer."

—Romance Reviews Today

The MacLean Curse Series

"Delightfully humorous, poignant, and highly satisfying novels: that's what Hawkins always delivers."
—*Romantic Times*

"A delicious flirtation.... Humor, folklore, and sizzling love scenes lend [*Much Ado About Marriage*] the perfect incentive for not wanting to put it down."
—*Winter Haven News Chief* (Florida)

"*The Laird Who Loved Me* is delightful in every way."
—Reader To Reader

"Fast, sensual, and brilliant.... *To Catch a Highlander* is romance at its best!"
—Romance and More

"*How to Abduct a Highland Lord* is laced with passion and drama, and with its wonderfully romantic and thrilling ending, it's a story you don't want to miss!"
—JoyfullyReviewed

and Karen Hawkins

"Always funny and sexy, a Karen Hawkins book is a sure delight!"
—bestselling author Victoria Alexander

"Karen Hawkins writes fast, fun, and sexy stories that are a perfect read for a rainy day, a sunny day, or any day at all!"
—bestselling author Christina Dodd

"Karen Hawkins will make you laugh and touch your heart."
—bestselling author Rachel Gibson

All the titles in the Hurst Amulet series and The MacLean Curse series are also available as eBooks

ALSO BY KAREN HAWKINS

Available from Pocket Books

KAREN HAWKINS

A Most Dangerous Profession

Pocket Books

New York   London   Toronto   Sydney   New Delhi

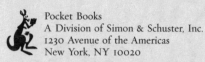

Pocket Books
A Division of Simon & Schuster, Inc.
1230 Avenue of the Americas
New York, NY 10020

This book is a work of fiction. Names, characters, places, and incidents either are products of the author's imagination or are used fictitiously. Any resemblance to actual events or locales or persons, living or dead, is entirely coincidental.

First Pocket Books paperback edition November 2011

POCKET and colophon are registered trademarks of Simon & Schuster, Inc.

For information about special discounts for bulk purchases, please contact Simon & Schuster Special Sales at 1-866-506-1949 or business@simonandschuster.com.

The Simon & Schuster Speakers Bureau can bring authors to your live event. For more information or to book an event contact the Simon & Schuster Speakers Bureau at 1-866-248-3049 or visit our website at www.simonspeakers.com.

Cover illustration by Alan Ayers, hand lettering by Ron Zinn

Manufactured in the United States of America

10 9 8 7 6 5 4 3 2 1

ISBN 978-1-4391-7594-1
ISBN 978-1-4391-7602-3 (ebook)

For my husband, aka Hot Cop, who knows me well and loves me still.

You are the heart of my heart.

Dear Reader,

In this book, there is a reference to a woman named Princess Caraboo who was one of the most notable shysters throughout history. In 1817, she managed to convince many people—some of them quite high in society—that she was a lost princess from an exotic land who'd been kidnapped by pirates. According to "Princess Caraboo," a title given to her by her avid supporters and an even more eager press, after weeks of imprisonment, she'd escaped the pirates' evil clutches by jumping overboard and swimming to shore, where she was found wandering through the parish of Almondsbury, near Bristol.

There's not enough room on this page to give the details of her entire deceit, but suffice it to say that she was not a princess, nor had she ever been kidnapped from an exotic land by pirates. The impostor's real name was Mary Willcocks Baker, and she was the daughter of a very poor family and had spent most of her life wandering from job to job and practicing the art of deception.

If you want to read more about the outrageous Princess Caraboo (and I encourage you to do so), look online for *Caraboo: A Narrative of a Singular Imposition* by John Matthew Gutch. Written in 1817, it gives a detailed account of how she came to be the darling of society, and how her deceit was unmasked.

I hope you enjoy learning about Princess Caraboo as much as I did. She's a fascinating creature in the footnotes of history.

All best,
Karen

A
Most Dangerous
Profession

CHAPTER I

A letter dated two weeks ago from Mary Hurst to her brother Michael.

The Hurst men are scattered to the winds. You're being held by a horrid sulfi who won't release you until we deliver the mysterious onyx box you purchased, which he fancies; William is braving the seas on his way to attempt to free you; and Robert is— *(A large ink blot mars this portion of the letter.)*

To be honest, we don't know where Robert is. The last we heard, he was chasing a beautiful redhead through the wilds of Scotland in an attempt to unravel a mystery.

Oddly enough, of the three of you, I'm most worried about Robert.

Bonnyrigg, Scotland
July 16, 1822

M r. Bancroft stepped onto the wide stone terrace and sighed at the thick mist that swirled about the trees and low lake. "Scotland!" he puffed out in disgust as he bent to wipe fat droplets of water from his shoes yet again with a handkerchief already limp from the damp air. "Who on earth would wish to live in a climate like this?"

Sighing, he reached into his pocket for a cigar, imagining the blessed warmth about to envelop him. He pulled out the cigar and frowned at the feel of it. "It's damp! Damn this sodden, wet, thick-misted, sopping mess of a—"

"Softly, my dear Bancroft."

The banker spun in surprise. "Mr. Hurst! Why—I—I—" The banker cast a glance at the house. "You're a bit early. The sale doesn't begin until this afternoon, and we're not yet ready—"

"Let me guess. Things aren't yet displayed, some aren't even unpacked, the cases aren't yet lit, et cetera, et cetera, et cetera." Robert Hurst hung a silver-topped cane over his arm and removed his gloves. "Am I correct?"

Mr. Bancroft nodded, silently admiring Hurst's perfectly fitted overcoat. It made Bancroft uneasily aware of his own inexpensive, ill-fitting coat.

Hurst leisurely withdrew his monocle from his left breast pocket and viewed the house that rose behind them from the mist. "So this is the famed MacDonald House. A pity it's not for sale, too."

"The new viscount would have sold it if it hadn't been encumbered. As it is, he will have to be content with selling the contents." Bancroft sent a sly look at Hurst. "I'm not surprised to find *you* here, sir. There are many interesting artifacts from ancient Greece, Egypt, Mesopotamia—"

"I know exactly what's to be sold," Hurst said drily, his dark blue eyes gleaming with amusement. "I received your letter last week and you were quite thorough in your catalogue, which I greatly appreciated."

Bancroft chuckled. "I shouldn't have given you such an advantage, but we've worked together so often that I felt it only fair."

"I am honored," Mr. Hurst said gravely,

swinging his monocle to and fro from one finger. "Just as the Earl of Erroll was honored to receive his copy of the exact same letter."

Bancroft's smile froze in place. "M-my lord?"

"And Lord Kildrew, Mr. Bartholomew, and God knows how many others."

"Oh. I didn't— That is to say, I never meant anyone to think—"

"Please, there's no need to explain things to me," Hurst said in a soothing tone. "You only wished to ensure a good number of bidders, which will be difficult in this godforsaken part of the country. Scotland is so . . . Scottish."

The banker gave a relieved chuckle. "Yes! That's it, exactly!" Feeling a sudden warmth at his visitor's understanding air, Bancroft placed his hand on Mr. Hurst's arm. "I promise you that if I'd had my way, I would have only notified *you,* sir."

Mr. Hurst raised his monocle and eyed the hand upon his arm.

Face aflame, Bancroft quickly removed it.

"Just so." Mr. Hurst lowered his monocle and tapped it gently on his palm. "It's a pity your letter came to the attention of so many. While I didn't allow such an egregious error to discourage me from attending, others weren't so unaffected."

Mr. Bancroft tried not to look as crestfallen as he felt. "Indeed, sir?"

"My new brother-in-law, the Earl of Erroll, was adamant that he had better things to do than attend."

"Oh. Oh, no."

"Yes, indeed. Lord Yeltstome swore he'd never come to another of your auctions unless dragged there by wild horses, which I thought quite overstated."

Mr. Bancroft pulled out his damp handkerchief and wiped his even damper brow.

"Kildrew, Bartholomew, Childon, Maccomb, Southerland—all said similar things. I won't bore you with the details."

"Thank you," Bancroft said in a faint voice.

Mr. Hurst pursed his lips. "Now that I think on it, I may be the *only* buyer attending from London."

Mr. Bancroft cast a gloomy look at the thick fog that roiled knee-high across the lawn and now broached the terrace. He'd been at this house for two weeks and, other than two hours one glorious afternoon, had yet to see the sun. He didn't think his spirits could handle the weight of the disappointment that surely awaited him at this afternoon's sale. "The viscount has been relentless in demanding action, and that pressed me into acting hastily."

"That's exactly what I told the others. 'Count on it,' I said, 'Bancroft was *forced* to write those foolish letters. He would never be so devious as to trick us into thinking we were *all* his favorite client.'"

"Of course not. At least you came, sir. I am quite content with that."

"I came with gold in my pocket, too."

Bancroft brightened. Mr. Hurst was one of the premier buyers and sellers of antiquities in all of England. It was hard to credit that the handsome, fashionably dressed man was the son of a lowly vicar, as well as being an employee of the Home Office. It was yet another example of how times had changed in the last twenty years.

It used to be that men of fashion treated their civic obligations with disdain and one knew what to expect. Now it was almost required that every member of society have a cause, which meant that men of good breeding frequently mixed with their lessers. Certainly, twenty years ago it would have been unusual for the son of a vicar to win the label of "leader of fashion," and yet that was a very accurate description of Mr. Robert Hurst.

Of course, it had been rumored for years that Brummell himself had been the son of a valet. Brummell's true origins were shrouded in mystery, as he'd had the good taste not to flaunt them. Hurst and his siblings, on the other hand, seemed quite easy admitting their humble parentage. And astonishingly, despite having little to no dowries and no connections to society, Hurst's sisters had all married into the peerage. Of course, the Hursts were blessed with good looks and a seemingly un- limited amount of good taste, qualities often lack- ing in those born to the velvet.

Bancroft cast a surreptitious glance at Mr. Hurst, whose air quite rivaled that of the banished Brummell. Hurst was perhaps a bit more ap- proachable, which was a benefit to men like Ban- croft, for Hurst could be a valuable acquaintance.

"Mr. Hurst, I'm glad you made the trip to see the sale. You won't be disappointed."

"I'm prepared to be pleased."

"Excellent."

"However, the sale is not the reason I'm here today. There were actually two reasons I'm stand- ing before you. One is that I'm looking for a spe- cific item."

Bancroft perked up immediately. "Oh? And what might that be?"

"I'm seeking a small onyx box of some antiquity. I don't suppose you have any in your warehouses in London?"

"Not that I am aware of, but I will check my inventory the moment I return. Do you have details on the piece?"

"I have an excellent rendering. I'll have a copy sent to your office. Should you find the box, I assure you that I will be *most* generous."

The cold, misty day was already looking brighter. "I will be vigilant in finding your object. In the meantime, I hope you'll find some equally interesting objects at this sale. The late viscount was quite the collector."

"So I've heard. I saw him at many auctions, but I was never quite sure what he was attempting to collect. At one auction, he purchased a very boring Gilpin, and then a French silver set at the next. It will surprise me if there's anything I might wish to buy."

"I'm sure you'll be happy with some of the artifacts. If it will convince you of their quality, I'll allow you a quick look at the items. My assistant is even now putting them on display."

Hurst's gaze warmed. "Ah, yes. Miss MacJames, isn't it?"

"*Mrs.* MacJames," Bancroft said, unable to keep the disappointment from his voice. "She's worked with me for only a week, but she's very knowledgeable."

"Ah. I will take a look at those artifacts, thank you. Mrs. MacJames can assist me if I have any questions while you stay here and enjoy a cigar. I insist you try one of mine, from America. It's the finest tobacco to be had." Hurst flicked back a lace cuff, reached into his coat, and withdrew a small silver case. He snapped it open, removed a tobacco leaf, then handed a perfectly rolled cigar to Bancroft, its fragrant aroma tickling the banker's nose. "The loose leaf keeps the moisture in the case at the proper level."

The banker sniffed the cigar and rolled it between his fingers, sighing with pleasure. "I don't normally smoke while working, but it's so blasted cold here."

"I completely understand." Hurst returned the case to his coat and then touched his hat brim. "Enjoy your cigar. I shall return shortly."

"Please take your time! I'll just wait here and—" But Hurst had already crossed the terrace and entered the house, the door clicking closed behind him. It wasn't until Bancroft had almost finished the cigar that he realized that Hurst hadn't shared the second reason he'd made the trip from London.

CHAPTER 2

A letter from Michael Hurst to his brother Robert over a dozen years ago, after his first sale of an antiquity.

Robert, I'm astonished you received so much money for that small statuette. It appears that you were correct in your assumption that Egyptian artifacts are growing in popularity among the wealthy.

Your silver tongue has always won your way into the beds of London women. I now realize that it can be applied to more lucrative opportunities.

I shall send you more objects to sell. Pray apply your persuasive ability to raising funds for my future explorations with all of the enthusiasm and vigor that you use to capture those beautiful ballerinas, handsome opera singers, and seductive actresses.

*M*oira MacJames placed two coins on a black velvet cloth. She squinted at the second one, then lifted it to the light. "Athenian, but—" She tilted it to one side. "Ah. Just as I thought."

"A fake, hmm?"

She jerked upright at the deep, masculine voice, her gaze flying straight ahead to the ornate gilded mirror above the table. Instantly, she found herself looking into the dark blue eyes of Robert Hurst.

Her heart pounded in her throat as her gaze traveled over him. His fashionable coat was smooth over his broad shoulders and cut to reveal a narrow waist, while well-fitted trousers were tucked into ornate riding boots that encased long, powerful legs. He was wearing his black hair longer now, and it fell over his brow, emphasizing his eyes.

"How are you, Miss— Oh, it's *Mrs.* now, isn't it?" His voice and eyes mocked her.

Her cheeks burned and she struggled to calm

her scattered thoughts. *Damn it all, he knew I'd be here. But how? Until two weeks ago, I didn't even know that.*

The desire to run for her horse had to be tamped down. If she wished to escape from this man, she'd need a good head start and a lot of luck.

If there was one thing Moira was very good at it was judging the best way to make an escape. She not only had a talent for it, but also plenty of practice.

The first step was to keep him from knowing how much she wanted to run. She turned and gave him a smooth smile. "What a surprise to see you here." She gestured to the artifacts lined up for display. "Among dusty treasures, just like old times."

"Actually, it's nothing like old times. For one, I now know who—and what—you are."

She quirked a brow. "Bitter?"

"No, no. I've merely become a realist, my dear." He leaned gracefully upon an ornate silver-handled cane, his expression cool. "You can't be surprised to see me; I was invited to the sale."

Robert wouldn't carry a cane without a purpose. A hidden sword, perhaps? "I knew you'd be here. I just didn't think you'd arrive before the doors opened." At which time she'd be long gone, her pockets lined with a few particularly sellable pieces. Since she hadn't found the object she was searching for, she'd have to settle for something else to make her time worthwhile.

"I take that to mean that you planned to leave by the time I arrived. It's a good thing I came early."

Blast you, Robert. How do you always seem to know my intentions? I hate *that.* "If I had planned to leave, no one would blame me, since you were so unpleasant the last time we saw one another."

"Me?"

"You had me arrested."

"You were a spy and pretended to be Russian royalty. What else could I do?"

"I wasn't spying. I was simply collecting information about some business ventures for a foreign investor."

"Who was gathering information to manipulate the market and devalue our currency. *And* the information you passed on was stolen right from the desk of the Home Office. If you hadn't escaped you'd have gone to prison, and you know it."

"But I did escape, so there's nothing more to be said about it." Yet she thought about it frequently—especially the way Robert had coldly turned her over to the authorities, as if he hadn't cared for her one iota.

She reached down for the small velvet-lined

box that sat on the table. "Would you like to examine some of the items? These coins are quite rare. They're Athenian."

"And fake."

"One of them." She picked up the one in question. "It's an ancient fake, just as old as the original, which gives it value on its own." She caught the flicker of interest on his face.

"Rare, indeed. Not unheard of, but very unusual."

She held out the coin in the palm of her hand. "The condition is astounding."

He sauntered forward, produced a monocle, and regarded the coin.

He was so close, the scent of his soap tickled her nose. Like him, it was sophisticated, masculine, and elusive. The fragrance sent her memory tumbling back to a time when she'd held those broad shoulders, straddled his powerful thighs, and lowered herself onto—

"Fascinating." His deep voice sent a shiver straight through her. He turned his head so that his gaze was level with hers. "How much is the opening bid?"

Her fingers closed over the coin, aware that her nipples had betrayed her, beaded in anticipation. *How can he still affect me like this? It's been years. This won't do at all.*

She turned and replaced the coin, then stepped to one side to put some space between them. "If you wish to bid on it, you should begin low. Most collectors won't recognize the value of a fake that is this old."

"Trust me, I know the value of a good fake," he returned drily. "Better than most."

Her cheeks heated, and she forced herself to look away from his eyes. Her gaze took in his French cuffs, and the immaculate stitching of his coat. Many men used corsets to fit into their clothing, but Robert was blessed with an athletic body that didn't require such measures. She knew that body far, far too well.

She smoothed the black velvet about the coins and said lightly, "I don't suppose you'd be interested in saving us both time and just tell me what it is that you want from me?"

His jaw hardened. "You know exactly what I want."

"No, I don't," she returned, more sharply than she wished.

"It has to do with the onyx box." Robert's large hand, adorned with an ornate emerald ring, cupped the head of the cane as if he were ready to wield it. Though he carried himself with an air of ennui, his hands gave him away. They were strong, purposeful, and lightly calloused from all of the writing and riding that he did.

"I don't *have* your onyx box anymore, which you well know. Your brother William took it from me the last time we met. Why do you ask about the box?"

Robert's mouth thinned with anger. "There is more than one box and you know it. Why are you assisting that reprobate George Aniston?"

Her stomach tightened in a sick knot, yet she said smoothly, "I don't know a George Aniston."

"You know him." Robert moved so quickly that she didn't have time to whisk herself out of the way, his warm hand closing over her wrist as he towered over her, his eyes blazing into hers. "Don't play your games with me. You knew I and my family needed that onyx box to win my brother Michael's release, yet you still took it. And you did so at the behest of George Aniston. I can only be grateful that my brother and I managed to wrest it from you."

Which had been a bitter loss, too. She managed a cool shrug. "You have the box, so there can be no issue now."

"That would be true, if there were only one such box."

She tried to insert a bored tone into her voice. "I have no idea what you're talking about."

"Oh, but you do. For now I find you here, where rumors have it that another onyx box—an almost exact replica of the other—might be for sale. My dear, that cannot be a coincidence."

"Do you see such a box among the items? For I do not."

His brows lowered. "No, but it was rumored it would be here. And we both know it. Now, tell me why you are assisting George Aniston in this quest. I will have the truth."

She curled her fingers into the palms of her hands to hide their dampness. "My association with George Aniston is none of your concern."

"Oh, but it is, for he and I pursue the same object. I already have two of the onyx boxes. Now I want the same thing he does; the same thing you've chased here—the third and final one."

She'd give everything she possessed to defeat George Aniston. No one hated him more, and no one had more reason to beat the vile Aniston at his own game.

But first she had to extricate herself from her current situation. She eyed her wrist, still in Robert's steely grip, then shot him a look through her lashes. "You are hurting me."

"I doubt that." Yet he loosened his hold.

She almost winced. Not because he'd hurt her,

but because she recognized the inherent decency that was so much a part of him. That decency was also the reason she'd left him; he was a man who would do the right thing come hell or high water. Unfortunately, she hadn't wanted him to do the decent or right thing. No, her life was too complicated for that.

She set her jaw against an unexpected flash of sadness at the way fate had betrayed her. "You may release me."

He lifted his brows in silent disbelief and she frowned.

"Have I tried to strike out, attempted to flee, offered resistance of any kind at all?"

His gaze narrowed. "Not yet."

"I have remarkably little information for you, but I will tell you what I know. For a short while I was Aniston's messenger where Miss Beauchamp was concerned."

"He was blackmailing her."

So he had been. And he'd used Moira to further his evil purposes, damn his black heart. She'd hated delivering the blackmail letters to Marcail Beauchamp, a famed and talented actress. Miss Beauchamp hadn't been the usual brassy sort one expected to find in a theater, but was instead a very quiet and composed lady. It had been painful to deliver the poisonous communications from Aniston, but by that time, Moira was too deeply in Aniston's coils herself to do more than offer her unspoken pity.

But it wouldn't do to admit as much to Robert, so she shrugged as if she didn't feel the weight of his disapproval. "I didn't know what he was doing. I was told to deliver and receive various envelopes, which I did."

"Marcail believed you were afraid of him."

It showed? That shook Moira so much that she couldn't speak for a moment. How had Marcail seen through Moira's carefully displayed façade? Was it as she'd come to fear, that her heart was so engaged in this venture that she'd lost some of her abilities? If that were true, could she truly win her way free from Aniston's clutches?

Icy doubt made her stomach tighten until she felt she might wretch. She realized that Robert was watching closely and she forced her stiff lips into a tiny, bored smile that was more a sneer. "He's not a nice man."

"No, he's not. Why are you working for him?"

"He pays me well."

"No, that's not it." Robert loosened his hold a bit more. Though his strong fingers remained about her wrist, his thumb was now sliding across the delicate skin almost in a caress. "You are talented and resourceful and could find work anywhere, could be anyone you chose. Is Aniston blackmailing you, too?"

There it was, out in the light. Just as ugly in sound as it was in reality.

She swallowed hard. "It's a pity you and your brothers didn't put Aniston behind bars."

"If we'd found him, he would have been prosecuted. But what about you, Moira?" Robert leaned forward. "You haven't answered: Is he blackmailing you, too?"

The gentle words filled Moira's heart with such longing that tears filled her eyes. If only she could tell him, explain things, lean on him, *trust* him. But she already knew the cost of trust—and she couldn't take the risk.

Still, for one precious moment, she imagined how lovely it would be if she could. Lately there'd been many moments when she'd had to fight despair. *I'm so alone. If only I could trust that he wouldn't attempt to interfere with my life once he realizes the truth. But I can't. Robert is driven by his conscience and his pride. I could withstand one, but not both.*

I must do this alone.

She pulled her wrist from his grasp, turning away to swipe the tears from her eyes. "Don't be foolish. What could George Aniston possibly hold over my head? *I* don't have a reputation to protect and I have nothing of value that Aniston or anyone else might want. So pray stop suggesting that horrid man has a hold over me. As I've already explained, I'm in his employ and he pays me well. *Very* well. That's all there is to it." She watched as Robert's mouth hardened in distaste and she welcomed it. "That's all there is to say. I don't know anything more than that. And I damned well don't know anything about your precious onyx box."

"Then allow me to refresh your memory. There are three boxes. This last one seems to be missing . . . for now. The first two have already been in your possession. One of them, which my brother recovered, you took from Miss Beauchamp. The other I took from your lodgings in London."

"*You're* the one who—" She clamped her lips over the rest of the thought.

His smile couldn't be called "nice." "Oh yes, 'twas I who stole the box from your lodgings. I admit it freely. But only after you'd stolen it from someone else, a very befuddled professor, a researcher much addicted to Egyptian artifacts who thought you madly in love with him before you absconded in the dead of night with that particular piece of his collection."

Damn it, she should have known Robert had

been the one who'd stolen the box from her lodgings. But she couldn't afford to let him see how upset she was. Instead of railing as she wished, she lifted her chin and said in a cool tone, "I don't know what you're talking about." Denial was all she had left. A flicker of something crossed his face— was it disappointment?

"I don't believe you."

"Fine."

His face hardened. "No, it's not fine, Mrs. *MacJames.*" He almost spit the name. "I doubt you know your real name anymore, but I do. It's Moira MacAllister—*Hurst.*"

She shrugged against his anger. "I don't recognize that name."

White lines etched his mouth, and she knew he had only a thin rein on his temper. "Unfortunately, it's your real name. Thanks to your trickery years ago, we are married."

Moira glanced down at the thick rug. A horse was tied up just inside the stables; she'd left it there just in case something went amiss. Her gaze flickered to the boxes she hadn't yet unpacked. She'd already read through the inventory twice and was fairly certain the onyx box wasn't here, but she'd hoped to search for it herself. She wouldn't have that luxury now.

She looked back up to Robert. "I am surprised you haven't had our marriage set aside."

"I could have, if I'd wished the world to know my foolishness. It seemed more prudent to find you first and *then* take my tale to the authorities. It will be so much more amusing watching you explain your ruse."

"The world will still know," she pointed out.

His jaw tightened, and for the first time, a flicker of fear tightened her throat. He would never exact physical vengeance on a woman, but he wasn't above making her pay in other ways.

She turned to the open crate that rested on the table and pulled out a flat ivory box. "I hope you don't mind if I keep unpacking while you empty all of the dark pockets of my past. Mr. Bancroft is anxious that we begin on time." She placed the box on the table and opened it, displaying a number of small alabaster vases.

Moira's fingers slid over the smooth surface of the closest one, her heartbeat slowing as she allowed the sheer artistry of the piece to soak into her skin. She traced the perfect curve of the neck and followed the delicate flute with one finger. Immediately, everything else faded, her attention taken by the vases. They were exquisite in design and literally stole her breath. "Oh my." She traced the smallest one with her fingertips, aware that Robert was now leaning over her shoulder.

"Amazing."

She welcomed the awe in his deep voice. They'd both loved antiquities; it was one of the few things they'd shared other than physical pleasures. "I'd read the description, but seeing them—" She shook her head.

A faint smile on his lips, he reached past her, using his kerchief as he picked up one of the more delicate vases and examined it with the assurance of an expert. "What do you think these held?"

"As small as they are, I'd guess perfume or some other precious liquid."

"Yes, they're too small for olive oil."

"Which would have been plentiful in this time and not held in such valuable containers."

He pulled out his monocle and regarded another vase, his shoulder warm against Moira's. "Hm. 1200 A.D., I'd say."

"No, I think they're older than that." She caught the tremor in her voice and stepped away from him. "Look at the third one," she said quickly. "There's etching on it."

He held the etched surface toward the light.

A distant door opened and closed, footsteps echoing down a hallway and then disappearing.

Moira barely heard the noise as she leaned forward to see the etchings.

Robert turned as she moved and met her gaze. Their faces were level, her eyes inches from his. How could she have forgotten how compelling his eyes could be? Framed in thick lashes, the deep and mysterious blue of a sapphire, they captured her imagination and stole her composure. She wanted nothing more than to lean forward and . . .

Her gaze dropped to his mouth. Firm and masculine like a Greek statue's, it drew her like the sparkle of a diamond. Her breath came heavier as she leaned toward him, her lips closer and closer to his—

He turned and replaced the small vase. "It's beautiful; you rarely see alabaster of this purity." He lifted his monocle to examine it better. "You may be right; the etching does seem to indicate an earlier era."

Robert was surprised his voice sounded so normal, as his heart was thundering in his chest and his cock stood at full attention. But that was the way it always was with Moira. She infuriated, confounded, and seduced him, all at once.

He didn't know what it was about her, but he would have to watch himself closely to keep from falling for her tricks. He'd almost allowed himself to kiss her; it had taken all of his strength to turn away. Yet even now, he was tense with desire and far too aware of her.

She leaned forward, her red, silken hair already falling from its pins, one thick strand curled over her shoulder. "Did you see the inscription on the bottom of the box that holds the vases?"

Even saying something businesslike, she sounded seductive. He forced himself to turn his gaze on the ivory box and its contents. "I don't see an inscription—ah. Wait." He moved to one side so that the light caught the faint lines. "I thought this might be Roman, but I can see now that it's Greek." He peered at it through his monocle, then finally turned to her. "It's an unusual—"

The room was empty.

"Damnation!" He raced to the door and almost ran into Mr. Bancroft, who was just entering.

"Ah, Mr. Hurst!" The man's gaze flickered to the table behind Robert. "I see Mrs. MacJames showed you the box and vases. Astonishing, aren't th—"

"Where is she?"

Mr. Bancroft blinked and then peered past Robert. "She isn't here? But I thought—"

"She left. Did you see her?"

"No. I just came in from the terrace, and the hall was quite empty."

Robert cursed. He whirled back to the room, his gaze sweeping over the long windows. Could she have gone through them? No, he would have heard them open. *Where the hell is she? She can't disappear in a puff of smoke. She had to—* His gaze locked onto a faint line in the patterned wallpaper. In a trice he was at the hidden door, searching for the latch. "How do you open this?"

Bancroft had followed him across the room and now shook his head. "I don't know. I'd never noticed that doorway, and—"

Click. Robert had found the hidden latch and the door swung open, a hidden entrance for servants who might need quicker access in order to efficiently meet their master's and mistress's needs.

Robert ducked his head and raced into the small hallway, which quickly grew dark. The passage was narrow, the flagstone floor worn smooth with use, and the faint scent of freshly baked bread let him know where the final door would open. He had to duck his head so as not to hit the wide timbers that occasionally appeared as he made his way. He rushed along and turned a corner, the light disappearing completely. But Robert maintained his speed by the simple expediency of trailing his hands along each side.

Urgency pressed him forward. He couldn't let her escape.

"Mr. Hurst!" Bancroft called after him. "When you see Mrs. MacJames, please remind her that the items must be ready soon and . . ." The voice faded as Robert ran down the twisting hallway.

The fool. Moira MacAllister was gone and would never reappear. She *had* to know something about the onyx box; he'd seen a flicker in her gaze.

Robert cursed as he stumbled down a step, twice bumping his head painfully when an especially low beam crossed the ceiling. The hallway ended at a small door that swung open to reveal the kitchens.

At his entrance, several undercooks turned and stared in astonishment.

One stepped forward. "Pardon, *monsieur,* but you are lost, no?"

Robert brushed a cobweb from his shoulder. "Did you see a woman come out this door?"

"*Oui,*" gulped the cook. "She ran through and went on to the stables."

"How do you know she was heading for the stables?"

"Because she took an apple for her horse."

Robert muttered his thanks and ran out the door. The stables were set across the small cobblestone courtyard, and he rushed inside and collared the first groom he saw. "Have you seen Mrs. MacJames?"

At the man's blank stare, Robert added, "An attractive redhead."

The groom's expression cleared and he said in a thick Scottish brogue, "Och, tha' one. She had a mount already saddled and took off like the hounds o' hell were after her."

"Blast it!" Robert looked out the stable doors toward the long drive that led up to the house. "Send someone for my carriage. I left my groom walking the horses in the drive and—"

"Lor' love ye, guv'nor, but ye'll no' catch her in a carriage. She dinna go down the drive, but tha' way." The man nodded over Robert's shoulder.

He turned and his heart sank as he faced the wide fields that led into a thick copse of woods.

"Aye," the groom continued, admiration coloring his voice. "She took tha' horse right o'er the fence and through the field. Tha' lassie rides like the wind. She's a crackin' good horsewoman."

"She's a royal pain in the ass."

The groom chuckled. "Och, most women are."

Robert walked out toward the high fence that bordered the field, his gaze on the copse of trees. The wind stirred their leaves, but no other movement enlivened the moment. He fisted his hands, struggling to contain the anger that threatened to choke him.

She'd escaped yet again.

With a muffled curse, he turned on his heel and strode to his carriage.

CHAPTER 3

A letter from Robert Hurst to his solicitor on the first anniversary of his marriage.

Enclosed you will find payment for researching the questions I had regarding my unfortunate marriage. While there are options available to release me from it, all of them seem likely to result in public embarrassment.

I do not find that acceptable.

Therefore, I've decided not to pursue any action at the moment. My "wife," after tricking me into giving her my name, has since blessed me with her absence. If I must be saddled with such a scheming gypsy, at least she has the good sense to stay far, far away.

*T*hick fog hung over the degenerate alleys and narrow dockside streets of Edinburgh, as if to hide their shame. Dampness clung to the cobblestone, trailing up walls and wisping against Moira's skin like clammy, ghostly fingers.

She tried to shake the gloominess from her mind, but the dank mist suited her feelings exactly. It had been over a week since her run-in with Robert Hurst, yet those few moments had changed something, made her vulnerable in a way she hated. Without even trying, he'd made her feel as weak-kneed as a new bride. Moira was many things, but weak was not one of them. And right now, she had to be stronger than she'd ever been before.

Robert was still here in Scotland, trying to discover her direction. He'd never find it, though. She was always thorough in hiding her trail.

She tugged her hood over her head, hiding her face in the shadows, and paused on a corner to squint into the mist. She'd already gotten lost once; she couldn't afford to do so again.

From an alleyway came the sound of raucous, drunken laughter as two men stumbled into the street. One of them noticed her and made a comment that sent his companion into guffaws of laughter. She ignored them and hurried on, her head down.

She turned a corner and pulled her cloak tighter as she stepped around a ragged figure crumpled on the ground, reeking of gin and unwashed flesh. She paused and looked at the poor figure. Did the man or woman—it was difficult to tell among the rags and matted hair—need assistance? Had they been attacked and perhaps left for dead? There were thieves and worse about.

She slipped her hand to the small pistol strapped to her waist under her cloak. It was a lovely pistol with delicate scrolling etched along the grip, the barrel slender and short. The pistol was so small that it was of use at only very close range. Still, she was more than proficient in its use and had found it more than sufficient for protection. With a careful glance into the shadows, Moira bent to shake the bony shoulder.

The figure stirred, revealing a woman's dirty face.

Moira knelt beside her. "Are you well, missus?"

The woman blinked rapidly and then coughed loudly. "Och, I jus' falled." She waved Moira on, as if annoyed to have been awakened, then tucked herself into a tighter ball in the middle of the walk.

Moira returned her pistol to its sheath and continued on her way. As she reached the corner, the huge clock that overshadowed the square tolled, deep and melodious.

I'm late! God, no! Her heart thudded sickly in her throat as she dashed down the street to the churchyard. Beside the low iron gate sat a large black coach, malevolent in the mist. Moira pressed a hand to her chest, her heart beating with a lonely, deep ache.

I must be calm. I must control this situation and stay strong.

Hands fisted at her sides, she walked across the courtyard. As she approached the coach, she pushed back her hood and smoothed her hair. The mist parted and the coachman yelled for her to halt.

The crest seemed to leer down at her, a red sun overlaid by a stag wearing a circlet of white heather. She hated that crest, yet longed to see it with all of her heart.

The coachman climbed down from his seat

past two burly footmen, and went to the door. He knocked briskly upon the curtained panel. A moment later, it swung open and a man stepped out.

George Aniston was dressed like the veriest dandy; his blond locks combed just so, his cravat an impressive size and set with a glittering ruby, his knitted trousers striped in the current fashion.

His petulant scowl made him look half his age. "You're late."

"The mist confused me. If I could have come by carriage—"

"You know the rules." His voice was as youthful as his figure, his face as smooth as a schoolboy's. When she'd first met him, she'd made the mistake of thinking him weak, foolish, and lacking in capabilities.

She'd only made that mistake once.

"So the box wasn't there, was it?" he asked.

"You don't look surprised." *Of course, he already knew it wasn't there.* She hid the bite of disappointment. Knowledge was power, but with Aniston she could never get ahead. He always knew. It was one of the things that made him so dangerous.

"After you left town, I received word that the artifact I seek was sold to a collector in the highlands."

"So Bancroft never had it." Anger simmered through her. "You sent me on a wild-goose chase."

He shrugged. "I can send you on any sort of a chase I wish. I *own* you."

No, you don't. No one *owns me. Ever.* She burned to rage at him, but there was more at stake than her pride. She said in a tight voice, "I could have done more good elsewhere."

"Perhaps. I sent you to fetch a different onyx box almost a month ago. If I remember correctly, you failed at that small service, too."

He called making her an accessory to blackmail a "small service," and she feared that to him, it was nothing more.

She met his gaze evenly. "Don't blame me for that. You didn't tell me Miss Beauchamp had William Hurst with her."

The heavy lids drooped over the icy blue eyes. "I didn't expect that development. Still, I would have thought that for someone with your . . . skills, a little surprise like that wouldn't have been insurmountable. And then there was the time you told me that you'd found one of the boxes in a collection in Edinburgh, but then found you were mistaken." His gaze narrowed. "I still find that tale difficult to believe."

"It wasn't the same style of box. It was gold and

onyx, but far too large." She met his gaze steadily though it cost her dearly. She hadn't dared tell him the truth—that she'd had one of his precious boxes in her grasp and it had disappeared from her lodgings. Of course, now she knew what had happened, but at the time she'd had no good explanation as to why the box had gone missing and couldn't risk him thinking that she'd sold it, or worse, and so she'd lied.

"Do you or do you not wish to end this debt between us?"

"Debt?" Her voice was sharp and bitter. "You *stole* from me; I don't *owe* you anything!"

His mouth tightened and before she could say another word, he was before her, his words hissing through his teeth. "Don't you *ever* speak to me like that again. I *own* you, worthless fool that you are, and I won't take such disrespectful behavior!"

She yearned to use her pistol but she dared not. Not only because of the footmen, who were obviously just paid thugs, but also because Aniston was right. She was completely at his mercy. She couldn't afford to allow her emotions to lead her into making a mistake. The man was mad and seemed to be sliding further and further into it.

So she would do anything, say anything, pretend anything, steal anything that he asked. But in the end, she would win.

She nodded. "I'm sorry. I was irritated at being sent on a pointless mission."

He eyed her narrowly but finally nodded, satisfied with her contrite expression. "That's better. You seem to forget that I hold what's most precious to you in the palm of my hand." He held out his bare hand, the skin eerily white in the mist. "Do you want me to finish this?" He closed his hand tightly, as if crushing the very air.

She swallowed convulsively. "I want to finish this so that we're both satisfied. But you must understand this: the loss of the onyx box was not my fault. I did what I said I would do. But not only was Captain Hurst there, but his brother as well and—"

"Hold. His brother? Which one?"

She cursed her slip of tongue. *This is why I mustn't get angry. I lose my concentration and make mistakes.* "Robert Hurst. It seems that every time you send me to fetch an onyx box, I run into him."

Aniston appeared intrigued. "Ah! He was at Bancroft's sale, too?"

"Of course he was there; some of the artifacts were quite impressive."

"Did he mention the onyx box?"

"Yes. He was hoping to find another there, as were we."

Aniston nodded slowly. "Interesting. *Very* inter-esting."

"I was most unhappy to see him. He is a signifi-cant force."

Aniston murmured, "Yes, he is." He rubbed his chin. "So the Hursts are still pursuing the onyx boxes."

"It seems so. Just how many are there?"

"Three."

Damn it. He always *knows.* She wet her dry lips. "So Hurst has one, and this unknown buyer has the other. Where's the third?"

"I haven't found it yet, but I will."

Ah ha! He doesn't know that the Hursts have already recovered it. Though she wasn't certain how the in-formation was useful, it soothed her to know that Aniston wasn't as all-powerful as she'd thought him to be.

Aniston turned his cool gaze upon her now. "Leave the final box to me. I will discover its loca-tion soon enough. Meanwhile, you will fetch the one that was recently purchased by this buyer."

"So you know who has it?"

"Sir Lachlan Ross. I have a carriage waiting to take you first thing in the morn—"

"*No.*"

Aniston's mouth tightened and Moira hurried

to add, "Please. I just returned and it's been weeks since I—" Her hands curled into fists. "Aniston, you *promised* I could see her when I returned."

Aniston's gaze narrowed. "But you were not successful."

"You know it wasn't my fault."

He pursed his lips but then gestured toward his coach. "Fine. You may see her."

Moira's heart thudded hard. "She—she's here?"

He nodded to his coachman, who rapped upon the door panel. It opened and a sharp-faced woman climbed from the carriage, pausing to say sharply to someone inside, "I said put that down and come!"

Moira's world spun slowly, the beat of her heart so loud it drowned out all thoughts. A small foot appeared in the doorway, followed by a tousle-headed child of five years of age. The girl had long dark hair and blue eyes surrounded by thick lashes. She had a cherubic face, round with rosy lips and a snub nose.

The child's expression darkened on seeing Aniston. But when her gaze flickered past him to Moira, it was as if the sun had broken through the clouds.

"Mama!" The small child jerked her hand free from the nurse's as she ran forward.

"Och!" the nurse exclaimed, stomping forward. "You little brat, come back here!"

But Moira was faster. With a sob, she reached Rowena and scooped her little body up, enveloping the child in her arms.

Aniston lifted an indifferent hand to the nurse. "Let them have their moment. After all, they get so few."

Moira buried her face in the girl's neck as the child burst into tears and wailed, "I-I w-want t-to g-go h-home!"

"So do I, sweetheart." Moira held her daughter close, rubbing her cheek against the child's silky hair and kissing every inch of the dear, dear face.

She would have given her life to take Rowena home with her right now, and for a wild moment, she thought about picking up the child and running into the mist. But she'd tried that once, and she—and Rowena—had paid horribly.

Moira caught Aniston's cold gaze over Rowena's head and realized that the coachman was standing to one side, pistol already drawn.

Swallowing hard, Moira set the child back on the ground and stooped before her. The little face was tear streaked, the eyes red-rimmed as she hiccupped, "M-Mama, p-please t-take m-me with y-you."

Moira's heart ached even more. But she couldn't afford weakness right now. *These few moments may be all she has to support her until I can come for her.* Moira brushed Rowena's hair from her forehead and said in a calm voice, "Not this time, sweetheart, but soon. Very soon."

"B-b-but I d-d-on't want to go b-b-back! Miss Kimble *hitted* me and—"

Moira pulled the child closer, looking over her head at the nurse. "You *hit* her?"

The nurse looked uneasy and glanced at Aniston. He shrugged and dusted imaginary lint from his sleeve.

Seeing him so unmoved, the nurse sniffed and said in a cocky voice, "I dinna hit the lass when she's quiet, but some days she's whiny and willna listen weel, so I pop her upon the head and—"

Moira straightened.

The nurse squeaked and took two hurried steps behind Aniston.

He frowned and tugged his cloak closer. "Pray watch where you're walking, foolish woman. I don't want your dirt upon my good cloak."

"She had better watch more than that," Moira said furiously. Rowena's thin body trembled, her small hands clinging so tightly around Moira's leg that she couldn't have moved if she'd wanted to.

Moira fixed her gaze on the nurse. "If this child comes to any harm under your care, there is no one in this world who will protect you. Not this cretin"—she jerked her head toward Aniston—"not the constable, not the devil himself."

The nurse paled and glanced at Aniston, who said in an amused voice, "She is most likely telling the truth about that. She has certain abilities." His cruel gaze then narrowed on Moira. "Of course, she can't do anything right *now*, can she?"

Moira met his gaze steadily. "We two are almost finished."

"We will end this when I say so, and not before."

There was nothing more to be said. Heart heavy, Moira gave Rowena a hug and then gently disentangled the child's arms. "Ah, sweetling, I am so glad to see you." She pulled out a handkerchief and wiped her daughter's face. "Are you well?"

Rowena nodded, hiccupping. "I-I am learning to read."

Moira's heart ached. She'd wished to teach the child to read; it was yet another thing stolen from them. "Who is teaching you to read?"

"Mrs. Kimble. When she's not mad, she likes a good story."

Surprised, Moira looked at the nurse, who

turned red and mumbled, "She's a bright 'un and takes to readin' faster than me own bairns ever did."

"Thank you," Moira said quietly. "Thank you very much."

After a surprised moment, the woman's hard face softened. "Ye're welcome. I will make sure I dinna smack her head, but 'twasn't done in spite."

"I appreciate that, but 'tis best if it isn't done at all." Moira kissed Rowena's cheek. "We will be together soon. I promise."

"But you said last time—"

"I know. Something changed, sweetheart. I need to leave just one more time—"

"Noooo!" Tears spilled down her cheeks again, but Rowena's face was set with determination. "*Please*, Mama, take me with you. I will be good and I won't make any noise and—"

Moira swooped the girl to her. "Sweetling, you *are* a good child. I can't take you with me because it will be much too dangerous. But I promise that this will be the *last* time." She met Aniston's gaze. "I swear it."

Aniston's cold smile did nothing to ease her fear.

Collecting herself, Moira stood, Rowena held tightly against her. At her movement, the coachman cocked his pistol.

She turned her full scorn upon him. "Put that down. It could accidentally go off, and then where would your master be? God knows I wouldn't do his bidding unless forced."

Aniston flicked a finger and the coachman, red with anger, disarmed the pistol.

"I've had enough drama for one day," Aniston said. "It's time for Rowena to leave now." He turned to the nurse. "Take her."

The nurse gingerly approached Moira. "I'll put her in the coach now, mistress."

Moira bent down and hugged her daughter once more. "Be very brave," she whispered in Rowena's ear. "And read well for Mrs. Kimble. The next time I see you, you can show me all you've learned."

Through sniffles, Rowena nodded.

It took every ounce of strength Moira had to make herself reach down and peel her daughter's fingers from her own. With the release of each small finger, Moira's heart broke a bit more.

She gently pressed Rowena's hand into the nurse's with a beseeching look. "Treat her well," she whispered. "If you do, you will be compensated beyond your wildest dreams."

The nurse's face lit up and she said in a low voice, "I'll treat her as if she were me own bairn."

"No, you will treat her like *my* daughter, something you will *never* forget."

The woman said in a grudging tone, "Fine, then. I'll no' hit her."

It wasn't much of a promise, but it was all Moira had. She watched as Rowena was placed back into the carriage, the nurse following.

Moira turned to Aniston. "This is the final errand I run for you," she snapped. "Once this is done, I want Rowena back. If you don't—"

"Pray don't bother me with your empty threats. I decide when this is over, not you. Find the box, Moira, and I will consider letting that be your final task." Aniston's gaze flickered over her. "My carriage will fetch you in the morning to begin the journey."

"How am I to get this box from Ross?"

Aniston looked amused. "*You* are the expert on procuring things, not I. You'll find a way to get the box. I'm sure of it."

"Then I need more information. Who this man is, where he lives, how to reach him—"

"The coachman will know the route to Balnagown Castle. It's in the highlands. It will take a week and a half to reach there, perhaps longer. What else do you need to know?"

"Why did Ross purchase the box? Does he know its value?"

"I don't think so. He bought it for his private collection. He has a very large one, from what I've heard, and fancies himself an expert."

"Is he?"

"He thinks so, but I don't believe *you'd* consider him so. You know so much more about antiquities than other people." There was grudging respect in Aniston's voice.

"What more do you know of him?"

"He's wealthy, unmarried, and childless. They say he has a very fine stable. And he's been in two duels in the last year." Aniston shrugged. "I know nothing else."

Moira frowned. "Two duels? What were they over? Gaming debts?"

"Other men's wives."

"Both times?"

"Yes."

Finally, something she could use. "I'll leave in the morning. I'm staying at the George."

"I know where you're staying," he returned coolly before he turned and walked toward the carriage. As one of the footmen opened the door, Aniston paused. "One more thing: if you fail to bring me the box this time, I won't be as patient as I've been in the past."

"I won't fail—providing your information is

better than what you gave me on Bancroft and Miss Beauchamp."

Aniston's mouth thinned. "Just find the damn box." He climbed inside his coach, and the door closed smartly behind him.

Moira watched, her jaw clenched. She'd fetch Aniston's damned box—but he wouldn't get it until he'd released Rowena.

The coachman hied the horses and the coach lumbered forward, swallowed by the mist before the sound of the creaking wheels had faded.

A sob caught in Moira's throat, but she swallowed it and lifted her chin. She would find a way to win Rowena back. And once the child was safe, Moira would follow her blood legacy and finish this game. Aniston might think he held all the cards, but she'd only begun to play.

When this ends, not even God will be able to help George Aniston.

CHAPTER 4

A letter to Robert Hurst from his sister Triona Hurst Mac-Lean upon his going to Eton to study as a youth.

Father told me you weren't taking your studies as seriously as he'd hoped, but then that's not surprising. He's a difficult taskmaster; no one could fulfill his hopes with their studies and still have time for things like food and sleep.

Father may worry about you, but I don't. I know of no one more driven than you. Considering you're but a lad of sixteen, that's a serious statement indeed. It makes me wonder where you'll end up once you're a man grown. The world has no boundaries for someone who savors success and is willing to work for it.

*R*obert stretched out his legs and admired the reflection of the flames in the gloss of his boots. "I wondered when you'd return."

The man who stood before him on the thick library rug merely grinned. He was a small man with wizened features and shrewd blue eyes. His back was visibly crooked, yet he moved with an unusually quick walk. "Ye said not t' bother ye until we had some information, so I waited until we was certain."

"So you found her?"

"Aye. Ye said she had a taste fer luxury and so she does. She's at the George, sir."

Robert smiled now. *Aha, Moira. I know you too well.* "Good work, Stewart."

"Thank ye, sir. She is using the name of Mrs. Randolph. Och, and she's turned into a brunette, sir. I almost didna recognize her, except she smiled at the porter and—" Stewart's face reddened.

"I quite understand." Moira MacAllister wasn't the sort of woman one forgot. It wasn't just that she was beautiful, though she was, spectacularly so. It was the combination of her looks, her spirit, and her vibrancy. One never forgot how she looked, but more important, one never forgot how she made you feel. Just one smile could grab your soul . . . and she would extract it if you weren't careful.

Fortunately, Robert was careful. He wasn't as immune as he wished—the way she'd affected him at Bancroft's sale proved that—but that had been a momentary lapse. He was protected by years of outrage at her perfidy and lies. "Ask Leeds to watch Mrs. Randolph this evening. I have information that she won't leave until the morning, anyway."

Stewart blinked. "But, sir, I can—"

"Mr. Stewart, you are one of the few men I trust with my most clandestine efforts. However, this is no ordinary woman. She charms like a cobra and she's managed to escape more than once by using that charm. I won't have that happening again."

"Sir, I can assure you that I'm no' likely to become a slave to a woman, beautiful or no'."

"I'm gratified to hear that. But where this particular woman is concerned, I'll take no chances. Take Leeds to the inn and make sure he sees her before you leave, so he knows whom he is to watch. Then you are to return here to prepare for a journey tomorrow."

"Yes, sir," Stewart replied stiffly. "Will there be anything else?"

Robert eyed his offended servant and said softly, "Yes, you can cease being so dramatic."

Stewart flushed and bowed. "Yes, sir. I'll take Leeds to the inn right now."

"And tell him I may visit our little thief before the night is out. I have some questions that need answers and I must start my journey come morning."

"Aye, sir. Am I to come with ye?"

"Yes. You'll be playing the part of my groom. Leeds will be a footman. I shall take two more footmen and an undergroom, as well."

"Very good, sir. If I might be so bold, is Buffoon a-comin', too?"

Robert sighed. "Stewart, I've told you many times that my valet's name is 'Buffon,' which is a highly regarded French name."

"Beggin' yer pardon, sir, but I dinna care wha' the French think."

Robert hid a grin. "Why do you ask about Buffon?"

"It just seems tha' whenever we bring yer valet along, we end up in more mischief than usual," Stewart said in a distinctly morose voice.

"You think him bad luck?"

"Aye. I also think he's a whey-faced, weak-kneed, poufy-shirted fool."

"Pray don't hold back," Robert said politely. "You can tell me what you *really* think of my valet."

Stewart broke into a reluctant grin. "Sorry fer bein' so forward, sir, but that valet o' yers is nothin' but a Frenchified piece o' lace."

"I know. That's why I take him with me."

Stewart blinked. "I beg yer pardon?"

"People judge one by one's servants. When they see Buffon they assume that I, too, am a whey-faced, weak-kneed, poufy-shirted fool. That ruse has helped me on more than one occasion."

"I ne'er thought o' tha'."

"Which is why I will ask you to do less thinking and more doing." Robert waved a hand toward the door. "Off with you, Stewart. And tell Leeds to keep a sharp eye on Mrs. Randolph. She has been known to disappear from locked rooms."

"Och, sir, have no fear. Leeds is as good at watchin' as I am." Stewart gave a smart bow and left the study.

Robert regarded the closed door for a long time before he rose and went to his desk. There, he sat and, using a key hidden under an inkwell, unlocked a drawer and pulled out a leather folio holding a thick stack of papers. The dispatches told the exact locations of Miss Moira MacAllister, as well as whom she spoke to, for how long, and—where they could—what about.

The first report was from two months before Robert had met her years ago. The last one had been added late last night.

Robert closed the folio and sat back in his chair. He'd never worked so hard to keep up with anyone in his life—not for personal, nor professional reasons.

Yet despite the many papers in the thick folio, he knew a lot of information was missing. "You're hiding something, Moira MacAllister, I could feel it in your voice. Whatever it is, I'll find out."

Leeds was already retired for the night, but at Stewart's slight prod, the ex-soldier was wide-awake in an instant. He donned his street clothes and pulled a cap low over his broad face, then they rode to the inn.

The George was one of the best inns in Edinburgh, with over eighteen guest rooms furnished with the best of everything.

Leeds looked about the inn yard, visually marking doors and windows. "'Tis a big hotel. Wish't it were a mite smaller. Who is this miss we're watchin'?"

"A Miss Moira MacAllister, though she's goin' by the name o' Mrs. Randolph. She tol' the innkeeper she was waitin' on her husband to join her."

Leeds scratched his chin. "No husband?"

"Nary a one as far as I can see. I think she pretends she's married to keep men away."

"Lor', the people the master consorts with. I think his work fer the Home Office is more than he lets on. Don't ye think so, Stewart?"

"The master dinna pay either o' us t' think," Stewart said sourly. "He pays us to *do*."

"A bit out o' sorts, are ye?"

"Aye, the master was a bit harsh this evening. He was sure I was fallin' under the spell of—" Stewart broke off as a woman passed before a downstairs window. The George had a private general room for the fairer sex, where they could take tea or meet together. "That was her; she's in the lower sitting room."

The woman passed the window again, pausing this time to lift the sash and look outside, presumably at the threatening weather. Her dark hair was piled upon her head, contrasting with the creamy whiteness of her skin. The light from a lantern lit her face and showed that her eyes were delicately slanted, her eyebrows tilted to an exotic angle, her nose straight and patrician. But it was her mouth that caught a man's attention. Something about the curve of her full lips suggested sensual pleasures best not spoken aloud.

"Gor'," Leeds choked out.

Stewart nodded.

"Sweet gor'." Leeds breathed again.

Stewart punched Leeds in the shoulder.

"Ow!" Leeds rubbed his arm, looking offended. "What was tha' fer?"

"Tha' was to remind ye to keep yerself professional at all times. Mr. Hurst says she's a seductress, and if she can get ye under her spell—" He scowled. "I think she might be a witch. So watch ye'self and dinna get cocky, or ye'll come to a great fall."

Leeds's eyes had widened and he sent an almost fearful glance at the now empty window. "How do I protect meself from a witch?"

"Dinna let her gaze fall upon ye. But if it do, make certain she dinna think ye're payin' her any heed. So long as she dinna think ye're followin' her or out to harm her, ye'll be fine. But if she sees ye—" Stewart shook his head.

Leeds gulped and nodded. "I'll stay low to the wall, I will."

"Good. Note who comes to see her, and find out their names and such. If she leaves, follow her, but be discreet. Send word to Mr. Hurst when ye discover her direction."

"What if she leaves town altogether?"

"She won't; Mr. Hurst says she's due to leave tomorrow morning. He's goin' to visit her this evenin', though, so dinna be surprised to see him. In the mornin' we'll be travelin' with Mr. Hurst."

Leeds brightened. "Where are we goin'?"

"I dinna know, but I'll be a groom and ye'll be a footman. Buffon will be comin', too."

"That lace-bowed jackanapes?" Leeds sighed. "I suppose there's no help fer it. How does Mr. Hurst know so much about this woman's plans?"

"How does he know anythin'? He's a smart one, he is. One o' the best. And I've a feelin' that whatever important business Mr. Hurst is upon, this woman might be a big part o' it. She might be a spy."

Leeds looked every bit as impressed as Stewart wished. "Och, I'll no' leave me post."

Satisfied he'd done his best to convince Leeds of the importance of their work, Stewart bid him good night and disappeared into the darkness.

CHAPTER 5

Diary entry by Michael Hurst as he waits for his release from captivity.

Yesterday I discovered that my assistant, Miss Smythe-Haughton, has initiated a hare-brained scheme to charm my captor in the hopes of winning my release without the onyx box. I dislike her undertaking such an endeavor and expressed my displeasure, which she ignored. While the box is a crucial link to finding the long-lost Hurst Amulet, that cannot justify her putting herself at such risk. Especially when I saw the expression on the sulfi's face when she attempted—of all the witless things—to dance for him during dinner.

Miss Smythe-Haughton might be a crack cryptographer and have a way with winning support from the locals, and she may be the only woman I know who can ride camels as if born to it, but the woman dances like a lame bear. Since the sulfi did not order her beaten, I must surmise that he has an excellent sense of humor.

$\mathcal{A}$n hour later, Robert rode into the inn yard. He cast a quick glance around and saw Leeds idly grooming a horse in direct sight of the door.

Leeds flicked Robert a glance from beneath the brim of his hat and nodded toward the wide door.

Robert touched the brim of his own hat and dismounted, tossing the reins and a coin to a waiting linkboy before entering the inn.

Mr. King, the proprietor, bustled forward. "Och, if 'tisn't Mr. Hurst! How good to see ye, sir."

"And you. I trust you're busy this time of year."

"Filled every room," the innkeeper said proudly.

"Excellent." Robert removed his hat and set it upon the hall table, his gloves neatly placed across the brim, and then allowed the innkeeper to assist him in removing his greatcoat. "I came to visit a certain guest of yours, and I must ask for your discretion."

Knowing well how generously "discretion" could

pay, Mr. King beamed. "Indeed, sir, I'll no' breathe a word. Which guest are you wishin' to visit?"

Robert took a shiny guinea from his pocket and dropped it into the landlord's hand. "Her name is Mrs. Randolph. If you'll give me the room direction, I shall announce myself."

"Ah, Mrs. Randolph. She's a loverly woman. In fact," he added archly, "the porter just delivered her bath. She's in room seven, top of the stairs to the right."

"Thank you. Do you happen to have an extra key?"

"Of course!" The landlord scurried to a small room off the foyer and returned with a large iron key. "Here ye are, Mr. Hurst. If ye need anything else, jus' say th' word."

"Thank you." Robert took the key and crossed the foyer. So Moira still had a weakness for a hot bath. He wondered what other things about her were the same. Did she still enjoy warm, buttered bread? Reading the morning paper over hot tea and crumpets? Lolling in bed until the afternoon?

Of course, Moira's idea of lolling was rather vigorous, and the memories warmed him as he headed up the stairs.

After he found her room, he pressed his ear to the door. He heard humming, followed by a splash.

Good. She won't have that damned pistol on her. Still, he'd take no chances. He pulled out his small silver mounted pistol and checked it quickly. Then he slipped his key into the lock, turned it, and swung the door open.

Moira was indeed naked and glorious in the bath . . . and holding a pistol aimed right at his heart. "What an unpleasant surprise," she murmured, her smooth voice at odds with the anger that sparkled in her green eyes. "May I suggest that the next time you decide to surprise a person, that you have your pistol ready *before* you get to their door? I heard the chamber click."

He closed and locked the door behind him, his own pistol held steady. "You heard that, hm?"

"Barely, but it was enough."

He noted that water dripped from her fingers. "Do you think you can fire accurately with a wet hand?"

"I am willing to try. In fact," she smiled as she lowered the pistol so that it pointed to his crotch, "we could up the stakes a bit just to make it interesting."

"No, thank you. I prefer not to tempt fate, especially where my, er, *parts* are concerned." A faint quiver of amusement crossed her face and to his chagrin, he found himself smiling in return. "It seems we're at an impasse."

"Again. It's getting a bit old. Sooner or later, one of us will have to best the other."

"One would think." He crossed to a chair and sat. "Very comfortable."

"I don't want you comfortable. Robert, please leave."

He merely uncocked his pistol and replaced it into his coat pocket.

Moira's lips tightened, a flash of disappointment crossing her expressive face. Robert hid a grin. By putting his gun away and sitting so innocuously in a chair a good distance from her, he'd removed himself as an immediate threat. For all of her faults, Moira would never shoot someone without a damn good reason.

Of course, if she *had* perceived him as a danger, she'd have shot him without a qualm and with deadly accuracy.

She sighed and set her own pistol on the small chair beside the tub. "Stay if you must. I'm going to finish my bath."

"Feel free."

"You are too kind." Her voice dripped with sarcasm. "I can't think of how to thank you."

"Oh, I can think of a way." His gaze traveled over her. She was indeed now a brunette, though the tub reflected the copper light of her hair through the dyed strands. She'd piled her waist-length hair on her head and pinned it there, but there was no containing the wealth of silken tendrils, and several had found their way to her creamy shoulders, where they clung as if afraid to let go.

Robert realized he was staring, and dropped his gaze to her pistol. "Still armed everywhere you go? That must be a weighty habit."

"It serves." She soaped a large sponge. "So why are you here?"

Robert stretched his legs out and crossed them at the ankle. "I came to tell you that your journey tomorrow has been canceled."

Her green gaze locked on his. "How did you know I was going on a journey?"

"I know many things."

"Oh, for the love of Saint Christopher, stop being so damn mysterious." She rubbed the sponge along one elegant arm. "It's annoying."

He chuckled. "I knew you were leaving because I discovered George Aniston's lair yesterday and I've been having him watched. One of my men overheard him instruct his groom to bring a coach to you in the morning."

"Oh."

"Oh, indeed. Why are you still working for George Aniston?"

She placed her slender foot on the edge of the tub and began to wash her leg.

She had wonderfully long legs. They were outstanding, too—curved just so, exquisitely feminine and made for wrapping about a man's waist.

Robert shifted and forced his gaze back to her face. What were they talking about? Oh, yes. "Moira, enough of this. Tell me about Aniston."

"Why should I? I don't owe you anything, and you don't owe me."

"I would agree, except for one little fact: you tricked me into marriage."

She sighed. "That was years ago. And I've never asked for a penny in support."

"That's the curious part. It made me wonder why you even went to all of that trouble."

She hesitated. "I had my reasons."

"Which are?"

She slanted him a look before rinsing the soap from her legs.

It was all Robert could do not to react to the way she was slowly pouring water over her smooth, silken skin. He'd forgotten that it was almost impossible to keep a sane thought in his head when she was naked. Thank God the deep tub covered more than it revealed. All he could see were her head, shoulders, one arm, and one long leg. But even that was distracting in the ex-treme.

He collected his thoughts. "I've been looking for you all these years. The least you can do is an-swer a few simple questions."

"So ask them. But I'm going to get out of the tub first. It's getting cold."

"No, you can get out when I leave. If it's getting cold, then answer quickly. You went through an elaborate ruse to get me to marry you."

She'd charmed him into dressing as the King of Hearts to her Queen for a fancy dress ball at Vauxhall Gardens. It had been a foolish costume, but she'd been adamant about wearing them and he'd allowed it because he was already under her spell.

That had been his almost-ruin. The Home Office had grown suspicious of Moira, who had somehow convinced all of London that she was a Russian princess. Because of his connections to the *ton* through his sisters, who'd all married quite well, Robert had been asked to discover what he could about this mysterious woman.

It had been his first major assignment and he'd thrown his heart into it. Perhaps too much so. The instant his eyes had met hers, something had flared between them—and was flaring between them right now. Try as he might, he couldn't keep his eyes off her glistening shoulders as they rose above the edge of the huge tub.

He shifted in his chair. "As far as weddings go, ours was a paltry affair."

She chuckled low. "Don't be bitter. The gardens were lovely and . . ." Her smile faded. "You looked very handsome."

And she'd looked like a fairy that night, her eyes sparkling more brightly than the diamonds about her neck. "I was a bloody fool."

Something flickered in her gaze but she merely shrugged. "Nonsense. It was an elaborate deception and you didn't expect such a thing. How could you?"

He must have asked himself that question a thousand times. While wandering Vauxhall's famed dark gardens, they'd run into an obviously drunk man dressed as a vicar, who swore they were the most beautiful couple he'd seen that night. He then demanded to be allowed to "marry" them.

Robert had thought the man mad, but Moira had laughed and teased him that he was afraid. Drunk from both her beauty and the fact he was embarking upon his first assignment, he'd agreed to the unthinkable—to allow the "vicar" to marry the two of them on the spot. The vicar was quick to comply and even produced a false marriage license, demanding that it be signed.

Moira's green gaze met his as she swiped at a curl across her cheek. "How did you discover that silly wedding wasn't a mockery? I didn't think you'd give it a second thought."

"When you disappeared the next morning, I began to investigate everything you'd said and done. That night kept coming back to me. Something about it . . . it seemed wrong somehow." How Moira must have laughed at his naïveté. "To my surprise, I found the marriage license. You went to a lot of trouble to make our false marriage seem valid."

Her lashes dropped to shadow her expression. "I knew you would be angry, but—"

He waited, but when she didn't offer more he said sharply, "But what?"

She looked away and waved a hand as if banishing an annoying insect. "It was fun while it lasted."

He scowled. "Which part? The bedding? Or the sham of a relationship that never was? Frankly, neither was all that memorable to me. If I didn't feel that you'd stolen something from me, I would never think of either."

Color stained her cheeks and her lips folded into a straight line. "There was nothing wrong with our performances in bed. I still cherish those memories."

So that hurts, does it? Good. He couldn't help being pleased. "When all was said and done, I found myself the most sorry for the vicar."

At her surprised look, Robert added, "I found him not long after you disappeared. He told me how you'd contacted him and offered him a fortune to do this one thing. How he said no, but you were determined."

"He said yes quick enough once we began talking money," she said sharply.

"His little sister was ill. He needed it to pay for her care."

A shadow crossed Moira's face. "I didn't know."

"He admitted that. But that's neither here nor there. You set everything in motion, including posting banns and filing the license, so that our marriage appeared to be legal."

She began to speak, but he held up a hand. "I realize I could have it set aside, but only if I was willing to face public scrutiny. You knew I wouldn't do it. Why, Moira? Why go to so much trouble?"

"Perhaps I just wished for a husband—someone to watch over me."

"You ran off immediately after. I saw you two

weeks later, when I caught up with you in Bath, but you escaped again. So no, you didn't want someone to watch over you."

She sent him a hard look. "I still can't believe you turned me over to the authorities."

"You were a spy."

"Which was why you were assigned to woo me in the first place, wasn't it?" Her cool, disdainful voice held another emotion, but he couldn't quite identify it.

"In the beginning, that is why I began to pursue you. But after the second month, no."

Her gaze slashed across the room. "Don't tell me you 'cared,' for I won't believe it. If you'd cared, you wouldn't have had me arrested."

He set his jaw. "My feelings for you didn't change the fact that you'd been filching information for a foreign government."

"By the time you caught up with me, I had quit," she returned hotly. "I wanted to begin anew, and this time I wanted to do things right."

"I wish I could believe that. But truth hasn't been your strong point, has it?"

"I've only done what I felt needed to be done."

"Such a short sentence, yet such a long meaning. You used me, Moira. You tricked me into giving you my name and then you left. You may be angry that I tracked you down and then turned you over to the Home Office, but it was no less than you deserved."

"I didn't stay captive for long."

"No. I shouldn't have allowed anyone else to guard you but me. Apparently I am the only man in England able to withstand your charms."

Her face pink, she shifted in the tub, water glistening on her bare shoulders. "I didn't think you'd ever realize our marriage at Vauxhall was in earnest."

"You didn't know me as well as you thought. But your actions presented a conundrum as there was no reason why you'd go to such lengths." Robert paused. "Later on, though, a thought occurred."

Her gaze was locked with his and he had the impression that she held her breath.

"Moira, where's our child?"

CHAPTER 6

A note slipped into a birthday gift from Robert Hurst to his brother Michael for his sixteenth birthday.

Since you are so enamored of travel tomes, I have sent you these. Consider them your birthday gift, as I ate the Turkish delight I had purchased for you last month from a London confectionery shop.

I'm sure you will prefer the books anyway, so enjoy your dry, dusty tomes and I hope they sweeten that soured disposition of yours.

*M*oira couldn't breathe. How had he guessed the truth?

He cocked a brow at her. "Well? Do we have a child or not?"

"Don't be silly." She dipped the sponge into the water to give herself time to think. "Us, with a child? I can't even imagine it."

He frowned, his gaze narrowing. "There is no child?"

"No. I'm not a very maternal sort of woman. What would I do with a brat?" Even saying the words seemed a betrayal to Rowena.

"I don't know if I believe you."

She forced a chuckle. "Feel free to search my luggage, my apartment, whatever you wish. I prefer my life unfettered, as do you, I thought."

He was silent a moment, his gaze assessing her. "So you tricked me into marrying you because . . ."

"It was a challenge. I just wished to see if I could do it."

"*Ma chère*, allow me to disabuse you of the notion that that makes any sense. You tricked me and left me for some purpose. The only purpose you could have is that you were with child."

For one wild moment Moira thought about telling him the truth, but even as she had the thought, her sponge slipped from her fingers onto the floor. The splash brought her back to her senses. She was so close to getting Rowena back; all she needed was that damn onyx box. There was no need to deal with this complication.

What if he decides he wants to keep her? Moira's heart stuttered. *I can't get her back only to lose her again!*

The courts would never be kind to a woman alone, especially with her dubious history. Robert had connections in the government and he would use them to his benefit. *I can't chance it. He must never know about Rowena.*

Moira leaned over the edge of the tub for the dropped sponge, stretching to reach it. When she slid back into the water, she caught the faint flush on Robert's face.

So you aren't immune to me.

Watching him from under her lashes, she pulled her hair to one side and laid an arm on the rim of the tub, baring her breast.

His lips tightened slightly, a significant response

for a man who was always in control. Satisfaction buoyed her. "Perhaps I married you because I knew it would inflame you," she said calmly, rubbing the lavender soap on the sponge and then circling it around her breast.

This time he visibly caught his breath. *You aren't made of stone, are you?*

"Stop that right now."

"Stop what?"

"Distracting me. I know what you're doing and it's not going to work. If you don't wish to discuss why you tricked me into marriage, then let's talk of something else."

"Please, let's."

"Good. Tell me about George Aniston. Why is that scoundrel in your life? And don't pretend you're in his employ. I know you and if there's one thing you possess, it's pride. You'd never work for a worm like him."

Suddenly, Moira was tired . . . tired of dissembling, tired of always being wary, tired of hating George Aniston and yet having to be polite to him while having to be hateful to Robert, when all she really wanted to do was—

No, don't, she told herself severely. "As you've already guessed, I'm assisting Aniston in collecting the onyx boxes."

"That tells me what, not why." Robert leaned forward and she was struck by his strength. Despite his lace and fine clothing, there was no mistaking that he was a man through and through. He'd proven that to her between the sheets and in other ways as well. He might look a dandy, but he was hard-bodied, cool-mannered, and deadly when the situation warranted it. Anyone who thought differently was a fool.

He fixed his blue, blue gaze upon her now. "Moira, whatever Aniston has over you, it can't be worth degrading yourself to doing his bidding. Nothing is worth that."

Oh, but there is, she thought, her chest tight with anguish. "There's nothing to tell you about Aniston. He and I've done business a few times. That's all."

"So you're friendly."

"*No.*" The word cracked through the air.

Robert's brows rose and she knew she'd betrayed her feelings too much.

She scowled. "He's a cheat and no friend of mine. He never has been."

"I can see that." Robert's soft voice held a wealth of meaning. "Then why do you assist him? It can't be the money, for you're quite capable of making money whenever you wish. You're very resourceful."

She sighed. Perhaps part of the truth would assuage his curiosity. "Aniston is blackmailing me. He specializes in that low art."

"True. He was using it against my sister-in-law, from whom you stole the first onyx box."

"Miss Beauchamp is married to William?"

"Yes, though she keeps her maiden name for her career upon the stage."

"Her marriage must be a blow to Lord Covington. Wasn't she his mistress?"

"In name only. Covington is more likely to get engaged to George Aniston, if his preferences are any indication."

Moira started. "Covington and Aniston are lovers?"

"For almost two years. Covington dropped Aniston after his blackmail schemes were revealed. It was then revealed that not only was Aniston blackmailing Miss Beauchamp, but he was also pledging Covington's funds around town and had run up a huge number of bills. Once Covington dropped Aniston, he was forced to leave London or be thrown into debtor's prison.

"Which brings us back to: Why is Aniston blackmailing you? Forgive me if I indulge in some speculation, but you seem to be unable to share the truth." Robert templed his hands, resting his fingers against his chin, his dark blue eyes agleam. "You say Aniston is holding something over your head in order to secure your very considerable services."

"Yes." More or less.

"Hmm. Forgive me for stating the obvious, but it's not as if you have a reputation to uphold or a family to protect. And I cannot imagine you abide him for the money. As you said, you had retired, so I'm assuming you had sufficient funds stashed away to do so."

She didn't answer, and he smiled. "I know for a fact that you did retire, because there has been no mention of you for over five years in any investigation run by the Home Office."

"I could have been overseas," she said waspishly, hating that he had deduced so much from so little.

"I had people watching even there. You disappeared and then about six months ago, there you were, back in business and in a big way. There has to be a reason."

"Perhaps I was bored."

He shook his head. "No, Aniston has something he is holding over you, forcing you to fetch and scheme for him. Something significant."

She puffed a frustrated sigh. "I'm done with this conversation. If you'll excuse me, I must get out of this cold water." She grasped the sides of the tub and stood, water running down her skin, her nipples peaking in the cold air.

Robert had thought he was completely under control, but the sight of her naked body glistening, as if she were Venus arising from the ocean, made his heart stop. Every drop caught his attention as they slowly ran down the top of her full breasts, slid down the flat plane of her stomach, then caressed the smooth curve of her hips and thighs.

Robert's body tightened, his cock hardening.

She wrung her wet hair over the tub, then flipped it over one shoulder before she picked up a towel and dried herself.

"I don't know that brunette hair is your best look. It makes you appear a bit witchy."

She slipped on a silk robe. "It will fade within two weeks." She rubbed the towel on her hair and showed him the faint dark smear left upon the cloth. "See?"

The long robe belted about her narrow waist, her hair wrapped in a towel, she sauntered across the room to take the settee next to him.

She had no shame. Nothing but the thin silk of the robe separated her from him, a maddening thought.

As if she knew, she tucked her legs beside her

into the settee, the movement tugging the robe open so that the deep cleavage between her breasts was revealed. The thin robe clung to her damp skin and her nipples were clearly outlined.

No other woman he knew was so comfortable being nearly nude before a male. Not the opera singer he'd sponsored for a year, not the ballet dancer, nor the actress. Or the many others he'd bedded.

Only Moira.

"Enough of this," he snapped. "I can see you're not going to be honest about your connection to Aniston. There is another reason I came here. There's no need to visit Ross tomorrow, as you were instructed. That onyx box will be mine."

Her lashes flickered, then she shrugged. "Perhaps."

"*Ma chère,* I'm doing you a favor—there's no need for you to waste your time. If I see you in the highlands, I will personally tie you up, put you in my coach, and have you delivered to the Home Office to face the charges of treason which still await."

She leaned back, sleek and elegant. "Am I to suppose that you've already found a way to acquire the box?"

"Ross and I have already agreed upon a price. I have but to deliver the funds and it is mine."

Robert saw the fleeting disappointment in her eyes. *Good. That's all I need.* He stood. "I believe I've been quite clear. You'll inform Aniston that the onyx box is not available to him."

"And if I can't?"

"Tell him now or tell him later, after you have failed to fetch the box. It doesn't matter."

Very real fear crossed her face, surprising him. *What in the hell is she hiding?* Moira was no coward, so if she feared Aniston, then she had good reason.

Robert grasped her wrist and hauled her to her feet, the scent of lavender tickling his nose, her body pressed to his. His temperature rose, his breath quickening as his body reacted to her. *This is not why I pulled her into my arms.*

He held her away from him and gave her a little shake. "Damn it, stop being so stubborn. Tell me what hold that fool has over you."

Her gaze went to his and held it. "Why do you care?"

He didn't know why. He only knew that when he saw the fear in her eyes, he was overcome with the need to act, to take charge, to protect her.

Which was entirely foolish.

A look of amazement arose in her gaze. Then, before he knew what she was about, she slipped an arm about his neck, lifted onto her toes, and kissed him.

The kiss was bold, like Moira herself. She made full use of her curves, pressing against him as she pulled one of his hands to her hip.

Robert's resolve fled. God, she drove him mad with desire. He still wanted her, desired her, dreamed of her—he'd never stopped.

He wrapped himself around her, deepening the kiss, molding her to him, the thin silk urging him on.

She moaned, her thigh rubbing his rigid cock. Robert cupped her rounded ass and lifted her, carrying her to the bed, where he joined her on the coverlet, his hands roaming over her body like a starved man gorging himself. God, how he'd longed to have her like this. How he'd *dreamed* of it.

No other woman could inflame his passions as quickly as this one. She knew just where to touch, how to stroke; even her kisses were more intoxicating than any others.

He ran his hands up to her breasts and impatiently pushed aside her robe. Her creamy breasts were revealed, the dusky rose-colored nipples begging for attention. She didn't have the overly large breasts some men craved; hers were more delicate in size, fitting the palm of his hand perfectly.

He bent and captured one of her nipples between his lips, teasing her to gasping moans, his body aflame as she tugged at his trousers, releasing his shirt.

He slipped his knee between hers and opened her thighs. Her robe slipped even more, revealing her body to his hungry gaze. God, but she was seductive; he ached for her touch even as she gave it. Her hands never stilled, seeking, stroking, undoing buttons until she'd opened his breeches.

The feel of her hands on his bared waist brought him to his senses.

This was how she tricked me before. It is how she will trick me again. The thought was like ice water upon his passion.

He pushed himself away and looked down at her. She appeared somehow vulnerable, her eyes were half closed, her face flushed with desire, her lips swollen from his kisses. Her skin white against the blue silk robe, her dark hair making her eyes appear almost emerald.

Never had any woman worn the flush of passion better, yet Robert found the strength to leave her by remembering the last time she'd been like this, moaning beneath him. He'd been enthralled, enraptured . . . and at the end of that day, she'd tricked him into marriage and disappeared.

Ignoring the thundering of his heart, he rose from the bed and adjusted his clothing, saying with a coolness he was far from feeling, "I shall send my carriage in the morning to convey you wherever you wish. Just don't make the mistake of appearing at Ross's."

She sat upright, tightening her robe, her cheeks pink. "And what am I to tell Aniston?"

"The truth; that I informed you that it would be a wasted effort." He lifted his brows. "Or you can tell me what that cretin holds over you, and I will deal with him for you. However you wish it."

Her lashes dropped as she looked down at the robe sash between her fingers. "No. I will deal with Aniston. He is my problem, not yours."

Robert shrugged. "Have it as you will." He went to the door and unlocked it. "When I've retrieved that damned box, I'll return."

"I won't be here," she said sharply.

"Go where you will; I will find you nonetheless." He smiled. "I always have."

And with that he was gone, the door closing firmly behind him.

CHAPTER 7

A letter from Alexander MacLean to his brother-in-law, Robert Hurst.

The last time you came to visit Caitlyn, you wondered if there were some interesting research tomes in my library. Naturally your sister would not allow such an innocuous question to rest, and she has combed the shelves to make a list of all of the books that might be of interest to either you or any of your brothers. That is, she has combed all of the *lower* shelves. She left it to me to do the *higher* ones.

May I point out that the library is *very* large? And that this little task took me *hours*?

It would be easier to cut off my own leg than disappoint my wife, so I must ask that you refrain from ever wondering anything aloud in my house again. Like all of the Hursts, she has no concept of the word "no."

The luxuriously large coach lumbered down a narrow lane through the Scottish countryside. The verdant hills had given way to mountainous crags that loomed in the distance, white tipped against the gray sky.

Grasping a ceiling strap, Robert stretched his legs, glad that they were within two days of reaching Balnagown Castle, where Sir Lachlan Ross resided.

The last week had been interminable, the roads at times nearly impassable, the days filled with grayness and rain, the inns damp and inhospitable, the food too wretched to think about. He sighed, weary to the bone.

Still, it was worth it: soon he'd have the third and final onyx box in his possession. He smiled. *And then the real search for the Hurst Amulet will begin.*

Michael had always said the amulet should be in the possession of their family and he'd become obsessive about it. To Robert, it seemed to be family folklore more than anything else. Almost everything they knew could be labeled as fable and hearsay.

Robert wondered if Michael believed the tales that said the amulet had magical properties. According to the story, the amulet had been created by an ancestor, a white witch of great beauty. Then it had been stolen from her by the laird of the MacLean family. In return, she'd cursed the family so that whenever one of them lost their temper, storms would fly. "Ridiculous," Robert muttered.

Still, two of Robert's sisters, Triona and Caitlyn, had married into the MacLean family and, through the years, he'd caught bits of conversations that indicated that the curse existed. But that was foolishness. He was a practical man, one who dealt with facts and not far-fetched nonsense like curses and magical amulets. All he knew was this: there was a family heirloom that, through the ages, had gotten lost. Records proved that it had ended up in the possession of Queen Elizabeth, who had given it to a foreign emissary for reasons unknown, though some suggested she'd grown fearful of it. After that, the amulet had disappeared.

Robert reached under the seat and pulled out

his portmanteau. From a secret pocket on the side he removed first a small vial—a potion his sister-in-law had given him before he'd begun the mad chase after Moira, saying it would render the user unconscious, which he thought might be useful. He then removed a black velvet bag.

He replaced the vial in the secret pocket and opened the bag. Inside lay two onyx boxes, their odd engravings gleaming in the gray light. He spread the velvet across his lap and, flipping a few unseen latches, undid the boxes so that they lay completely flat. He placed them upon the velvet and turned them so that the inside surfaces were face up. Then, with a twist, he slid the two panels and clicked them together. They fit perfectly. He tilted the smooth surface so that the light found the etchings, which produced a map. Michael believed that the map would lead them not only to the lost Hurst Amulet, but to other treasures as well.

The map was why a sulfi had held Michael prisoner, demanding the return of the box he'd legitimately purchased. "It's also why George Aniston wants these," Robert murmured as he studied the map. It was the only reason Aniston would be persistent in trying to obtain them all; he had to know.

Did Moira know about the map? Robert traced

a wriggling line that was perhaps a river. He doubted Aniston would share such information; if the man had any sense, he'd be cautious around a woman of Moira's resourcefulness. She was much stronger and more devious than Aniston and, if cornered, would fight like a she-wolf.

Robert tilted the metal surface to a better angle, catching the gray light streaming from the window, noting that a mountain range appeared to take up almost half of the map. *What country could this be? It certainly wasn't Egypt; they had very few mountains there. Italy? Greece? Switzerland?*

The final panel held the key. He sighed and refolded the boxes, then slid them back into the velvet sack and into his portmanteau. As soon as he had the final box, he'd sprint back to London. Hopefully William would have secured Michael's freedom, and they'd all examine the map together. Michael's knowledge of ancient maps should enable him to decipher the markings.

The sound of thundering hooves announced an approaching rider. Robert banged on the roof. The coach immediately pulled to one side and stopped.

Robert leaned out the window, and smiled at the rider who'd just pulled up. "Ah, Leeds. You're early."

Leeds patted his lathered horse. "Ye expected me, sir?"

"Oh, yes. Miss MacAllister gave you the slip."

"Indeed she did, sir. Ye said to tell you if—"

"When's the last time you saw her?"

"Three days ago, sir. Just as ye said it would, Aniston's coach came fer her. And every day, she sent it away. The last day, she sent it off as usual, went back inside, and we ne'er saw her again.

"We thought she was still inside the George fer the day, but when she hadna come down fer dinner, I sent someone upstairs." Leeds shook his head. "She was gone."

"I warned you," Robert said, feeling an odd mixture of irritation and excitement. He shouldn't be excited, damn it.

"I don't understand, sir. She made quite a point o' sendin' off the coach, tellin' the coachman tha'—" Leeds caught Robert's dry smile and broke off.

"That's when she left, then. I daresay she sent the coach around the corner, then exited through the back door and went to meet it."

"We were watchin' the back door, sir."

"Perhaps she found an open window, and met the coach down the road, away from the inn. No matter. If she's escaped then you can be damned sure we'll see her again, for she's heading to Balna-gown Castle, too. What sort of coach did Aniston send?"

"It was a light one, sir. Made fer travelin' swiftly, no' comfort."

Robert glanced down the road behind them. "If she left three days ago, and if she has a lighter coach, she could catch up, though we still have a day or two before we need to worry. At least she's behind us, and there's only one road into Tain, the closest village to the castle, so she'll have to come this way."

"Aye, sir. I rode hell fer leather once't I knew she'd escaped."

"Good man." Robert noted the man's exhausted face. "Tie the horse on back and join Stewart on the box. We'll stop shortly to spend the night at some ill begotten inn. Stewart seems to know every damp bed this side of the Argyll River."

Leeds grinned. "Aye, sir."

Robert settled back into his seat. He wasn't the slightest bit surprised by the news. *So you didn't listen to a word I said, did you, Moira? Some things never change.*

He should be upset, but he realized that if she hadn't followed, he'd have been disappointed. Since their meeting at the George, he'd been plagued with memories of the feel of her beneath him on the bed. Every time he closed his eyes, he would see her delicious body stretched out on the coverlet—every delicate hollow, seductive shadow, and beckoning curve. Because of those memories, he'd found sleeping very unrestful, but far more interesting than usual.

He yawned. He could do with a nap now. Smiling, he settled into the corner and allowed the rocking of the coach to lull him to sleep.

An hour later, a loud rumble awoke Robert. He lifted his head and listened, frowning. *Surely that can't be Moira.*

A shout from the coach box made Robert unlatch the window and look out.

"'Tis her, sir!" Leeds yelled from his perch. "That's the coach Aniston sent!"

The small vehicle was obviously built for speed. Though lighter, it also lacked the stiff springs that made traveling in Robert's coach bearable and far more stable. *Little fool. If you've been traveling like that for days, I'll wager you're a mass of bruises from head to toe. Serves you right, too.*

"Shall we spring 'em, sir?" Stewart called.

Robert watched as the black coach drew nearer, its pace spanking. Aniston must have prepared the way with multiple teams if she'd sustained such a pace all the way from Edinburgh.

"Spring them!" Robert snapped. "And stay to the center of the road. Don't let her pass."

The coach lurched forward as Stewart hied the horses to a gallop. They were relatively fresh, as they'd been traveling slowly for the last two hours.

Robert's coach rumbled to full speed; Moira's coach approaching. He watched as the small coach began to close the gap, though there was no way to pass, as Stewart held the big coach to the dead center of the road.

"Take that," Robert said, catching sight of Moira's dark hair as she peered out of her window. He touched the brim of his hat, then settled back into his coach, chuckling. *That will teach her.*

The coach raced onward, hitting the deep ruts and rocking wildly. Robert took solace in the realization that Moira's ride would be much rougher. They rounded a corner and he heard Stewart yelling. Robert leaned back out of the window and saw Moira's coach swinging wildly to one side, trying to catch the gap between Robert's coach and the ditch to shoot past.

It was an insanely dangerous thing; she had to be mad! Robert gripped the window ledge with both hands and shouted a warning that was lost under the noise of thundering hooves.

Good God, woman, there's not enough room on this road for the two of us! He slid to the other side of the coach and looked down. A deep ditch lined the road, filled with icy water.

Grinding his teeth, Robert slid back to the other side as Moira's team found the gap they were seeking and surged forward, coming abreast of Robert. He could see the steam rising from their coats, smell the mud churned by their feet. Moira was leaning out the window, yelling up at her coachman, her hair tugged from its pins and streaming behind her.

The coachman lifted his whip and snapped it over the lead horse's ear, and Moira's coach jolted forward. Stewart cursed loudly, jockeying for position in the narrow road. Her wheels came dangerously close—if they collided, they'd both be in the ditch.

Damn it, someone is going to get hurt! Robert grabbed his cane and pounded it on the roof.

Stewart obediently began to slow and Moira's coach shot ahead. As she whisked by, Robert caught sight of her lips curved in a triumphant smile.

There was nothing he could do but sit back and

watch her coach race briskly by. It rounded a corner and—

Crack!

Moira's coach lurched, one wheel at an odd angle.

It was as if time held still. Robert saw that the wheel had broken, the axle exposed. The horses began to rear, trying to catch their balance as the coach swung wildly behind them. At the final moment, he saw Moira's white hand clutching the door frame as the coach flipped over into the deep ditch.

His heart thudded sickly and he flung open the door of his moving coach. He was already on the ground and running toward the overturned carriage by the time his had pulled to a halt.

The black coach was upon its side, one wheel still turning. The horses were tangled in the broken traces, whinnying and jumping madly.

A shaken groom was pulling himself out of the ditch, icy water dripping from him, his cheek a bloody mess.

"Leeds, see to those horses!" Robert yelled over his shoulder.

Leeds was down in a trice and running to calm the frightened team.

Robert reached the overturned coach. It lurched drunkenly in the ditch, tilted almost on its top, but it seemed stable, stopped from rolling over by the trunk of a heavy oak.

He climbed onto the tilted carriage, opened the door, and looked inside. Moira was crumpled in the corner, her eyes closed, a streak of blood vivid on her temple. At the sight of her chest moving up and down in smooth rhythm, his heartbeat slowed and reason returned.

He swung his legs inside as Stewart ran up.

"Is she alive, sir?"

"Yes, but she's injured. Find out where the closest village is. We need a surgeon."

Stewart hurried off.

Robert let himself down into the coach, carefully setting his feet on either side of Moira's crumpled form. Her yellow silk gown and pelisse made her paleness seem even more ominous. His heart thudded sickly when he saw that blood had soaked into her hair and spread to the coach cushions. "Damn it! You just had to best me, didn't you?"

He looked around for a piece of cloth to bind her wounds. The inside of the coach was topsy-turvy, the cushions and the contents of the seat boxes scattered. A foot warmer rested near Moira's head, the handle matching the shape of the bruise on her temple.

"That had better be all that's wrong," he said

through gritted teeth. "I won't have you die at my feet, damn it. Not after I spent so many years trying to find you, and now you just—" His throat tightened and he couldn't finish the sentence. He wasn't sure who or what he was threatening, but he meant every word.

He yanked off his gloves and examined her wounds, his heart sinking at the deep gash on her head. He tore a flounce from her gown and was wrapping it around her head when her eyes fluttered open.

She blinked up at him, wincing as she turned her head.

"Does it hurt?" he asked.

"Like the devil," she murmured, her hand pressing to her forehead.

"There was a coach accident. Do you remember?"

She closed her eyes. "No. I don't—" She grimaced.

"Does anything else hurt?"

"Just my head, but it—" Her brows knit in pain.

"Don't move." He looked above him at the open door. "*Leeds!*"

Leeds's stocky face appeared in the doorway overhead. "Aye, sir." He caught sight of Moira. "Och, they's a lot o' blood, isna' there?"

"Yes," Robert said tensely. "Is there a village nearby?"

"Nay. A farmer stopped by and said there's no town fer another ten miles, but the local squire's no' far off. Stewart's gone there fer help."

"Bring my portmanteau from the coach. I've medicine in it."

"Yes, sir!" Leeds was gone in a trice, quickly returning with the portmanteau. He lowered it through the doorway to Robert.

"How are the horses?"

"Two are scraped up and one is lame, though I dinna think 'tis serious."

"Good. Unhook them and rub them down as well as you can. The ones that aren't injured will need to be walked while we wait for help."

"Aye, sir."

"As soon as someone comes from the squire's house, we'll rig up a sling and get Miss MacAllister out of here."

"Yes, sir!" With that, Leeds was gone and Robert pulled the vial from the secret compartment in his portmanteau.

"I don't need a sling; I can climb," she said faintly.

"For once in your blasted life, you'll do what I tell you to do." According to Marcail, the potion in the vial would make a person sleep. With any luck, it would put Moira to sleep long enough that they could move her without causing her too much pain. He held the vial to the light and wondered about the dosage. His sister-in-law hadn't said, and he was leery of using too much. He'd start with a sip and go from there.

He slipped his arm under Moira's shoulders, lifted her gently, and held the vial to her lips. "Drink some of this."

"What is it?"

"It will help the pain. Careful, it probably tastes horrid."

She sipped it cautiously, then took a bigger sip. "It's sweet."

"Good." He held the vial to the light. She'd taken half of it, but perhaps that would be enough. "Let me know how you feel."

"Very well." She closed her eyes.

He waited, studying her profile, noting her pale skin. Outside, Leeds instructed the men to walk the horses. A moment later he heard his own carriage being moved up the road, probably to keep the lane from being blocked.

She sighed, and he glanced at her again. To his surprise, the tense expression on her face had relaxed and her breathing was smoother.

"Moira?"

She opened her eyes, offering a sleepy, almost seductive smile. "Yes?" Her voice was low and rich and slid over him like a pair of warm hands.

Bloody hell, what's in that potion? He cleared his throat. "Feel better?"

"Ohhhh, yessss." She closed her eyes again, her lips still curved in a smile. "Muuuuch better."

Good God, whatever was in that vial was potent.

She laughed, the sound sultry. "I can't believe the coach didn't take the corner. It didn't look that sharp. I shouldn't have pressed the driver."

"No, you shouldn't have."

She peeped at him through her lashes. "If it had been anyone else but you, I'd have never made the attempt. You are my one weakness."

Oh ho. Apparently the potion also reduces inhibitions. That's interesting. "I don't wish to be anyone's weakness."

"Well, you are. You, Robert Hurst, are my one, big, grand weakness." She blinked slowly, her thick lashes casting shadows over her eyes and making them appear deep forest green. "I wonder how many other women think that about you? Probably hundreds."

"I doubt that," he said absently, noting that blood was beginning to soak through the bandage on her head. *Damn it, where's Stewart?*

"I don't doubt it," she returned, her lips turned into a sulky pout. "How many women have you seduced since I left? A dozen? Two dozen? Or are your conquests too numerous to count?"

He started to reply, but she continued, "I used to think about you with all of those conquests whenever I missed you."

"You missed me?"

"Dreadfully. I don't know why, because you weren't in love with me. You never pretended you were. But I—" She blinked, as if realizing that she'd said too much.

"Moira, does your head hurt anymore?"

She paused, then smiled. "No! Not at all."

That was good news. He would have to thank Marcail for the tonic, and ask her about the interesting side effects.

"In fact," Moira added, "I feel wooooonderful."

"That's good because we will need to move you soon. It might hurt."

"That's all right. It can't be worse than having a ba—" She stopped, her eyes slowly locking with his.

Silence stretched between them. Finally, he said, "Baby." He was unable to believe the words he'd just said. "*Our* baby."

"No. *My* baby," she replied stubbornly.

Robert didn't know what to say. His worst fears had been realized. This was why he'd searched so long for her, why he'd never given up.

I have a child. Good God, what do I do now? "Where is this child?"

Moira's lips quivered, and tears filled her eyes.

The truth hit him like a blow to the stomach. "*Aniston*. He's taken—"

Moira held out a hand, as if to stop his words.

"Damn that man! That's what he is holding over you, isn't it?"

"Yes. He stole her from my home while I was gone seeing to the sale of some land."

"You were living in Scotland all of this time?"

"Yes. I bought a small house in a village near Edinburgh within two weeks of our last meeting. I had tucked away a good bit of money and we had very few needs. She and I were so happy there— until Aniston stole her away."

He had a daughter. "How long has that cretin had her?"

"Almost six months now. Sh-she's growing up without me, and I don't even know if she's safe or—" Moira pressed a hand to her mouth.

"And you've tried to rescue her." It wasn't a question; he knew her too well.

"I've tried everything. Aniston keeps her locked away somewhere and only rarely allows me to see her. He is very careful to come fully armed and with a number of men. Once I tried to escape with her, but he caught us and never again allowed me to see her unless we were guarded. If I wish to see her, I must do as I'm told. Aniston thinks he's defeated me." Her eyes flashed emerald fire. "But I will *never* give up trying."

Robert closed his eyes, fury surging through him. Aniston had their daughter—*his* daughter. *When I finally get my hands on that—*

But now was not the time for useless fury. Moira was injured.

"We will deal with Aniston later," he managed to say through clenched teeth.

"We can't." A tear slid from the corner of her eye and trailed down her cheek. "I have to get this box and return it to him. I saw her just last week and the nurse hits her, and I—" A sob wracked Moira's body.

When he next saw Aniston, Robert would take great pleasure in ripping the man apart.

Moira gulped a sob and Robert noticed that the bandage he'd made for her head was now soaked through with blood. He cursed and ripped two more flounces from her gown and tied them more tightly over the other bandage. They slowed the flow immediately, though she winced. "I'm sorry if that's uncomfortable. You're bleeding. It had to be done."

"It doesn't matter. Nothing matters. Only Rowena." Moira's voice was softer than a whisper.

"You matter as well, *ma chère*. Once I kill Aniston, Rowena will need her mother more than ever. Meanwhile, we need to get you to a doctor." He glanced impatiently at the door swinging open over their head. "I wish Stewart would return."

"Robert, you understand now why I must have that box? I have no choice."

"We'll talk about the damned box when you're better."

"You are so kind," she said. "Few people know that about you, but I do. So kind, and so afraid anyone might see it."

"That's the tonic talking," he said. "I don't know what's in it, but it makes you very silly."

"You're always kind to me," she said drowsily as she captured his wrist and brushed her lips over the back of his hand.

A wave of lust answered her innocent gesture and he pulled his hand free. "Stop that."

She smiled. "You understand me. No one else ever does."

"We understand one another. Although I

wonder why you didn't tell me about our daughter before now."

"You didn't want a child."

"No, but I—"

"I did." Her gaze met his, clear and honest. "So I didn't tell you about our daughter because I wished to keep her to myself, without any interference from you."

Robert frowned. He should be thankful to hear the truth, regardless of how damning it was to his pride.

This tonic had many uses indeed. It would have taken him weeks, perhaps months, to get so much honesty out of her. "Moira, shouldn't that have been my decision, too?"

Her brows lowered. "Robert, if I'd told you, you would have been upset and thought it a trick and always wondered if she was really yours."

Moira was right; he would have wondered. "Is she?"

"Yes." Moira yawned, suddenly looking very sleepy. "You can see it now, but not when she was younger. She grows more like you every day, which is . . . most unfair. Since I've been the one . . . doing all of the . . . work." Moira's eyes closed as the tonic claimed her.

"Even asleep, you are the most infuriating

woman I've ever met," Robert told her. With relief, he heard Stewart's voice and another one, loud and aristocratic. *Help has arrived.*

His head spinning with the shocking fact that he was a father, Robert climbed from the coach to organize Moira's rescue.

CHAPTER 8

A letter from Michael Hurst upon his older brother, Robert, gaining a position with the Home Office.

Now that you're with the secretary's office, I'm sure people are asking you right and left to espouse their causes. Fortunately for you, I have no cause except to find the Hurst Amulet. You've mocked my ambition, but I'd give up life and limb and honor to restore it where it belongs, with our family.

I know you're now shaking your head, but trust me on this, brother mine: it's good to have a purpose in life, and much more amusing than merely existing from day to day. When you get bored playing hide-and-seek with disreputable persons, I suggest you, too, find a purpose for your life. It may be just the thing to settle your restless spirit.

S he awoke slowly, blinking in the darkness of the huge, gray coach. It was cold. Shivering, she looked at her hands, neatly gloved, her feet shod in plain, brown shoes like those worn by housemaids. That's odd. I don't remember purchasing those.

Disoriented, she looked out the window of the coach. The scenery was idyllic and peaceful. Green hills, blue lakes, summer sun splashing over beautiful fields of flowers. And approaching in the distance, a child riding a big black stallion.

She leaned forward. Was that Rowena? As if in answer the child waved, and Moira waved back, laughing as Rowena rode the magnificent horse up to the coach.

Moira was happy, content that her child was so close and safe. If she reached through the window, she could touch Rowena's flowing hair . . . but then the carriage began to rumble forward faster, the beautiful horse falling behind.

Moira tried to lean out the window, but she couldn't. The scenery sped by faster and faster until it was a blur, Rowena falling farther and farther behind.

Moira wanted to call out, but her voice had frozen. The

coach began to rock, lurching wildly side to side. She gripped the edge of her seat, clutching it desperately as it overturned and she sailed through the air and—

She gasped, opening her eyes to a darkened room lit only by a fire in a large, ornate fireplace. She blinked, her heart still pounding. *It was just a dream.*

Panting, she rested on the mound of pillows, feeling drained and weak. *What's happened to me? Where am I? Where's Rowena?*

Her fingers clutched the thick sheets and she absently noted the fine coverlet, the heavy blue bed curtains. Wherever she was, it was a luxurious bedchamber.

She turned her head, gasping when pain shot through her temple. She closed her eyes and pressed a hand to her forehead, finding a thick bandage there. *My head. What happened? I was ... I was chasing Robert, trying to get ahead to gain the onyx box and—* Oh. Memories of the crash filled her mind, of pain in her head and Robert's face looking into hers, concern in his deep blue eyes.

And Rowena? Moira desperately searched her memory, biting her lip when she remembered. *Rowena is still being held by Aniston.*

Tears threatened, but Moira fought them off. Her head ached and her eyes were hot and uncomfortable, and she was so thirsty that her lips and tongue felt swollen.

She lifted her head and saw Robert asleep in a chair beside her bed, his head slumped to one side. He was disheveled and unshaven, several days' worth of beard upon his face.

It was one of the few times she'd seen Robert less than perfectly attired, too. His coat was slung over the back of the settee, his shirt open at the throat, and his loosened cravat had been tossed aside. As she watched, he stirred but didn't awaken, his thick lashes resting on his cheeks.

It was a sin for a man to have such lashes, she decided irritably, kicking a little where her night rail was twisted about her legs. She was so hot and uncomfortable and—

"You're awake." Robert's voice startled her as he came to stand beside the bed. His shirt-sleeves had been rolled up to reveal strong, muscular forearms.

"Yes," she croaked, pressing a hand to her throat. "I'm awake. I'm hot and my head hurts and I'm so very thirsty and—"

He chuckled, and to her surprise, he pressed a kiss to her forehead.

The unexpectedly tender gesture made tears well once again. She didn't know what to say.

Apparently Robert didn't either, for he abruptly turned away and poured her a glass of water. "You gave us all quite a scare."

"How long have we been here?"

"Almost five days. Do you remember anything?"

"I remember trying to pass your coach and the accident."

He held the glass to her lips and allowed her a cautious sip.

"You hit your head and lost consciousness in the coach. After I brought you here, you caught a fever. There was one day when we didn't know if—" He set the glass aside and put a cloth into a water basin. After wringing it out, he brought it back to the bed.

She took the cloth. "You are too kind." She rubbed it over her face, her hands shaking like a blancmange. The coolness felt heavenly and she closed her eyes, savoring it. Finally she sighed and handed the cloth back to him. "Thank you."

"You're welcome." He placed his hand on her forehead. "The physician was right; he said you'd turned a corner."

I don't remember a thing. "Where are we?"

"We are the guests of Squire MacDonald and his wife, Anne. The coach overturned half a mile from the drive leading to their house, which was fortunate for us." He glanced around the well-appointed room. "The house is very nice. *They've* been very nice, as well. The squire is very fond of brandy, so I'll send him a case in thanks."

"I shall do the same," she said, wondering at Robert's solicitude. A thought struck her like an icy hand. *Did I talk while unconscious? Did I tell him about Rowena? Please God, no.* She pressed a hand over her rapidly beating heart. "May I have something more to drink?"

"If you're up to sitting, I shall pour you some of the lemonade that our hostess provided before she retired for the night. She seemed certain you would awake this evening." He paused. "I informed our hosts that we are man and wife."

"Oh? You didn't think they'd welcome us otherwise?"

"I wanted no questions as to the propriety of my being in your sickroom."

"Why *are* you in my sickroom?"

"Who else would tend you? The squire's wife who, while a kind soul, is a stranger?"

"I hadn't thought about it, but I didn't expect you to do it." Moira put her hands to her sides and struggled to sit. "I'm weak as a kitten."

"Allow me." Robert slipped an arm about her shoulder and helped her, his strong arm warm against her back. Then he moved to one side to stack pillows behind her. "Better?"

She let out a relieved sigh. "Yes, thank you."

"Good." He flicked a short glance at her and then said, "You can take some tonic while you are sitting up."

"I feel fine. A little weak, is all. I'm sure that once I have something to eat and drink—"

"You also need your rest, and the tonic will help you sleep." He picked up a small vial and a waiting spoon and prepared a dose. "You like this; you said it was sweet."

She took the tonic, more to get him to move away from the bed than any other reason. It was disturbing to see him mussed and unshaven, looking more masculine than ever. "Mmm. It is sweet."

He went to fetch her the promised lemonade, and she eyed it thirstily. "After I drink that, I shall get out of bed."

"You'll get up when I say you will, and not before."

"You've become overbearing."

"I've always been overbearing."

She couldn't argue with that. She took the glass, but her hand trembled so much that he quickly rescued it from her.

"Allow me." He held the glass to her lips and tilted it for her. Her dry lips burned on contact with the lemonade, but she'd never tasted anything so wonderful in her life.

When she finished, she sighed with satisfaction. "That was lovely."

He returned the glass to the small table. "Shall I read to you while you rest?"

"I'm really not tired."

"Mm-hmm." He lowered himself into the small chair, the wood creaking in protest.

Beginning to feel the effects of the tonic, she sent him a glance under her lashes and watched as he tried to get comfortable. Robert had grown more muscular over the years, his arms and shoulders wider and more powerful. "You are very healthy," she said aloud. "*Very.*" She stirred as a restless feeling settled over her.

His amused gaze found hers. "Feeling the tonic, are you?"

"Yessss. I suppose I am." Every sense seemed heightened. The thick sheets were soft against her legs, the counterpane's design seemed more prominent under her fingertips, the lemonade scent tickled her nose, and she could hear her own breath. Every moment seemed clear, and oddly sensual. She pulled at the neck of her night rail, which seemed too tight.

Her gaze flickered to Robert and focused on his

firm mouth. He'd always been a sensual kisser, teasing and nipping and driving her mad with— *Stop thinking about that!* "So . . . have you been here with me the entire time?"

"Yes."

"Without starched cravats, I see."

His lips twitched. "Despite the arrival of my portmanteau and my valet, I've been too busy to do more than wash and change."

"Your valet must feel slighted."

"You have no idea. Buffon believes my appearance is a reflection of his value. Needless to say, his sensibilities are a bit bruised."

"Buffon . . . I should have known you'd have a French valet. No English valet would allow you to wear so many ruffles."

"My valet will never dress me, nor does he attempt to press his style upon me, be he English or else."

She eyed him now. "I wish you'd take off that shirt."

His brows rose. "Why?"

"The wrinkles make my head hurt. My eyes try to trace them and it's impossible." He started to reply, but she abruptly said, "I'm surprised you didn't continue after the box. You had a head start."

He stretched his long legs before him, his gaze hooded. "I didn't wish to leave until I knew you were well. I'm sure you would have done the same for me."

I wouldn't have waited on you.

She caught his amused gaze and realized that she hadn't been thinking to herself at all. "I . . . I said that aloud, didn't I?"

"Yes. The tonic has an interesting effect on you. You become more . . . honest."

"I'm always honest."

He raised his brows, and she felt compelled to amend, "Well, *most* of the time. Sometimes a lie is necessary—especially when a person has a secret." She knew she should quit talking, but she couldn't. "I wish I didn't have so many secrets—far more than the average woman."

"You've never been honest with me. I've found out more about you in the short time you've been under the influence of that tonic, than when we were living in each other's pockets."

"What have I told you?"

A self-satisfied smile settled on his mouth. "All sorts of interesting things."

She pressed her fingers to her lips. Had she told him about Rowena? "Were any of the things I told you very surprising?"

"Very."

"I didn't mention anything really unusual, did I? Because if I did, it was probably untrue. This tonic makes me feel very odd, and who knows what I might have made up while—"

"Moira, you told me about our daughter."

Oh God, no. But one look at his stern face told her he knew.

"You also called for her during your fever. I know all about Rowena."

"I see," she said wearily. The tonic no longer made her senses stronger. Now it was dulling them and making it difficult to think.

"Don't look so forlorn. It explains a lot: why you are so determined to obtain that onyx box, and why you've been working for Aniston."

"I *hate* that man."

Robert's jaw tightened. "So do I."

For a moment, they were united.

She closed her eyes to rest and heard Robert say, as if from a long way off, "I've made some decisions about our pursuit of the box."

She forced herself to look at him, though her eyelids were as heavy as anvils. "Yes?"

His gaze flickered over her face and he chuckled. "I'll give you the details when you awaken from your nap."

"We should . . . leave . . . right away." Her lips had gotten difficult to move.

"We'll see about that."

"Are you worried . . . that I might still beat you to Ross's?"

Robert looked inordinately amused. "If we were to leave this room at the exact same second, I would reach our destination first."

"I was . . . beating you . . . before . . . the accident."

"You wouldn't have *had* an accident if you hadn't been pushing so hard." His brows lowered. "You took a very foolish chance."

She'd have taken a million other, more dangerous chances to win Rowena's release. She started to say so, but her mind was already slipping away. And within seconds, she was fast asleep.

CHAPTER 9

From the diary of Michael Hurst, awaiting his release from the sulfi holding him hostage.

I've received word that William is on his way with the onyx box. I hate to give it up, but what must be, must be. I hope he also remembers the port I requested last month. Being in such close quarters with Miss Smythe-Haughton is taking a toll. Despite my warnings she has tried to develop a friendship with my captor, with dire consequences. The man now thinks himself enamored of her and has offered to purchase her.

I must admit, I am sorely tempted. I certainly hope William remembers the port.

$\mathcal{T}$he next time Moira awoke, the sun was well up in the afternoon sky. In Robert's place by the bed was an overly cheery maid named Firtha, who began to flit about the room and chatter nonstop in a way that made Moira's mood even less sunny.

With Firtha's help, Moira washed and changed into a fresh gown. Though the simple tasks tired her, she felt much better. She should be ready to travel come morning. "Firtha, I'm starving."

"Och, miss, I'll ha' a tray brought immediately." Firtha rang a bell and asked the answering footman to bring some luncheon, while Moira moved to a comfortable chair by the crackling fireplace. She hoped for a little peace with her meal, but with her tray came her hostess.

Lady Anne was a broad-faced woman dressed in a new frilly gown that reflected last year's fashions to perfection. Obviously glad for some company other than servants, she welcomed Moira and then recounted the exciting events of the day of the accident, asking a myriad of questions.

Moira answered every inquiry politely, glad that as the conversation continued, her hostess seemed quite content to carry on both sides. That left Moira to her own thoughts.

Perhaps the time had come to include Robert in her plans to obtain the onyx box. She had a risky idea of how to retrieve it without Lord Ross being any the wiser, and a little help would be welcome. But the truly big question, the one that burned in her heart, was how did Robert feel about Rowena? Once they freed her, would he wish for custody? Panic immediately began to rise at the thought.

I can't think about that now; I've got to get that box to win her freedom. And the sooner I speak to Robert about it, the better. She picked up her teacup and waited for her hostess to pause for a breath. "Lady Anne, I would like to visit my husband before dinner. We need to plan our travel now that one of the coaches is gone and—" She stopped at Lady Anne's incredulous gaze.

"But my dear, I thought you knew. Mr. Hurst already left."

Moira set the teacup into the dish so hard that it rattled. "What?"

"He didn't say good-bye, but left us a very nice letter." Lady Anne grimaced. "Oh, dear, he left you a letter, too. I should have thought of it, but I was so happy to see you sitting up that— Firtha! Pray go downstairs to the front hall and bring back the letter addressed to Mrs. Hurst."

The maid dipped a curtsy and left while Moira curled her hands about the arms of her chair in frustration. *He left me a letter? Why in hell didn't he just wake me up and tell me he was leaving?* But she knew the answer: she would have argued and he didn't wish to hear her objections. *The coward!*

Lady Anne sighed. "I can see you're upset, and no wonder. Men can be so impatient."

"What time did he leave?"

"Early this morning. I'm surprised I didn't hear his coach being brought around, for my bedchamber is right off the main courtyard and I'm a notoriously light sleeper. If he hadn't left a note we would never have known he was gone until breakfast."

"He can be very impulsive." *And arrogant, and a great pain in the ass, too.*

Lady Anne must have noticed that Moira's teeth were clenched, for the older lady looked uneasy. "He said he wouldn't be long—just a week or a little more."

"Ha! With the roads the way they are? He's mad."

"Oh, dear." Lady Anne fidgeted with the brocade trim on one of her sleeves. "I do hope—"

Firtha returned and handed a neatly addressed note to Moira.

She ripped it open.

Moira,

I'm off to fetch the onyx box. I'll return as soon as possible and we'll make plans to retrieve Rowena. Rest easy; come what may, I shall not allow Ross to keep the artifact. Aniston's fate, too, is sealed, though he does not know it.

I know you would have preferred to travel along for this adventure, but I work better on my own. In the meantime, stay with the squire and his wife. I shall bring another coach with me for our return to Edinburgh.

Yours,
Hurst

Moira refolded the letter, resisting the unladylike temptation to wad it into a ball and stomp it into flatness.

Lady Anne cleared her throat. "I hope the letter explains everything to your satisfaction."

Moira tucked the note into the pocket of her gown and managed to say fairly calmly, "Hurst has continued on our journey and will see about hiring another coach, since we lost one of ours."

"Ah. I suppose that explains why he took all of the horses with him."

Moira's teacup was halfway to her lips, but at that, she lowered it. "I'm sorry, did you say . . . he took *all* of the horses?"

"Yes. And all of the footmen and coachmen, too." Lady Anne's brow lowered. "I still can't believe we didn't hear them! That's quite a retinue."

Moira managed a smile, though it cost her dearly. Oh, the things she'd have to say to Robert the next time she saw him. She didn't know exactly when that would be, but it would be far sooner than he thought.

"There, there," Lady Anne said bracingly. "Don't look so gloomy. You needn't fear that you'll languish here while waiting for your husband." Lady Anne patted Moira's hand, as if conferring a treat upon a child. "The squire and I are quite well thought of in the neighborhood, and we're planning a quiet little dinner party for your amusement once you feel more the thing. We won't have dancing—I fear that would tire you too much—just a nice, snug little dinner party and some music. Mrs. MacDunnon's oldest daughter is coming. She recently returned from

Rome, where she took singing lessons from La Cabrini!"

On and on Lady Anne went, describing in endless detail all of the things she thought would amuse a woman of the world, which she plainly thought Moira to be. Though she longed to scream, Moira murmured, "How delightful!" at appropriate intervals.

Lady Anne took this for encouragement. While her hostess babbled on, Moira planned her escape. If Robert thought he could just leave her behind, he was a fool.

She interrupted, "I beg your pardon, Lady Anne, but I think I should return to my bed."

"Oh, dear! It's your first day up and you must be tired, yet here I'm babbling on and on." Lady Anne stood. "I'll leave you to rest. If you want anything, just ring the bell and Firtha will see to it."

"Thank you. That's so kind of you, but I think I'll sleep for the rest of the afternoon."

"Very well, my dear. If you're up to it, we dine at seven."

"I look forward to meeting the squire. Do you think I might have a bath before dinner?"

"Of course! I'll send one up now and Firtha will come back at six to help you dress. No late city hours for us here in the country!" With an arch look Lady Anne finally left, Firtha following with the luncheon tray.

Moira waited for the door to close. Then she crossed to the wardrobe, collected a small trunk, and placed it on the bed. It was a large and heavy case, made with iron bands and a heavy wood bottom, all covered with leather. She reached inside, flipped two hidden latches, and removed a thin false bottom. Inside was a complete suit of clothing befitting a gentleman of fashion, a dark wig, a packet of hairpins, and a fat pouch of coins.

She counted the coins, replaced the items, and returned the portmanteau to the wardrobe floor. Perhaps Robert had done her a favor. A lady of fashion traveling in a coach would need two days to reach her destination. A gentleman on a good horse traveling ventre à terre could make the same trip much quicker.

But she was still weak from her illness, so rest was crucial. She slipped back into bed. She'd sleep the rest of the afternoon to conserve her energy, then eat dinner with the squire and his wife. But as soon as her host and hostess were abed, she'd make her way to the stables, and borrow a horse. To assuage her conscience, she'd leave her hosts a letter and a generous portion of the coins.

She snuggled under the covers and curled onto her side, examining her plan for flaws.

It will work. She settled against her pillows and almost immediately fell asleep, dreaming of riding pell-mell across the moors, chasing a black-haired devil with eyes of blue.

CHAPTER 10

A letter to Michael Hurst from his sister Lady Caitlyn Hurst MacLean, two years ago.

Of all the Hursts, you are the most like our grandmother, Mam. No one believes in magic and amulets more. Do you remember the tales she used to frighten us with when we were children? Not for her the soft stories of princesses and knights and good deeds. No, she always told the stories where witches ate bad little children and evil kings ruled their countries by placing a horrid curse upon those who dared rebuke them.

Like the Brothers Grimm, she delighted in sharing the darker side of the world. You loved those stories while the rest of us cowered in fear. Perhaps that's why you're the explorer among us; you savor the things we seek to avoid.

*L*ater that same afternoon, Leeds wiped the blood from his nose and looked about the tack room. "Och, tha' finishes it."

"Aye," Stewart agreed, holding a handkerchief to his cut ear. "'Twas no' so hard. After all, they're but Sassenachs."

He looked at the six footmen and two coachmen who were now trussed and tied up along one wall. He and Leeds might be sporting some bruises, but the footmen and coachmen were far worse for wear, only two of them even conscious.

"Ye could see Mr. Hurst's Scottish lineage in the way he fought tonight," Leeds said.

Stewart cast a cautious glance at the closed door before he leaned forward to say, "There's no' many men as can fight like Mr. Hurst, fer all he wears them Frenchified clothes."

Leeds nodded. "He do dress like he couldna' lift a fork, much less make a fist."

"But when he makes a fist—" Stewart shook his head in admiration. "'Tis somethin' to see."

The door to the tack room opened and Mr. Hurst walked in. He had already tugged his gloves back on, his cane tucked under one arm, his cravat back in perfect repair. Only the faint scrape along his jaw indicated he'd been involved in a glorious altercation. "You've tied them securely?"

"Aye, sir," Stewart said. "Leeds tied 'em, and I checked the lashin's meself."

"Good. Thank you for assisting me."

"Och, now," Leeds said, grinning. "'Twas a pleasure."

"Aye," Stewart said, cracking his knuckles. "'Twas more fun than havin' to put up the horses."

Robert had to laugh at their enthusiasm. "It was a good fight."

"Wha' are we to do wit' them now, sir?" Stewart asked.

"We'll hold them here until morning, when we'll put them on the mail coach and send them back to Edinburgh to their damned master.

"It's a pity we won't be there to see Aniston's face when his servants are returned to him."

Stewart rubbed his chin. "Ye seem a mite put out by this Aniston fellow."

"'Put out' isn't the phrase I'd use." Robert couldn't keep the bitterness from his voice. Just the thought of Aniston made his chest tighten as if a vise were upon it.

Stewart cleared his throat. "Sir, just to be certain . . . are we to send them back *alive*?"

"Of course you're to send them back alive! I just don't want any of them to follow us. And this will send Aniston a message he'll not forget.

"You may leave them for now; just lock the door and keep the key with you. I won't have someone stumbling upon them and letting them all go."

"What if the servants from the inn need to get into the tack room?" Stewart asked.

"I've already spoken to the landlord. He was more than glad to make a few extra coins by renting us this space for the short time we'll need it."

"Yes, sir," Leeds said. "We'll sleep in the next room so we can keep an eye upon them."

"Excellent. I shall go inside and bespeak a room. Buffon should arrive within the hour with my luggage. We should reach Balnagown Castle by nightfall tomorrow." The real work would begin then, and Robert was looking forward to it. "When Buffon arrives, take care of his coach and horses, but do not allow him to unpack my luggage. I have all I need in my portmanteau."

Leeds and Stewart looked pleased at the prospect of telling Buffon what to do.

Robert left and went out to the inn yard. The inn had been a welcome surprise, much larger than they'd anticipated, considering how far north they'd traveled. The two-storied timbered building dated to the sixteenth century, a style Robert rather liked. He entered the front hall and, upon finding the innkeeper, obtained the use of a private parlor.

The room he was escorted to was cozy, the ceiling so low that he was in danger of banging his head on the broad beams. A welcoming fire crackled in the grate and several well-stuffed chairs sat nearby, while a small table with two chairs were tucked beside a window that overlooked the inn yard.

Robert was glad to strip off his coat and gloves and warm himself by the fire. The innkeeper further endeared himself by producing a decanter of very tolerable brandy, which Robert enjoyed as he awaited his valet's arrival.

He sipped the amber liquid, savoring its warmth, and wondered how Moira was faring. She would be angry that he'd left her behind, but he'd had no choice.

I have a daughter. The thought rang through him.

His entire life had changed since he'd found out. Yet he didn't feel different; he didn't feel like a father. While he was worried about the child, it was more because of her innocence than the fact that she was his.

Was that normal? He sighed and took another sip of brandy. *I don't know what a father should feel. Damn Moira for keeping this from me. I deserved to know.*

Yet he couldn't entirely blame her. Their relationship had been based on lies. She'd been living in London, pretending to be the daughter of a Russian prince. She was very, very good and few people had realized her deception. She'd become the darling of society, welcomed into the homes of the wealthiest and most powerful.

Before long, someone in the Home Office had noticed a slow leak of financial information. After some research, they'd realized that the Russian princess was neither Russian nor a princess, and Robert was sent to investigate by pretending to become one of her admirers.

He had expected to be unimpressed with such a sham. But what he'd found was an amazingly beautiful and intelligent woman who was as charming as she was false. But beneath that falseness, he sensed something else—an almost desperate vulnerability. Who was she? Who was she working for? And how was she able to fool so many people?

The more he'd attempted to learn, the deeper he'd become involved. There was a spark between them from their first meeting and eventually they'd succumbed to it.

Robert now admitted that the attraction had been growing into something more, which was why he'd been so furious when she'd disappeared. He'd foolishly hoped that she would begin to trust him, and tell him the truth about herself and her past. Instead, she'd arranged their sham marriage and then disappeared without a word, taking with her important documents she'd stolen from a high-ranking government official.

The Home Office had demanded an explanation, and Robert hadn't had one. He'd been too involved in trying to discover who the real Moira MacAllister was, to notice her side activities. Furious at being made a fool of, he'd set out to find her, using all of his resources. After days of near misses, he'd finally caught up with her at a small inn by the docks in Dover. There, her defiant attitude and seeming unconcern had infuriated him even more. He'd reclaimed the stolen papers and, to prove that she meant nothing to him, had left her in the care of another man from the Home Office to deliver her to face charges.

An hour later, the agent had been thoroughly bamboozled and locked in a closet, and Moira was gone.

Robert had never stopped looking for her. As the years progressed, he'd convinced himself that it was just professional pride and curiosity about her motives in tricking him in such a way that drove him on, but now he had to face a few facts about himself—none of which were pleasant. His anger with Moira had nothing to do with his job with the Home Office, and everything to do with the growing feelings he'd had for her when she'd left.

Discovering now that she'd been carrying his child when she'd left, and that she hadn't bothered to tell him, added to his fury and confusion.

After I get my hands on that damned box and settle the issue with Aniston, she and I are due for a long, long talk.

He settled deeper in his chair, wishing he hadn't had to leave her at the squire's. No doubt she thought to set out after him, which was why he'd not only taken all of the horses, but also gone through her clothing and portmanteau to make certain she had no funds to hire a carriage.

"Let her feel the sting of being left behind for once," he murmured, sipping the brandy. It served her right.

A coach pulled up outside, the traces rattling.

Robert stood and crossed to the window, glad to see it was Buffon's. Robert's luggage—two large trunks and a number of smaller cases—was strapped to the top, so that it was almost as tall as it was long.

Stewart approached as the coach came to a stop and immediately engaged the valet in an energetic discussion. As Robert watched them, a rider on a large bay trotted into the inn yard, garnering no more than a passing glance from the arguing servants. The man guided his horse around the coach toward the stable.

As the gentleman pulled his horse to a halt he turned his head, his profile in stark relief against the dark stable door.

"Damn it!" Robert slammed his glass onto the table, the brandy sloshing out as he stalked out of the parlor.

CHAPTER II

A diary entry from Michael Hurst the day he discovered the first onyx box.

I wasn't impressed with the onyx box itself when I purchased it, for it was the parchment inside that excited me: a rare reference to the Hurst Amulet. I thought the parchment the true treasure, as there are dozens of such boxes and neither the piece nor its age were particularly notable.

But this morning, after I placed the parchment in a safe location, I prepared to toss the box into a crate to be sent back to England to be sold, and something caught my eye. One side seemed a little thicker than the others. To my surprise, it opened and revealed—I cannot trust myself to write it here, but I think I now know why I've been unable to find that damned amulet here in Egypt.

Someone removed it long, long ago.

*M*oira wearily contemplated dismounting her horse, her legs trembling with fatigue. Her escape had been flawless; no one had seen her and she'd quickly caught up to Buffon's coach, which had led her here.

But other errors had been made. First, she was much weaker than she realized, which had become apparent as the hours passed.

Second, she'd assumed that Robert's valet, being of such a prim and precise nature, would travel timidly. But either he had the constitution of a workhorse, or his commitment to his employer's appearance was fanatical, for Buffon had only stopped when forced by the needs of the horses. Which had left Moira riding much longer than she'd expected.

She patted her horse's neck. "No doubt you're as tired as I am, aren't you, girl?" The mare whickered softly. "Well, there's no rest until this saddle is off, is there?"

Gathering herself, Moira swung out of the saddle. As her boots hit the cobbled yard, she knew she'd made a mistake. Her knees buckled instantly, and if she hadn't been holding on to the saddle she'd have fallen to her knees.

She set her teeth and forced her weak legs upright. They locked in place like a tin soldier's; only by leaning against her mount was she able to stand.

Behind her, she could hear the altercation between Robert's valet and a groom. Thankful for the diversion, Moira rested her forehead against her horse's neck. "Now what do I do?" If she tried to walk, she feared she might fall. But she couldn't stay here much longer; someone was bound to see her, and while her costume was good enough to stave off instant recognition, it wouldn't withstand close scrutiny.

She'd just have to grit her teeth and try to make it to the stables. Once there, she could find a place to rest away from prying eyes.

She took a deep breath, pushed away from the horse and took its reins, trying to ignore her trembling legs. "Ready?" she asked the mare. "Let's go."

She managed three steps before her knees buckled again, pitching her forward. Moira threw out her hands to catch herself, but strong arms swept her from the air, and she was tossed over a shoulder like a sack of grain.

Moira knew it was Robert the second she settled against his broad back, his arm around her thighs as he walked easily toward the inn. "Stewart," Robert called as he walked past his astounded groom, "take care of the lady's horse."

The groom, a small, wizened man with an oddly shaped figure blinked. "Lady?"

Buffon, a tall, well-favored man and considerably younger than she'd expected, looked down at the groom with disdain and said with a heavy French accent, "*Oui*, it is a lady. Can you not see? Ah, but all you see are the trousers and not the shape, eh?" He flipped a dismissive hand toward the red-faced groom. "Pah, you English who cannot tell the difference between a man and a woman. I wonder that you manage to have children."

As Robert carried her into the inn, the innkeeper stared in amazement.

"What a surprise," Robert said smoothly. "It appears that my wife has come to visit."

"But I—" Moira began.

Robert slapped her bottom. "She was supposed to stay put at the home of our acquaintance. She can stay in my room; there's no need to prepare another."

The innkeeper, clearly sensing more largesse, nodded. "Yes, sir! I put ye in room number two, at the end of the hall at the top o' the stairs."

"Good. We'll wait in the parlor until then. My wife has recently been ill, and she's still not strong. If you've some gruel and some bread, that would be most welcome."

"Robert, no!" Moira protested. She lifted her head to tell the innkeeper, "I dislike gruel and would rather have something else. Do you have—"

"She'll have gruel." With that pronouncement, Robert went into the small parlor. Ducking the beams, he carried her to the fireplace and unceremoniously dumped her into a chair.

Seeing his grim expression, she said, "You shouldn't have left me."

The words sounded sulky, but she didn't care. She was so tired, her back and legs afire, and now Robert had just ignominiously scooped her up and paraded her before the entire population of the inn.

"Idiot. You're so tired you can barely sit upright." He went to a small table and picked up a glass and brought it to her. "Here. Drink this."

"It's not more of your tonic, is it?"

"No, it's brandy."

She took the glass and, by dint of supporting her

wrist with her other hand, managed to sip it without trembling too badly. The first sip warmed her, the second smoothed her tattered nerves, and the third sip made her lean back in the chair and sigh. "Thank you." Some of her tiredness seemed to melt away.

"You're welcome." He plucked her hat off and tossed it aside. "Now I can see your eyes." He took the chair opposite hers, his dark blue gaze hard. "You're a fool to have come all this way. Less than a week ago a fever nearly killed you."

"Robert, this isn't your fight; it's mine. I will do whatever I must to get that box, and my daughter, sick or not."

"She's *my* daughter, too."

Moira rested her head against the tall back of the chair. "This is too important for us to argue over. I came here to you, because I think we'll do better if we work together."

"I can get the box without your help. I've already made arrangements through Ross's Edinburgh agent to purchase it."

"As did I," she replied. "Before I left town."

Robert paused. "Mr. Gulliver?"

"At number four High Street. A rather unctuous man with a tendency to sneeze."

Robert muttered a curse. "That arse sold the box to both of us!"

"Yes." She took another sip of the brandy. "Did you ever wonder why Ross, who isn't well known in the world of antiquities, possesses such a unique item?"

Robert shrugged. "I assumed he'd somehow recognized its value."

"No. He purchased it because it is easy to reproduce."

"Ah, he sells copies."

"Yes. I recognized Mr. Gulliver, though he didn't know me, since I was veiled. He used to go by the name of Comte Constanti. Before that, he was a well-known forger of Greek statuary."

"Bloody hell. You knew this when I caught up to you in Edinburgh. Why didn't you tell me this before?"

"Because you *left* me at the squire's before we could discuss it." She placed the empty glass at the table by her elbow, glad that her trembling had stopped. "If you had taken me with you, I'd have shared my information."

"I was coming back to get you."

"*After* you'd retrieved the wrong box." She lifted her brows and waited.

Robert regarded her for a long moment. "I suppose you think I owe you an apology."

"Several."

"A pity. You're not going to get a single one. You were ill and still aren't well enough to travel."

"Nonsense. I'm tired, but only because your valet apparently feels he is very important to your comfort and he pushed the coachmen the entire way. I rode almost nonstop, and I didn't expect that."

Robert sighed. "Buffon thinks I can't pull a shirt on without his assistance."

A soft knock preceded the innkeeper's wife, who brought in a small tray with a bowl of gruel and a glass of milk. When she caught sight of Moira wearing trousers, she gasped.

Robert smoothly cut in. "My wife's love of a good joke sometimes betrays her sense of decorum."

"I see," the woman said primly. She set the tray before Moira and said in a disapproving voice, "There, miss, some gruel fer ye."

Moira looked at the thin, watery gray gruel and tried not to curl her nose. "That's very kind. This will serve as a beginning. Do you have anything else to eat in the kitchen?"

The woman looked surprised. "Och, o' course we do. We've a braised goose, some hard cheese, a bit o' haggis, and—"

"The gruel will be enough for my wife,"

Robert broke in. "I'll have some of the goose, please."

"Actually, no goose," Moira countered. "My husband's stomach is a bit off, but fortunately he *loves* good haggis. And I've heard yours is excellent."

"So I think, madam. I make it meself, and I add cracked pepper, too." Her chin firmed. "Me husband's mither says I have too heavy a hand wi' th' pepper mill, but I use th' recipe from me beloved mither, and 'tis a guid recipe."

Moira said in a warm voice, "I'm sure it's quite tasty. We'll have that, of course."

The woman beamed. "Then ye'll see fer yeself. Will there be anythin' else?"

"No, thank you. I'm sure the haggis will be more than enough."

Robert turned to countermand her order, but the innkeeper's wife was already out the door. "Blast it! Now I'll be stuck with that damned haggis."

Moira's gurgling laugh caught him unaware. He'd been shocked to see her in the courtyard, and even more so when she'd collapsed before him. He should have known she wouldn't stay at the squire's house, damn it. Even when choices weren't available, Moira made them.

Robert watched her now, noting that the

corner of a bandage peeked from under her braid at her temple, a bit of a bruise showing at the edge. "How's that hard head of yours?"

She made a face. "I had the devil of a headache this morning, but it's better now."

He didn't believe a word she said, for though her color was better, there were delicate blue circles below her eyes, and the tension in her shoulders told him she was still in pain. "You look tired. You will go to bed as soon as we've had our delicious haggis."

"We? I'm going to eat this miraculously healing gruel." She lifted the bowl, put a spoonful in her mouth, and grimaced. "That is horrid."

"If you don't eat the gruel, then you have to eat the haggis. I won't have you going to bed without some food."

She replaced the gruel on the tray. "I'd rather have haggis. I couldn't help requesting it; you should have seen your face when she mentioned it." Moira chuckled.

Robert gave her a reluctant smile. "I shall eat it."

"As will I." She regarded him from under her lashes. "I wonder which of us will manage to eat the most?"

"Is that a challenge?"

"Of course."

Heat stirred in him at her challenge. "And the winner of this haggis-eating contest will get what?"

"Oh, I don't know . . . What do you suggest?"

He shrugged, though his body had an immediate answer. He wanted more of *her*. More of her caresses, more of her silken hair beneath his fingers, more of her body in his bed. "Bragging rights will be enough."

"Fine, then. We'll see who can stomach the most for bragging rights *and* for the thicker blanket in the coach tomorrow."

His smile disappeared. "You will not be accompanying me tomorrow."

"Of course I will. Why else do you think I traveled this distance?"

"Moira, no. You're still injured—"

"I rode for hours and suffered no ill effects."

"I had to carry you from your mount."

Her cheeks pinkened. "My legs were stiff, that's all. If I'd traveled by coach with you as *should* have happened, I wouldn't be exhausted right now. A good night's sleep, and I'll be as strong as ever."

"I'm not taking you with me, and that's that."

Her hands fisted on her knees, her green eyes sparkling. "Robert, have you forgotten that my daughter is in the hands of a madman?"

"That's my daughter, too," he said sharply.

"You don't even know her. Don't try to tell me that you care about her, for I won't believe it."

Robert muttered a curse. "That does not alleviate my responsibility, which I take very seriously. From the moment I became aware that Rowena was my child, she became my concern, like it or not."

"That's so generous of you." Moira's voice was laced with sarcasm.

"It's all I have," he said quietly. "I'm being honest, Moira. You can't ask for more." He could see her struggling to understand.

"You admit you have no feelings for her, yet you still wish to help gain her release. I don't understand how you can feel one, but not the other."

"She's my family," he said simply.

"So?"

He saw the puzzlement in Moira's eyes. *How could she not understand that— Ah. Once again, I realize how little I know her.* "Do you have a family?"

Her expression closed, and she shrugged carelessly. "Doesn't everyone?"

"You didn't answer my question. We've never really discussed our pasts."

She leaned back in her chair, looking wilted and too tired to argue. Her exhaustion could work in his favor. "Tell me about your family, Moira."

"You first," she said, her expression showing her reluctance.

If that was what it took, then he'd do it. "I was raised in an old vicarage called Wythburn. Father is retired, so now he and Mother spend their time traveling and writing very, very long letters full of advice."

Moira's lips twitched. "They sound lovely."

"They are. In addition to them, I have three sisters and two brothers. All of my sisters are married, and I like their husbands well enough. One of my brothers recently married, which leaves only Michael unwed. I don't think he'll ever marry; he's too enamored of his wandering lifestyle."

She eyed him thoughtfully. "I can't imagine you as the son of a vicar."

"Father instilled in us all a love of reading and letters, which has kept us connected though we live far apart."

"You always seemed close to your siblings."

Is that envy I hear? Interesting. "We lived in the country, and there weren't many other children around, so we spent a lot of time in each other's company."

"Were you bored?"

"Not at all. We made up plays, became champion cricket players, had races, and swam in the lake. We were very close, especially since we had to band together to protect ourselves from Father."

Her eyes widened. "Was he mean?"

"No. Worse. He is an expert at making one feel guilty."

Her brow creased. "I don't understand. Is that bad?"

"Oh, yes, there is nothing worse. Father forced us to discuss literature at the dinner table, and if we hadn't read his latest 'suggested' reading—" Robert shuddered.

Moira chuckled. "It couldn't be as bad as all that."

"Oh, it was. He's a scholar, so our dinners were rife with discussions of the *Iliad* and *Odyssey* rather than hunting and horses, which would have been my preference."

"You couldn't change the topic?"

"And disappoint Father? *No one* could look as sad as he could. And he was such a good person that you felt horrid for causing even one sad frown."

Her eyes twinkled. "I would wager ten quid that you still managed to hold your own."

He smiled. "You would win that wager. Much to the disgust of my siblings, I worked hard to match my father's scholarship. I curried his favor more than any of them."

"Though you didn't love it?"

"Not at first; it was a childish ploy for approval. But now I'm glad I did it. I find myself still reading those classics, admiring them in new ways. So my father's evil plan worked—he bred an army of scholars, for we're all bookish—even William, the sea captain."

She lifted her brows. "That's a bit dismissive. It takes a lot of knowledge to sail a ship. You must read charts, understand astronomy, decipher the weather—most of the sea captains I've known are extremely capable."

"I didn't mean to be disparaging. It's my brother's chosen field, so it's my job to mock it."

She chuckled. "And does he do the same for you?"

"When he's not calling me a 'fop' and a 'lace-edged puffin,' he is quite capable of pulling out a few well-chosen insults, some of them from the bard himself."

"That will be most useful, since he's now married to an actress. I once saw Miss Beauchamp perform. She is a remarkable actress."

"She is, and my brother supports her desire to remain on the stage."

"He must be very sure of her, for I cannot imagine a career more fraught with illicit invitations."

"Other than ours? A false princess and a spy?"

She nodded, a shadow crossing her face. "You can get lost, pretending to be someone you're not."

"Very true." He watched her for a moment. "Now that I've bared my soul, tell me about your family."

Her lashes lowered as she regarded her riding boots. "There's not much to tell. My mother was a mill worker and had me when she was only fifteen. Supposedly, my father was the mill owner's son. He swore that he'd never touched my mother, though she bore the proof. When my mother's parents found out she was with child, they threw her out of their house and pretended she'd never been born."

"Families should stand by one another, through difficulties and triumphs."

She tilted her head, her expression grave. "Is that what your family would have done?"

"Yes."

"I would never abandon Rowena in such a way, no matter the circumstances. I don't think my mother would have, either. I don't remember much about her, as she died before I turned five. After that, I lived in an orphanage until I was ten."

"And?"

"One day, a very tall and elegantly dressed

woman came to the workhouse where we spent our days—"

"Workhouse?" His jaw tightened. He knew something of workhouses, of the brutal treatment that children, especially orphans, received in those places.

"Yes, I worked a loom with two other girls. This woman looked at all of us, as if selecting a horse. When she saw me, she stopped and said, 'This is the one.' I was told to pack my few belongings, that I was going 'home.'"

"Who was the woman?"

"Her name was Talaitha Tigani and she was a gypsy."

"Out of the frying pan and into the fire."

"No. Her daughter had died at an early age, drowned in a pond. Aunt Talaitha missed having a daughter, so after a few years she picked one. Me."

"So you became the daughter of a gypsy. It must have been an exciting life, especially after working a loom for hours every day," Robert said thoughtfully. "That explains why four walls aren't enough to hold you."

Moira smiled. "Talaitha taught me everything she knew: how to pick pockets, open locked doors, make charms—"

"And make people believe you were whomever you wished to be."

"Yes. Especially that."

It explained so much. "And so you became a Princess Caraboo." He smiled at the outrage on Moira's face. Princess Caraboo's real name was Mary Baker. Several years ago she had appeared on the steps of the house of a magistrate. Because she wore a turban, seemed unable to communicate except in an unrecognized language, and behaved in a number of bizarre ways, it was decided that she was a lost foreigner. People came from miles around, attempting to decipher the mystery.

A jackanapes eager to get involved in the mystery pretended to understand her "language" and interpreted her tale. He told her compassionate hosts that she was a kidnapped princess, stolen away from her homeland by pirates, and that she had escaped their ship and swum to shore. The romantic story made the unknown woman into "Princess Caraboo," and she was feted until a newspaper ran her story and her description was recognized by several people who knew the real Mary Baker. Caught in her lie, Mary confessed to all. It was a huge embarrassment for her hosts, and she was banished to America.

"Princess Caraboo was an amateur, pretending

to be from some made-up country," Moira scoffed. "*I* convinced the Russian ambassador that I was a princess from his own country."

"Thank goodness they have so many."

"That was a boon. He kept asking for specifics, and I had to put him off repeatedly. Meanwhile more and more members of the *ton* began to receive me. Eventually it became easier for him to believe the deception, too."

"You were accepted everywhere, even by the prince."

"People see foreign royals as exotic and exciting, so I was giving them something they wanted. As I speak very good Russian, it was relatively easy. I was invited everywhere, to elaborate dinners and luncheons, and modistes all along Bond Street begged me to use their services without charge."

"That rapacious lot gave away their services for free?"

"They profited from their gifts, as it brought them more business."

"Ah, of course. They could announce that they were *the* modiste dressing the beautiful Princess Alexandria."

"And then raise their prices accordingly." She smiled. "It was fun and exciting, while it lasted."

"You were very convincing. You must have traveled extensively to have managed that."

"Aunt Talaitha and I traveled all over Europe, especially Russia, where she has many friends. She was determined I should be accomplished; she taught me Greek and Latin, history, philosophy, even some mathematics. She said a brain was all we had between us and starvation, so it was important to feed the brain first."

"She sounds like a remarkable woman."

"She was. Very much so."

He caught the sadness in Moira's eyes. "She is gone?"

"Two years ago. She came to live with me when I had Rowena. The Scottish winters were too damp for her and—" A noise out in the hall caught her attention. "I believe our haggis is arriving."

Within seconds, the clattering in the hallway turned into the innkeeper's wife and her daughter, a plump young miss. Robert tried to hide his impatience, but when he caught Moira's unguarded expression, he realized it was for the best. Though he was fascinated to finally meet the real Moira MacAllister, she needed food and sleep.

After the women had deposited their platters and utensils, the innkeeper's wife beckoned them to the table. "That's a lovely sight, if I say so meself. There's yer haggis with tatties and neet, in a malt whiskey sauce. If'n ye need anything else, ye've but to ask."

With that, they left Robert and Moira alone.

He went to the table and pulled out a chair for her. "Shall we?"

Moira stood, and though she still wasn't steady on her feet, she appeared stronger for having rested. As she walked toward him, he had a new appreciation for her outfit. To fool people into believing her a male, she'd bound her chest and then dressed in the French fashion of an exaggerated collar, bunched trousers, and wide coattail, which was a perfect way to hide a female form. Her hair, wrapped about her head in a thick braid easily hidden by a hat, was close to its natural red. Another good wash and the dye would disappear completely.

He held her chair and then took the seat opposite, saying in an aggrieved tone, "You had to ask for haggis."

Feeling comforted by the intimacy of the small parlor, Moira chuckled. "Afraid?"

He sent her a flat look and ate a piece of haggis.

His face flushed, and a faint sheen appeared on his forehead. She eyed her own plate with misgiving and poked at the haggis with her fork. The grayish blob, already removed from the stomach in which it had been cooked, crumbled apart, and a spicy odor like sausage lifted from it. *Pretend it is sausage,* she told herself.

She took a forkful, closed her eyes, and put it in her mouth.

A moment later, she was gasping and reaching for her glass of water. "The pepper!" she said when she could finally speak, her voice cracking in protest.

Robert nodded in sympathy. "My brother-in-law Alexander MacLean takes great delight in forcing me to eat all sorts of Scottish foods, though he knows that my grandmother is more Scottish than he. I've had all sorts of haggis, which comes in an amazing variety, some much stronger than others, which is why I rarely ask for it. But this one . . . I've never seen so much pepper in a haggis."

"I should have ordered the goose."

He looked at his plate. "I'm glad I didn't serve myself a generous portion."

She had to laugh and managed another bite, glad to find that the roasted potatoes were more to her liking. She confined herself to that side of her plate. All in all, it was a filling meal, made pleasant by the warm fire and Robert, who kept up a steady

stream of conversation, telling stories about growing up in the old vicarage.

She could almost see it nestled among the trees
and hear the laughter of children as they played
pranks and tried to stay out of trouble with their
overly sensitive father.

It made her think about the quiet life she'd lived
with Rowena the last five years, tucked away in a
remote village. Their small cottage was surrounded
by a low stone wall, far away from the crazed madness that had once been Moira's life. She'd thought
the isolation was a good thing, but hearing Robert's tales of his adventures with his brothers and
sisters, she wondered if she'd overprotected Rowena. *When I have her back, I'll make sure I'm preparing her
for the real world.*

Robert embarked on a story about his twin sisters, Triona and Caitlyn, and how they'd attempted
to use the barn loft as a place to escape their trou-
blesome brothers, only to fall through the hay trap
just as their older brother, William, was romancing
a milkmaid.

Across the table, Robert watched Moira
chuckle sleepily. She was so tired, yet refused to
admit it. *She's such a stubborn woman. Why do I find that
so appealing?*

He softened his voice as he told childhood tales,

speaking slower and in a more soothing tone, willing her to relax, to rest.

Within a few minutes her eyes began to flutter, and soon her head tilted down, sleep finally claiming her.

He smiled, proud of his efforts. *My sisters are just as stubborn. Perhaps that's why I like Moira so much.*

Her fork slipped from her fingers, and he caught it before it hit the table. He quietly set the fork beside her plate, then lifted her into his arms and carried her to their bedchamber.

CHAPTER 12

A letter to Robert Hurst from his brother Michael, after finding a mention of the lost Hurst Amulet in an ancient inventory list for the household of Queen Elizabeth.

What I know thus far about the Hurst Amulet fascinates me, and makes my resolve to find it even firmer. The origins of the amulet are still a mystery. Our Mam would have the amulet steeped with the magic of fairies, embellished with a curse or two, and stolen from a white witch, but I'm long past the age of believing in something I can neither see nor touch.

Still, it is interesting to note how many people—some of them very powerful—have had the amulet in their possession, only to quickly give it away, as if it had burned their fingers. It is odd and does make one think.

*M*oira awoke slowly to sunlight streaming across the bed and warming her shoulders. She moved over to savor more of the warmth and found that the entire side of the bed was warm, even where there was no light. She lifted up on her elbow and noted an indention on the mattress. *Robert.*

She looked about the room, trying to collect her thoughts. *The inn. Dinner with Robert. And . . .* Nothing else came to mind.

She didn't remember arriving in her bedchamber, undressing to her chemise, or even climbing into bed.

I didn't drink that much brandy. Did I fall asleep?

She must have; there was no other explanation. She rested her head on her hand as she looked at the pillow beside hers. It gave her a pang to realize that he'd been so close and she'd been oblivious. She'd been waking to an empty bed for so long, it felt odd to share one. Of course, in her own house, sometimes Rowena would come running into her room in the mornings. Moira could see her daughter's excited face as she raced into the room and begged to be lifted into the bed.

Moira cleared her suddenly clogged throat. Where was Rowena now? An instant image of her daughter sleeping, her long dark lashes on the crest of her cheeks, filled Moira's mind. She crossed her arms and imagined Rowena there, snuggled against her, her dear little heart beating against Moira's. Tears rose, and Moira bit her lip to keep from crying.

No crying. Just get the box. Then, when you have her back, you will make Aniston pay. Focus on that and nothing else.

After a few moments the tears subsided, though the weight of them still pressed behind her eyes. She would never grow used to being away from Rowena. Her fury at Aniston carried her on whenever despair threatened.

Her jaw set, she shoved herself upright, her braid swinging forward.

The sound of horses clopping into the inn yard made her twist toward the window, the covers falling away and the air cool against her short chemise. She climbed from the bed and went to the window. Robert's groom and another man were harnessing the team. *Damn it, Robert! You will not leave without me!*

She reached for her clothes, then paused. She needed the saddlebags from her horse, where she'd packed two gowns and a comb. Though the gown would be horridly wrinkled, it would be better for travel than the men's clothing she'd worn yesterday. She took the lace-edged shirt and tugged it on, buttoning it at the neck. Perhaps she could call the maid to fetch the saddlebags and—

A knock sounded on her door. *Ah, the maid! Perhaps she brought breakfast, too. I can take something with me—* Moira opened the door, standing behind it as she buttoned her shirt. "Please send someone to fetch my saddle—"

Her saddlebags thunked onto the floor in front of her and the door was pushed closed.

Moira blinked up at Robert, who was already shaved and dressed. He looked so like his usual calm, cool self, dressed in the height of fashion, that she had to stem a flicker of frustration.

"Good morning," he said, his gaze flickering over her. "I like that shirt."

Her face blazed and she hurried to carry the saddlebags to the bed, where she opened one and pulled out a neatly wrapped brown package. "I saw the horses being hitched and thought you meant to leave."

"I am sending my men on an errand. I thought

the mail coach stopped here, but it doesn't come this far north, so my men are going off to meet up with it."

"The mail coach? Why?"

"That was Aniston's coach you were traveling in, so I knew the servants were his. I won't have them spying on us. Yesterday, Leeds and Stewart and I convinced Aniston's men that they were no longer needed and I'm sending them all back to him."

She couldn't fault Robert's logic. "I wish I could see Aniston's reaction when they return."

Robert's blue eyes gleamed. "So do I. Meanwhile, I brought your clothing and ordered you a bath." His gaze flickered to her hair. "The innkeeper said it would take an hour for the water to be brought, so you've time to eat breakfast, should you wish."

"Thank you." She undid the ribbon that tied the brown paper package together. "I didn't mean to sleep so late."

"You needed it, but I'm glad you're up now. We've much to do before we chase down this onyx box."

His smile warmed her, and she could think of nothing coherent to say. She didn't want to examine too closely her happiness at having Robert with her for this task.

She turned her attention to the package. A moment later, she shook out the folds of a round gown of pale green muslin trimmed in darker green silk ribbons. "I'll need to send for my trunks and—" She paused when his smile widened. "You already did that, too?"

"I sent a man at dawn. He is to fetch your trunks from the squire's and rush them to us at Balnagown Castle. He should arrive shortly after we do."

"You've thought of everything."

"I try. I trust you have everything in your trunks that you need for this expedition?"

"Yes." She peeped up at him. "We'll be good partners." Satisfaction filled her words.

"We shall see." He settled into the chair by the fireplace. Robert couldn't help admiring the sight of Moira in just a chemise and the white shirt. When she crossed to the washstand the sun lit her from behind, and for a startling instant her long, graceful legs were perfectly silhouetted before she crossed into the shadow and the white material became opaque once more.

Damn. Robert shifted uncomfortably in the chair. Though Moira had slept through the night, he hadn't. He'd been agonizingly aware of the warm curves pressed against his back—a back he'd turned to prevent his traitorous body from reacting even more than it had.

Though he could have asked for another room, he'd wished to make certain she was well—or so he'd told himself. The truth was that he'd wanted to feel her body against his once again, even if it was just his back pressed to hers.

She reached up to undo the shirt, pausing when she caught his gaze.

He waved a hand. "Pray don't let me stop you. I wish to discuss our plans once we arrive at Balnagown."

Her cheeks warmed. "Of course." She tugged the shirt over her head and tossed it to the floor.

The fine lawn chemise offered very little in the way of modesty. The thin material clung to every slope and curve, hugging her skin like a lover's hands, hinting at the shadows that lay beneath.

His body ached with a new flush of desire, and he glanced at the beckoning bed. *Don't think of that now,* he told himself sternly, but his cock was already hard and ready.

She spread the gown over a chair by the bed and pulled more items from the saddlebags—a silver comb, a packet of hairpins, and some stockings. "I have a plan to get the real box, not the fake one Ross is likely to try to foist on us."

"Oh?"

"Yes, but it will be much easier with help. Before I left Edinburgh, I asked about Ross from several people who knew him well and I found out some very interesting things."

"Such as?"

"For one, he enjoys pursuing married women."

Robert's gaze locked on her. "I didn't know that."

"He's been in two duels, both over married women. I think he collects them like he collects objects d'art."

"Interesting."

"It's his weakness. If we go to see him together and I present myself as your devoted wife, it will offer him a challenge—one I will make certain he can't resist."

"You will distract him while I search for the real onyx box."

"You're better able to recognize it. That was the one weakness of my plan: I wasn't certain I'd be able to tell the real onyx box from a well-executed fake."

He had to admit that it was a damn good plan. "Why do you believe that Ross keeps the original box in his castle?"

"For two reasons. First of all, because his

weakness is coveting what other people want. He's the sort to savor his triumphs, tiny though they may be, so he'd want it nearby to look at."

That made sense. "And the other reason?"

"He has bragged about his private collection to friends and acquaintances. He's even told people that he has his collection hidden in the castle, somewhere very secret. I think he has a vault somewhere, or a hidden room."

Robert was impressed. She had done an excellent job gathering important information. *It's a pity she doesn't work for the Home Office. They could use someone with her skills.* "You've convinced me. We'll fetch the box, leave Ross behind, and return to Edinburgh."

She beamed at him. "Working together, there's no possible way we can fail." She began to unbraid her hair. "Once we have the box, we can secure Rowena's freedom."

"I'll be damned if I calmly hand anything over to Aniston."

"Do not underestimate him," she returned sharply. "He is cruel. Cold. Calculating. He *likes* to inflict pain. Rowena's—" Her voice broke, but after a deep breath she continued, her eyes sparkling with tears. "I can't risk her safety."

"You really believe he'll injure her?"

"The only reason he hasn't harmed her yet is

that he knows that without her, he has no control over me."

The thought chilled Robert's heart. There were certain people who could kill without remorse. Some killed for sport, or for even less reason—it took little or nothing to lead them to it.

And such a man had his daughter—a daughter he'd never had the chance to meet or know. A knot formed in his throat: anger for what was, sadness for what had never been.

He realized Moira was watching him. "I will do nothing to harm our daughter," he said shortly.

She met his gaze for a long moment, then nodded. "I know." She sat on the edge of the bed and began to thread her fingers through her hair, untangling the thick strands.

Robert was mesmerized by the sight of her delicate white fingers sliding through her long tresses. Once she had unbraided it, she picked up the silver comb and began to run it through her hair. She caught his gaze and smiled. "You used to tease me about having silver combs. Do you remember?"

He remembered that and much more. He remembered her long legs, wrapped tightly about his hips. He remembered the lavender scent of her skin as he trailed his lips over her. He especially remembered how easy she was to arouse, and how he'd taken such pleasure in making her gasp for breath.

But all he said was, "You and I enjoy the finer things in life."

Her gaze flickered over him, approval in her gaze. "We do have that in common."

"I remember other things we had in common. More . . . interesting things."

Her thick lashes lowered over her eyes. "Perhaps."

"You pretended many things back then, but not that."

Her lips curved in a smile. "I found the physical aspects quite pleasing. I recall very clearly that you were very well"—her gaze flickered over him— "equipped for the part."

He almost grinned in return. Almost.

But for Moira, it was enough. She'd always felt a deep rapport with him, and that same understanding settled around them now, familiar, yet this time more fraught with tension.

There was so much between them, so much history and so much hurt, that though they could find moments of peace and agreement, a shadow still lurked overhead. Moira finished combing her hair, wishing things were easier somehow.

Robert's chair creaked as he stood. "If we're to

become partners in this, then I have a requirement of you." He came to stand beside her, and she was instantly aware of her lack of clothing and of the warmth emanating from him. He always seemed to simmer, his skin always warm, his gaze flickering from cool to hot with nothing more than a touch.

And oh, how she'd loved to touch him, to run her hands over his broad bare shoulders, the hard planes of his chest and stomach, and farther. The feeling was so powerful that she had to clear her throat before she could ask, "What requirement is that?"

"If we do this together, then I am the one who makes the final decisions. An army with two generals is bound to fail."

Right now, if he would only touch her, and ease the ache that was growing inside her with every second he stood so close, she would have agreed to anything . . .

Except that. "When I can, I'll do so, but—"

He placed a finger beneath her chin and lifted her face to his. "No 'buts.' Shall we seal our pact with a kiss?"

She saw the heat in his eyes, felt the hardness of his body. Though her mind said to resist, her body ignored the warning. She lifted on her toes to press her mouth to his.

That was all it took—the touch of his lips set
her aflame, unable and unwilling to pull back. She
wanted this, wanted him, *needed* to feel him. She'd
been alone so long, struggling against so much, that
it was heaven to just *feel*.

The second Moira's lips touched his, Robert
decided to have her then and there. He'd wanted
this since he'd found her naked in a copper tub by
the fire. Feeling her soft curves now, running his
hands over her, he regretted that he'd waited so
long.

He untied her chemise without breaking their
kiss, pulling back to tug it over her head, her hair
spilling back to her shoulders in a swath of silken
strands. She was so beautiful that it almost hurt to
see her.

She undid the button on his waistcoat and
tugged his shirttail from his trousers.

"Hold, *ma chère*." He sat down and tugged off his
boots, then stood.

She had his jacket off his shoulders in an instant. Laughing softly, he yanked off his cravat and
sent it sailing. The rest of his clothes soon followed.

Now naked, Robert slipped an arm about
Moira's waist and fell back upon the bed, taking
her with him. He captured her lips and kissed her

with abandon, delighting in her rapid breathing, flushed skin, and passion-darkened eyes. God, he loved being with a woman who enjoyed lovemaking. They had been apart for too long, and the fire between them burned too hotly for anything less than an explosive consummation.

She wriggled on him and murmured against his ear, "You feel so *good*."

"As do you." His hands roamed from her shoulders, down her back, to her waist, and then lower, cupping her against him.

She needed no more encouragement. She opened her legs, and he gasped at the intensity of the feeling as she slowly engulfed his turgid cock. She planted her hands on the mattress on either side of his head and moved urgently up and down, hot and slick.

Robert grabbed her waist, trying to slow her down. He wouldn't last much longer if she continued so. He lifted his hips slowly, and then planted himself deeply inside her.

She threw her head back with a gasp. Her fingers dug into his shoulders as she cried his name, succumbing to deep shudders of pleasure.

Sweat beaded Robert's forehead as he struggled for control, aching for release. When Moira slumped against him, he rolled atop of her, never breaking contact. Her legs locked behind the small of his back, and Robert began to move inside her, his gaze locked on her face. Her eyes were closed, ecstasy written on her lovely features as she moved with him, rocking her hips up to meet his thrusts. Her creamy skin was flushed, her lips swollen from his kisses. Every delicious inch of her belonged to *him*.

The intoxicating thought urged him on. Faster and faster he went, Moira's lips parting, her breath quickening. His heart thundered, his body damp as he drove into her again and again.

She suddenly arched under him, clutching his shoulders as she gasped his name, and Robert shuddered as a wave of heat tore through him. At the last second, he lifted himself free and rolled away as his passion spilled.

The mind-numbing pleasure left him gasping for breath. Moira lay on her back next to him, her palm on his chest. He realized one of his hands rested on her thigh, which quivered beneath his fingers.

Moira sighed deeply. "That was long overdue, my love."

"Yes."

They lay there as their breathing and their bodies slowly returned to normal. Robert couldn't think of a moment when he'd felt more sated. The sun warmed them pleasantly as the comforting sounds of dishes being set out in the common room below drifted into their room. Moira's lavender scent soothed him and he realized that if not for his concern for Rowena it would be easy to stay here and forget the world.

But there was no forgetting Rowena.

Moira evidently was thinking the same thing, for she rolled up on her elbow, her expression serious. "If we're to present the façade of a married couple to Ross, then this sort of thing is a good idea."

He laughed. "You're right." With a playful kiss on her nose, he rose to fetch one of the cloths on the washstand. He cleaned himself, then wet a clean cloth for her.

She thanked him while he went to pick up his clothes. "This cravat is ruined. Buffon will be devastated."

"I'm fairly certain my chemise will never be wearable again."

"Then we're even. My cravat for your chemise."

"So long as it's not your coat. I know how you prize them." She tossed the cloth to the washstand, then sat up and pulled the sheet over her.

"They *are* specially made and very expensive."

His eyes glinted with humor. "But if I had to make a choice between this and my best coats, the coats would lose."

"I'm glad to know I'm thought so highly of." Moira pushed her hair over her shoulder. "I would give up at least *two* chemises for this."

He chuckled and began to dress. "We always were good together in bed."

"Yes, we match well on that level." She pulled her knees up and clasped her arms about them, the sheet smooth over her skin.

He watched her every move, his gaze still heated.

Why, he's thinking about coming back to bed. She scooted to one side, surprised at the way her body, which still hummed with pleasure, readied at the thought.

A regretful look crossed his face as he picked up his trousers and pulled them on. "I wish I could spend the morning in bed, but the servants will bring your bath soon. I also have a few horses to sell before we leave."

"Oh?"

"I returned Aniston's men, but I kept his horses." Robert's smile glinted. "I hope he needs them badly." He pulled on his boots and then his coat.

She watched as he tossed the ruined cravat into a corner, then crossed to the wardrobe and removed his portmanteau to find another. His hair was mussed, his shirt open and loose, yet he still retained his air of fashion.

It is the way he carries himself, as if he doesn't give a damn what anyone thinks. There is no more powerful force than true unconcern.

He found a cravat and centered it about his neck, and then tied it with a few expert twists, securing it in place with a sapphire pin that matched his eyes. He tucked in his shirt, smoothed his waistcoat, and then ran his fingers through his dark hair.

She was a bit disgruntled that he could go from disheveled to perfection in such little time. It would take her several hours just to dry her hair.

He picked up his hat and opened the door. "I will return once I've seen to the sale of the horses. There's a farmer nearby who the innkeeper believes is looking for some good stock, so I shouldn't be long."

Moira leaned back against the pillows. "I shall enjoy my bath and then join you for lunch."

"Excellent." With a bow and a smoldering look at her, he was gone.

She listened to his booted feet go down the hall.

Soon after, his deep voice rang through the court-yard as he called to his groom.

Sighing, she snuggled into the pillows, her body aching pleasantly.

Tomorrow would bring new challenges, but at least she was no longer fighting this battle alone.

Chapter 13

Michael Hurst's diary, on hearing that his brother William is on his way.

I received word that William is to arrive within the month to secure my release. It's about bloody time. I've things to do, damn it!

While my lodgings are luxurious, I've been forced to endure the constant company of Miss Smythe-Haughton, which—because of my lack of female companionship—has caused me some discomfort.

Something rather odd happened last night. My assistant spent the afternoon in the harem, gathering information to help negotiate my release. Little did I know she was also using that time to learn the ways of the harem, including dressing in such a way that—well, I hardly know how to describe it.

I did not appreciate the way the sulfi began to look at her when she appeared so attired, and I now worry that more trouble is on the way. While the sulfi may allow *me* to go free once the box has been delivered, I'm not certain he'll do the same for Miss Smythe-Haughton.

The coach hit a rut in the muddy road and Moira winced as her knee banged against the edge of the opposite seat. "Ow! I hope we arrive soon."

Robert planted a foot against the seat Moira occupied to steady himself. "We're only a few miles from the inn where Ross said his agent would await me."

"Thank goodness. I'll be black and blue if the road gets any worse."

As if Stewart could hear her, the coach slowed and the rocking subsided.

Robert pushed back the leather curtain that covered the coach window. "The road is stone covered now and should be smoother." He peered into the distance and said with satisfaction, "We're beginning to climb, so we must be entering the mountains now."

Moira looked out the window, amazed at how the vista had changed over the last few hours.

Instead of heather-covered moors, purple mountains rose before them, fronted by deep, green valleys with sparkling blue lochs. The road looked like a ribbon, twisting around each curve as it climbed. "I've never been this far north. Have you?"

"No."

She nodded, lost in the beauty of the scenery. "It's a different world from Craigentinny."

He lifted a brow. "Is that your home?"

She shrugged and offered no more.

"That's hardly fair, seeing as how I've told you everything—including the time when I was stung by bees while trying to spy upon the neighbor's charming daughter."

She laughed.

"If I can tell you the most embarrassing of my childhood exploits for your merriment, the least you can do is share the mundane aspects of your own life."

Her lips twitched. "Fine. It's not very interesting, though. When I found out I was with child, I purchased a small cottage in Craigentinny. It's a pretty little hamlet an hour outside of Edinburgh."

"Why there?"

"It's close to where I was born, within a few miles of the mill my mother used to work at. It's the closest thing I had to home."

"I see."

"The cottage I purchased has only five rooms, but it's big enough for me and Rowena and a servant."

"It sounds snug."

A soft look crossed her face. "It is. Long ago, it was a hunting box for a local baron. There wasn't even a roof on it when I bought it, just stone walls. But with the help of some local artisans, it's now a very cozy little property."

Moira hadn't allowed herself to think about Claigsmore Cottage in the six months since Rowena had been stolen away; it hurt too much. But now, looking at the rolling land, it was hard not to think of her beloved home.

"I planted a small orchard behind the house. We've apple trees and a garden. Rowena is excited when it's time to harvest—" A crystal-clear image of Rowena holding up a large apple and laughing hit Moira like a punch. *What if I never see her again? What if we don't find the box? What if Aniston—*

She fought against the runaway thoughts, trying hard to recapture her control over her emotions.

Robert watched as her lashes lowered to hide her expression, and he knew instantly what had happened. His throat tightened. He didn't know what it was to love and then lose a child, but the expression on her face gave him a glimpse. "Moira, we will get her back. I swear it."

After a few more seconds, she gave a sharp nod. "I know we will." The words sounded like a challenge.

I need to give her something else to focus on. Robert crossed his arms and settled into his corner. "I do hope you're able to stay focused on our task, and won't be reduced to tears so often."

She stiffened. "I beg your pardon?"

"While I understand that you are upset, I hope it doesn't infringe upon our project. Having no partner is better than having a distracted one."

"I promise you that I will keep my emotions well in check. I usually do."

"Sometimes . . ." He let the word trail off. "I'm sure you do the best you can." He yawned. "I think I'll take a nap. You should do the same."

He could hear the anger in her silence. Her skirts rustled and she said in a flat voice, "I'm glad you can be so unconcerned that you can sleep."

He covered his mouth and yawned again. "Oh, I'll sleep well. Our little tryst this morning has left me a bit drained. I'm sure it made you feel the same."

Her cheeks pinkened, but she said in a stubborn tone, "Robert, we should discuss what we're going to do once we meet Ross's representative. If we wish to be a believable couple, then—"

"There's nothing to discuss. I'll tell them I'm there to fetch the box and that I brought my wife with me, which isn't unusual. Especially when they see that my wife is a beautiful, passionate redhead." He reached up to tweak his curtain closed, and then tipped his hat brim over his face. "It'll be as easy as that."

"But we must develop a history in case there are any questions."

"I don't plan on offering any details to Ross, so we don't need to discuss anything. I will do the talking, you will beam at me like a good wife, and all will be well."

Moira stiffened. "This is not how I define partnership."

"We're partners, just not equal ones. Someone has to be in charge, and I've been very clear that it will be me." He dropped his chin to his chest. "We only have a short while before we reach our destination. If you want a nap, you'd better take one now."

Moira glared at him. Did he really think she would sit back and allow him to boss her around? She'd thought she'd been very clear on that. "Robert, we have to—"

He snored. And not a real snore, either, but a pretend snore. His arms remained firmly crossed over his chest, his mouth—when not snoring—was closed, and even bore a faint smile.

Her brows lifted. He'd challenged her to give her something to think about other than Rowena. She didn't need his assistance in keeping her emotions under control; she did that very well on her own.

Her gaze narrowed at him. Yet for all of her irritation, she found herself admiring the cut of his jaw and the firm line of his mouth. A mouth that had recently driven her to distraction.

But she wasn't here to relive their interlude this morning. She glanced down at his riding boots, then placed one of her kid boots beside his large foot.

He didn't move, so she pressed her boot against the edge of his.

Robert shifted slightly, and slid his foot away.

Moira moved her foot against his again, and waited expectantly.

Nothing happened.

Well, that can be rectified. She lifted her foot over his and stomped.

"Ow!" He jerked upright and glared. "Blast you!"

"I wish to speak," she said primly.

"And I wish to sleep. You should do the same."

"I'm not sleepy."

He sighed. "Fine. What do you want to discuss?"

"How will we present ourselves? We know Ross likes to pursue married women. Should we be one of those unconcerned sorts of couples, or would that not be enough of a challenge to him?" She tapped her finger on her knee. "We can't be too obvious."

Robert shrugged. "I must take his measure. Then I'll know how to proceed, and you can follow my lead."

"I am perfectly able to lead this scheme myself," she said stiffly.

Robert hid his smile, glad to see her sadness replaced by firm resolution. It had been torture to see her so sad, which was only natural. Any man would be upset at seeing a beautiful woman on the verge of tears. *And after all, I was once wildly in love with her.*

The thought surprised him. *Where did that come from? I was madly in lust, not love. It was no more than that.*

She sent him a glance from under her lashes and he was instantly on his guard. "There is one thing I've been wondering. Something you haven't fully explained. In the beginning, you needed a specific onyx box to free your brother from his captor. But then things changed. Somehow you discovered that there were three such boxes, and now you want them all. Why is that? What is it about these three boxes that make them so valuable?"

He adjusted his hat so that it would shade his eyes. *Should I tell her? Can I really trust her?* He wanted to tell her everything, only it wasn't really his secret to share, but Michael's.

She fixed him with a firm stare. "We *are* partners."

He couldn't deny her reasoning so he shrugged. "Fine. I will tell you. There are three boxes, and if you know how to unlock them they open flat."

"To make a panel?"

"Exactly. And—when they are fitted together, they make a map."

Her eyes widened. "A treasure map?"

"Yes."

"So Aniston must know about the map. That explains why he's so determined to find it."

"He never mentioned a map to you?"

"No. But I knew there had to be something very special about the first box that he sent me to fetch, so when I had it in my possession, I examined it. But I never saw anything resembling a map."

"You have to know precisely what you are doing in order to open one."

"Ah. What kind of treasure do you think the map will lead to?"

Some part of him urged him on. If he wanted her to trust him, he had to show trust in her. "My brother Michael hopes that it will lead us to a lost family heirloom, the Hurst Amulet."

Her eyes lit with interest. "This just gets better and better."

"The amulet was in my family for centuries, until a member of the MacLean clan stole it and gifted it to Queen Elizabeth. She kept it for some years, but supposedly became fearful of its powers."

"An amulet with *powers?*" Her lips twitched. "You can't believe that."

"To be honest, I don't know what I believe. A telling number of people who came into contact with the amulet claimed that it had certain . . . abilities. Michael spent years researching it; he found many mentions of the amulet *and* its powers in old archives, even those in Elizabeth's court."

"What special power does the amulet supposedly possess?"

"Michael came upon one account where, at the queen's insistence, one of the queen's ladies-in-waiting wore the amulet. Afterward, the lady claimed to see her own future."

"That's too fantastical to believe."

"So I thought. She said that the amulet showed her whom she was to wed. Much to Queen Elizabeth's ire, the lady-in-waiting eloped with a courtier the very next day."

"She thought it would happen, so she made it so. There's not much magic in that, is there?"

Robert chuckled. "No, not when you put it that way."

Moira grinned back at him. "Since Elizabeth didn't approve of the wedding, I take it that she didn't care for the courtier, either?"

"Quite the opposite: he was one of Elizabeth's favorites, and she saw the elopement as an insult. She sent her guard to tear the lady-in-waiting from the arms of her new husband. Then she had them thrown into the tower for treason, and threatened them with beheading."

"Good God."

"One did not steal one of Elizabeth's flirts without consequences. She was a very jealous queen. Perhaps it had something to do with the color of her hair, for they say redheads are very passionate." He looked at Moira's hair, the deep red free from the dark dye that had covered it. "I would vouch for that."

"They also say redheads freckle, and I never have. What happened to the star-crossed lovers? Did they languish in the tower and die in each other's arms?"

"Fortunately, the lady-in-waiting was already carrying her new husband's child."

"That was quick."

He smiled. "Wasn't it? Elizabeth wasn't a monster and wouldn't allow a child to be born in the tower. She released the unhappy couple but banished them from court. According to the records, they lived a long and happy life far from the queen's attention."

"It that a true story?"

"It's well documented; Michael has the papers himself. But I don't believe the amulet is magic. Perhaps it simply holds heat, or trembles. I once saw a crystal that did both."

"So Aniston is searching for a treasure map that might lead to the lost Hurst Amulet, which supposedly tells the future," she mused. "Aniston's had some financial troubles, and if he can convince others that the amulet is magical, he could name his price."

"No one would be so foolish," Robert scoffed.

"You'd be surprised," she said drily. "There are many wealthy people who believe silly notions, including our king. George hasn't been the same since his daughter, Princess Charlotte, died. They say he holds séances in an effort to contact her and has become the pawn of charlatans. He would be ripe plucking for a man like Aniston."

Robert nodded. "I hadn't thought of that, but you're right. As you can see, this map could be very important."

"But didn't William take one of the boxes to Egypt to win Michael's freedom? The map won't be complete, then."

"It's a copy. As you pointed out before, it's a simple object and easy to falsify. We made certain the fake box still had a portion of the map inside, but with a few modifications." His grin was wicked.

"Very clever."

The coach turned then, and they entered the yard of a small inn. Stewart pulled the coach to a halt and Leeds jumped down to open the door. He lowered the step for Robert, and they spoke for a moment before Robert turned to help Moira down.

"Ross's agent will arrive shortly. Are you ready?"

"Oh yes." She smiled and took his hand. "I'm more than ready."

CHAPTER 14

A letter written yesterday to Robert Hurst from his brother-in-law Angus Hay, the Earl of Erroll.

I have no idea where to find you so I'm addressing this to your town house, hoping that you will find it before you leave Edinburgh. You asked what I knew about a certain Sir Ross of Balnagown. I've made inquiries and have much to report.

Robert, if you have any dealings with this man, have a care. I hear he is very volatile and his opponents have a tendency to mysteriously disappear and never be heard from again.

The inn was very small, only one floor, more of a tavern really. The windows were broad and low to the ground; the yard was neat and planted with flowers that bravely showed their face to the chilly Highland wind.

Robert took Moira's elbow and they walked inside. A broad-faced innkeeper met them on the threshold of the common room and introduced himself as MacKeith.

While Robert spoke with the innkeeper, Moira stripped off her gloves and wandered about the room. The area was quite large, with wide windows and good seating. Two long, well-scrubbed tables ran along the far wall for meals. There was a fat settee covered in deep-blue flowered chintz, and several chairs made in the Hepplewhite fashion. The broad mantel was decorated with a display of glassware, some of it quite lovely.

"Moira, MacKeith will warm our coats by the kitchen fire while we wait."

"That would be lovely." Moira allowed Robert to take her pelisse.

He handed it to the innkeeper. "Thank you, MacKeith."

"Och, 'tis me pleasure. Do ye need feed fer the horses?"

"And food for the men, too, please. We're here to meet with an agent of Sir Lachlan Ross's. Have you seen a Mr. Carmichael?"

"No' yet, though I was tol' t' expect ye. Would yer lady wife like some tea, or a small glass o' sherry?"

Moira hid a shudder. She hated sherry; it was so sweet, it made her teeth ache. "Do you have any scotch? I much prefer a glass of that."

The innkeeper looked impressed. "O' course we do. Can I offer ye a wee dram o' the water o' life, too, sir?"

"That would be excellent."

The sound of a carriage made the innkeeper turn to the window. "Och, there's Carmichael now—and Sir Lachlan is wit' him!"

Robert crossed the room to look out the window.

"I'll fetch yer scotch anon. I'm sure his lordship will wish fer a dram himself."

"Thank you." Robert didn't turn as the innkeeper hurried off. "Ross is riding a brute of a horse."

"Ah. Then I shall become a horse lover."

Robert smiled as he turned away from the window. "You are very quick. Are you ready?"

Moira smoothed her gown. "Oh, yes."

Out in the hallway, swift steps sounded. The door opened and a man entered. He was short set and incredibly fat, sporting three chins under a flushed face. He was dressed modestly, his neckcloth and sober coat befitting a solicitor.

His gaze flickered to Robert, and then blinked with surprise on finding Moira.

Robert bowed. "Good afternoon. I am Robert Hurst. I take it you are Carmichael?"

"Aye, so I am." The man bowed and said with a soft burr, "I'm Sir Lachlan Ross's man o' business." He cast an uncertain glance at Moira.

Robert flicked a careless finger in her direction. "My wife, Mrs. Hurst."

He offered no other introduction and after an awkward pause, the solicitor bowed in her direction and mumbled, "Pleased to meet ye."

She curtsied, then looked expectantly at Robert for a more formal introduction.

Robert pretended not to notice, studying the tip of his cane, as if the silver wasn't as polished as he liked.

Mr. Carmichael broke the silence with an

awkward laugh. "I'm certain ye're both tired from yer trip. Sir Lachlan wished to see a colt he's thinkin' o' purchasing, so he came as well. He'll be most anxious to—"

Heavy footsteps in the hallway announced the approach of Sir Lachlan. Robert stepped to the side, blocking Moira from the man's view.

Ross was expensively dressed, his boots polished until they shone. He was tall with broad shoulders, and gave off a vigorous air. His reddish brown hair was faded and streaked with white at each temple. His eyes were a startling blue, his nose beaked over a firm mouth, giving him the air of a hawk.

Ross's gaze flickered over Robert, touching upon the sapphire pin in his cravat and lingering on the sheen of his boots.

Robert didn't display any interest other than a mild lift of his brows.

Mr. Carmichael cleared his throat in a ponderous manner. "Sir Lachlan, this is Mr. Hurst, who has come to see about the artifact."

"Mr. Hurst." Ross bowed.

"Ross." Robert inclined his head with a distinct lack of enthusiasm.

Ross reddened, his jaw tightening in an ominous fashion. "I came to see a colt I'm purchasing or I'd have met you at my castle."

Robert shrugged. "This is as good of a place as any. Did you bring the box?"

"No, of course not. I didn't think you'd want to conduct business in a common taproom."

Ross's air of superiority disappeared when Robert looked about him in apparent surprise. "A taproom?" Robert pulled out his monocle and peered about the room, moving a few paces as he did so. "My dear Ross, you've been too long gone from town if you consider this a taproom."

Ross's heavy eyebrows lowered. "Now see here, Hurst, I didn't come here to—" His gaze locked on something past Robert's shoulder and all words disappeared from his lips.

Robert hid a smile and followed the man's gaze to where Moira stood, the sunlight from the window catching the red of her hair and limning the pure line of her cheek. "Oh. My wife, Mrs. Hurst. Moira, this is Ross of Balnagown Castle."

Ross bowed. "Mrs. Hurst, I didn't realize you were attending."

Moira dipped into a curtsy, looking engagingly graceful while holding out her left hand for Ross to kiss.

To Robert's astonishment, a simple gold wedding ring sparkled in the light. *Where the hell did she get that?* It was a masterly touch, one he hadn't thought of.

Ross hurried forward to take the proffered hand. Moira held her curtsy a moment longer than necessary, giving his lordship a nice look down her décolletage.

You are good, ma chère. Very good.

Moira stood, looking up at Ross through her lashes as if shy. "I shouldn't be here. I fear I foisted myself upon my poor husband."

"Yes, she did," Robert drawled in a bored tone.

"Sir Lachlan, I hope you don't mind, but I couldn't resist the chance to see your beautiful countryside. The highlands are so romantic! The mountains and lochs, even this little inn looks as if it belongs in a painting."

Ross beamed at the seemingly artless speech.

Robert smoothed the lace at his wrists and sighed impatiently. "Moira, please, don't monopolize Sir Lachlan." To Robert's amusement, Ross was still holding Moira's hand, one thumb rubbing her wedding ring, as if he was desirous of erasing it completely.

Ross collected himself with a visible effort. "Well, perhaps we should stay here a bit before we continue on. You must be tired from your journey."

Though Ross spoke to Moira, Robert said, "An excellent idea. I *am* a bit fatigued." He crossed to the fire and took the seat closest to it. "Ross, pray have a seat."

It was a rude move, since a gentleman would have seen his wife seated first.

Ross sent Robert a hard look and then made a point of offering the next best seat to Moira, who took it with a blush. *How does she do that?*

Ross sat down near Robert while Carmichael took a seat at the table, discreetly out of the way.

Robert stretched out his legs and examined the sheen of his boots. "I am delighted you made the trip here. I expected only Carmichael."

"It was a lovely day, perfect for a ride."

"You rode?" Robert lifted the monocle to Ross. "I thought Balnagown was still some distance."

"It is six miles down the road. I ride at least an hour every day. It keeps one fit."

"Riding is so . . . bouncy. It was uncomfortable enough getting here by coach. By the way, my luggage should be arriving later. Two more coaches, in fact."

Ross looked confused. "Two?"

"My clothes, sir," Robert said in a lofty tone.

"Oh. Of course, of course." He shot a glance at Moira. "Ladies do love to have *all* their pretty gowns with them."

"Oh, I brought only two trunks," Moira said artlessly. "Robert brought six."

Ross blinked. "Six?"

"It is so hard to know how to dress in the country," Robert said. "Will it be too cold? Or too warm? All one knows is that it will be 'too' something."

Moira added, "Hurst says that spring in Scotland is uncertain, and summer only slightly less so."

"It's a heathen land, *ma chère*," Robert said. "Which is why I didn't think you should come."

"Heathen?" Ross sent a dark look at Robert. "I must protest that, sir!"

"Oh, it's not worth the effort," Robert said easily.

Ross's flush deepened. "I think you'll find all of the same luxuries at Balnagown as you'd find anywhere in London." He turned to Moira. "Wait until you see Balnagown Castle. The lands about it are incomparable."

"I am glad I brought my riding habit, then. I love to ride, too, although *some* people do not." She shot a side-glance at Robert.

He yawned. "Yes, yes. I can only hope that Sir Lachlan will take you for a ride or two."

"I would be delighted," Ross said.

"It would be a boon to me, for I find horses a dead bore."

Ross looked as if he thought Robert was half mad. After a visible struggle he managed to say in a mild tone, "There are many excellent trails near Balnagown Castle. I'd be delighted to take Mrs. Hurst on the best ones."

Moira looked pleased. "I shall look forward to it."

"Providing the coaches make it here with your habit," Robert said, aggrievedly. "I wouldn't be a bit surprised if they became stuck in the mud. I've never seen worse roads."

Moira sniffed. "You're really worried about *your* clothes, not mine."

"I would be quite upset to lose the new shirts I just had made. The Belgian lace cost a fortune."

Ross's smile was only slightly less than contemptuous. "Mr. Hurst, you do live up to your reputation as a fashion plate."

"Thank you. I hope that you live up to yours." At Ross's startled expression, Robert added, "As an honest trader and businessman, of course."

"Of course."

The innkeeper returned with a small tray bearing four glasses and a decanter of scotch.

Mr. Carmichael stood and rubbed his hands together. "Ah, MacKeith, ye're a man after me own heart! A wee dram will warm the air."

Moira stood as well. "Please allow me to pour." She crossed to the tray.

The innkeeper turned to Ross. "Will ye be needin' yer dinner?"

Ross shook his head. "No, thank you. We won't be staying that long."

MacKeith bowed and left while Moira poured the whiskey and spoke quietly with Mr. Carmichael.

Robert turned to his host. "So, Ross, this artifact. I've been quite anxious to see if it's in as good repair as your agent said it is."

"Mr. Hurst, please. There will be time to discuss the artifact when we're at the castle."

"I take my collections very seriously. I appreciate beauty in all forms: a fine painting, a valuable object d'art"—he glanced at Moira—"a woman's white skin."

Ross's eyes gleamed. "It's refreshing to see a man who appreciates his wife's beauty."

"She is my newest acquisition. We've been married less than a month. She's almost virginal."

The man's nostrils flared at that tidbit. Moira's information was correct; Robert could almost feel Ross's interest churn. "It has been a most enjoyable few weeks. In fact— Ah, thank you, my dear." Robert took the glass that Moira handed him.

Moira turned and held a glass to Ross, bending just a bit so that her breasts pressed against the thin material of her gown, the thin ruffle of her chemise clearly visible.

Ross's gaze locked on her bosom as he took the drink.

Moira straightened, meeting Robert's gaze over Ross's head, and Robert held up his glass in a silent toast. She was quite subtle. Later, Ross would wonder if she'd been flirting or not and, in not knowing, would be even more intrigued.

Her eyes twinkled as she took her seat beside Robert and asked Ross about the horses in his stables. Ross enthusiastically embarked on a detailed listing of every horse he owned, had owned, and wished to own. Moira listened with a great air of interest, asking questions that showed her own knowledge, while Robert pretended utter boredom. It wasn't much of a stretch to do so, either.

Robert was actually delighted when, through the wide window, he saw Stewart leading the coach back into the inn yard. "Ah, the coach!" Robert stood, Moira following. "Ross, while I hesitate to break up such a delightful conversation, we should be on our way."

Ross reluctantly climbed to his feet. "Och, we should at that. I lost track of the time, talking about my horses."

"I quite understand," Moira said fervently.

Ross looked pleased as he bowed. He made several more unctuous statements while Robert led them all out into the hallway. He sent the innkeeper to fetch Moira's pelisse and, with a deft hand here, a smooth comment there, herded everyone into place and had them on the road in less than five minutes.

As soon as they were under way, Sir Lachlan leading the way on his large bay, Moira relaxed against the squabs. "That was a good beginning."

Robert set his cane against the far seat. "Indeed it was. I must admit that I underestimated your skills."

"You always did, my love." She slipped off her wedding ring and flipped it across the coach at Robert.

He caught it with one hand and examined it. "This was a nice touch. I fear I hadn't thought of it."

"Details are important."

He tossed the ring back. "Where did you get it?"

"I wore it when I was home, with Rowena. It was a good way to keep the gossips at bay."

"Since no husband was visible, I take it that the good people of Craigentinny believe you're a widow."

"Indeed they do." She replaced the ring on her finger. "So, have we hooked Ross well and good?"

"I believe so. By the way, we're newly married. I wanted him to think he would steal my bride fresh from the altar. I thought it would appeal to his prurient interest."

"And did it?"

"He was almost panting. I made him think you were only a few days shy of being a virgin."

"So he likes an innocent, does he?"

"I think the earl's about the challenge, seducing a man's beloved wife under his very nose—ordinarily a difficult thing to accomplish. And a newly married woman would be the most difficult to seduce of all."

"Very true." Moira pulled her gloves from her pocket and tugged them on. "I was surprised you were so obnoxious to our host." Robert's easy slip into the character of a spoiled man of the world had been done to perfection. "I wanted to slap you, even though I knew you were acting."

"It will sweeten the pot. If Ross enjoys seducing the wife of a man whose company he enjoys, imagine his joy at seducing the wife of a man he cannot stand. I wish to inspire the desire to humiliate me. The combination of desires should have him well primed to make a royal fool of himself."

"So I'm to charm and you're to disarm?"

"Well said, *ma chère*."

"I like how you think, Mr. Hurst."

"And I like how you played our host, Mrs. Hurst. He will rue the day he invited us to visit him."

Her heart warmed. It had been so very long since she'd had someone to work with, someone with whom to talk through her ideas and problems.

Her mind turned through the possibilities. "If we play this right, he will never know we have deceived him, which would keep him from raising an alarm."

"We'll do the best we can. It all depends on whether we can locate his secret hiding place without his knowing it."

"When we arrive at Balnagown, I'll finagle an early morning ride for tomorrow."

"Good. Keep him gone at least two hours. I'll start searching the more obvious locations. Meanwhile, I'll put my secret weapon to work uncovering information from the servants' quarters."

"Secret weapon?"

"Buffon. If anyone can ferret out good gossip, it is a Frenchman with an air of superiority. I don't know what it is about him, but the other servants fall over themselves to tell him the most inappropriate things."

She had to laugh. "He seems very disagreeable."

"He is. But he does much to establish me as a

worthless fop, while also obtaining the most valuable bits of information from the servants."

"Who know everything, regardless what their masters and mistresses think."

"Exactly."

"Robert, I actually feel . . . *hopeful*." At his surprised look, she said, "I haven't felt hope in so long. I owe you thanks."

"You can thank me once we have Rowena back." His expression softened. "I look forward to meeting her."

Moira's heart gave an odd jerk. She was beginning to realize that her decision to cut Robert from his own child's life had been made too hastily. She'd assumed many things, among them how he felt about having a child and whether he would be a good father, all without consulting Robert. At the time she'd been so certain she was doing the right thing, what was best for Rowena. Now she wasn't so certain.

Robert began to talk about various hidden places he'd found in previous cases, and Moira listened with growing appreciation for his resourcefulness. It would be wonderful if he could find the artifact and they could just slip away, though she knew better than to count on anything being easy. There were too many unknown factors.

But the nice thing was that she was no longer alone. Together, she and Robert would see this through to the end.

Moira twisted the ring on her finger. *Just a little longer, Rowena. Just a little longer.*

CHAPTER 15

A letter from Robert Hurst to his solicitor in London, following Moira's first disappearance.

Please continue looking for the woman in question. She has gone by many names—Moira Cunningham, Moira Bruce, Mary K. Poole, and Maria Chavez among them. Lately she has gone by Princess Alexandria Romanov.

While I believe her real name to be Moira MacAllister, I'm not yet certain. I am making inquiries to the four corners of the kingdom and hope to have more answers before long.

Whatever her name is, this woman crossed the wrong person. A Hurst never quits.

*B*alnagown Castle was located in the craggy highlands. Perched on a bluff covered in green ivy, a glass blue loch at its feet, the castle towered over the landscape.

Moira, who was leaning out the carriage window, pointed at the castle as they rounded a bend. "Oh, you must see it! It has one, two, three, *four* turrets!"

Robert, reclining in the corner, didn't bother to open his eyes. "I daresay it has an unwieldy number of windows, too. It wouldn't surprise me if Ross's servants are hard-pressed to keep them all clean."

Moira sat back and eyed him with reproach. "Must you ruin every romantic notion?"

"Only the ones involving clean windows."

"You're hopeless." She looked back out the window. "It's beautiful, but so isolated. How can he live here alone?"

"I think he is more comfortable surrounded

by adoring servants than by people of his own class."

The coach continued up the long, winding drive, the castle whisking in and out of sight behind the growing clouds. Moira glanced at Robert. The few times he bestirred himself to look out the window, he seemed genuinely unimpressed by the gorgeous castle. *What does impress him?*

There was no way to know. He was so carefully put together, so cautious about revealing himself—whether because of his position with the Home Office or some more personal reason—that it was frustratingly difficult to tell what he thought. She'd made her way in life by reading people, and was better at it than most, which made her inability to read Robert all the more annoying.

Perhaps that was part of their attraction: she was challenged by his closed façade, and he was challenged by the fact that she'd managed to escape him before and could do it again.

He crossed his arms over his broad chest, his chin sinking into the folds of his cravat, his expression so relaxed that she had no doubt he'd soon be fast asleep.

How can he sleep right now?

But that was Robert; always cool, never deeply engaged.

She wished she felt the same about him. Despite knowing the danger of caring too much, she was deeply intrigued by him. Of course, it didn't help that he looked like the romantic hero of every lending library novel she'd ever read: tall, handsome, and beautifully built. Even now, she imagined running her hands over his flat, rippled stomach and muscled arms . . .

She forced herself to look back out the window. She had to control herself if she wished to maintain her role for the next few days.

She cleared her throat. "Judging by this terrain, I should be able to keep Ross occupied for at least a three-hour ride, perhaps more."

Robert tilted his head back to regard her from beneath the brim of his hat. "That would be a very good start, but don't take any unacceptable risks."

"For Rowena, all risks are acceptable."

He narrowed his eyes. "Rowena will need you alive and well once this is over. From now on, you'll leave the risks to me."

Was that a flicker of relief in her green eyes? He couldn't be sure; her expressions were quick-silver, gone before he had time to register them all.

"Tell me, *ma chère,* can you play an avaricious collector?"

"A collector?"

"Yes, of all things Egyptian."

Her eyes brightened. "Ah. If I am excited by them, Ross will be encouraged to bring out his Egyptian antiquities."

"Exactly. You will be unimpressed by all jewels, artwork, and statuary, unless they're Egyptian."

"I can do that. I had a maid once who was crazed about exotic animals. She frequented Astley's so often that the ticket takers knew her name. Her eyes would glow when she talked about the elephant, the camel, and other beasts." Moira clasped her hands together, a blissful expression on her face.

Robert laughed. "Yes, that will do very well."

As quickly as it appeared, the blissful look was gone, replaced by a smug one. "Excellent. We will do this, Robert—I know we will!"

Robert's smile froze. She'd said "we" as if they were a true couple. He'd been very cautious not to examine the future; it seemed a dangerous thing to do.

The coach turned the final corner and the castle was revealed, thick white clouds settling about the turrets. Moira once again leaned out the window. "It really is a beautiful place."

Robert looked past her, impressed despite

himself. The castle seemed to come from a fairy tale, several stories tall, with well-defined turrets adorned by the Ross flag. Every window seemed to be open, and the wind teased out red and blue velvet curtains, adding splashes of color to the gray stone exterior. But it was the setting that made it truly breathtaking.

The grass about the castle was a riotous mass of wildflowers. Red, yellow, purple, and blue flowers bobbed in the breeze, dancing as if under some sort of spell, while the clouds swirled above.

"I wish Rowena could see this," Moira said, breathless.

Robert shot her a sharp look. For a moment, he wished he could show her Hurst House. Then he set his jaw and turned away. Hurst House was his secret and no one else's.

He'd purchased it four years ago on a whim. He'd been traveling between Edinburgh and London when a chance wrong turn had brought him to a beautiful old house, built in the late sixteenth century, of white stone with narrow windows. He'd purchased it immediately and then modernized it, adding water closets, running water, a roof cistern, and a kitchen that would make the most demanding chef quiver with pleasure.

He wasn't certain why he'd bought it, for it was fit to establish a dynasty. Yet he'd been intrigued, and continued to be so, working whenever he could with his man of business on the improvements. He hadn't even told his family about it, knowing they'd tease him mercilessly for such folly. He didn't blame them; had any of them purchased such a grand house, he'd have done the same.

He glanced at Moira again, wondering if she would like Hurst House's bucolic setting as much as Balnagown's. Hurst House was perched upon a low hill, majestic and gleaming, the white stone trimmed with thick green ivy, reflected in the series of glassy ponds that stretched before it, along with thick copses of trees.

He looked again at the gorgeous castle that towered above them, and an unusual sinking feeling gripped him. No one could compare Balnagown's splendor to the quiet majesty of Hurst House.

Not that it matters, he told himself sharply. *Moira will never see Hurst House—and why should she?*

"Oh, Robert, look!" Moira pointed up. "The stained glass in the top windows is breathtaking."

Indeed, the late afternoon sun caught the colored panes, which glittered as if magic. Robert silently damned every window of Ross's castle to Hades, at the same time deciding that Hurst House could use some fine stained glass, as well. He'd set his man of business on it as soon as possible.

The coach rumbled through a wide gate and into the cobbled drive. The shadow of the great building made Moira withdraw into the coach. "This says a lot about Ross that we didn't know," she said, her expression thoughtful.

The castle appeared to be in excellent repair, and a very large number of well-dressed servants scurried around in anticipation of their arrival. "Ross is extraordinarily wealthy."

She nodded. "Which explains why Aniston didn't try to simply purchase the artifact. Ross has no need of money."

"Which means that it would be impossible to purchase the real artifact—only a fake."

"Which he sells merely to prove that he can best his fellow man."

"That explains a lot. Since Aniston couldn't buy the original box outright, he sent you to fetch it for him." Robert had no illusions just how far Aniston expected Moira to go in her dealings with Ross. Robert clutched the handle of his cane tightly. *He and I will have a reckoning soon.*

The coach slowed to a stop, a swarm of footmen rushing to let down the steps.

Moira placed her gloved hand in Robert's. "We're going to have to play this very carefully. A man with Ross's resources will be unchecked out here in the middle of nowhere. He's like a king."

"Only not held to public opinion," Robert replied softly, assisting Moira down the steps. "We'll discuss this later."

Ross was handing his horse to a footman and hurried forward on seeing Robert and Moira alight.

Moira flashed her breathtaking smile. "Sir Lachlan, I was just telling my dear husband what a lovely castle you have! I am quite charmed. Pray tell me that there is at least one ghost!"

Ross laughed indulgently. "Oh, there are many of them. I shall tell you about them all at dinner tonight."

Robert pulled out his monocle and examined the castle with an absent air. "Yes, it's quite impressive." He dropped the monocle and let it swing against his waistcoat. "I do hope there's port in that large pile of rocks. I'm dying of thirst."

Ross bowed, tearing his gaze from Moira with obvious reluctance. "Mr. Hurst, I've some of the best port in all of England. I'll have a bottle delivered to your bedchamber."

"Thank you."

"I hope the coach ride wasn't too rough for you."

"No, no." Robert yawned behind one gloved hand. "Though I am a bit saddened there wasn't more of interest to see to pass the time. I slept the entire way."

Ross looked startled. "I thought you'd enjoy seeing the castle from the road and—"

Moira placed her hand on Ross's arm. "Oh, do *not* ask Hurst to express his interest in a mere *building*." She gave a merry trill of laughter. "My husband prefers a good cravat to architecture."

Though she was playing her part to perfection, Robert felt a flicker of annoyance. He met Ross's interested gaze with a shrug. "I'm afraid I don't enjoy a bucolic existence."

"Unless it has to do with fashion, gaming, or antiquities, Hurst is likely to be cursed with boredom," Moira said playfully.

"I also like port," Robert said loftily. "You cannot forget that."

Ross laughed and led the way inside, past the two footmen who held open the monstrous arched doors. "Och, Hurst, you'll find yourself with enough port to swim in. I have plenty of antiquities, too. But I've no patience with fashion and gaming."

More footmen came forward to take Moira's pelisse and gloves. As Robert handed over his gloves and hat, he saw that the great hall was resplendent with symbols of heraldry. An impressive display of flintlock pistols and muskets were arrayed upon the tall walls in an intricate circular design. A similar design on the opposite wall was comprised of swords of varying sizes.

"Goodness," Moira said, staring about wide-eyed. "You certainly have a lot of weapons. Have you used them all?"

Ross had handed his coat to a servant and turned to answer the question, dumbstruck as his gaze fixed on her with avid interest.

Robert almost chuckled. Moira had strategically placed herself in a pool of light that poured through a circular window. Her green gown seemed ethereal, and the golden light made her look like a fairy rising from a sunbeam.

But it wouldn't do to allow their host to see too much of her. Robert sighed. "I vow, I am exhausted."

"Of course." Ross turned to the waiting butler. "Escort Mr. Hurst to the blue suite and Mrs. Hurst"—his gaze lingered on her—"to the yellow suite."

The butler bowed and turned to leave, but

Robert forestalled him. "I beg your pardon, but is my wife's room close to mine?"

Ross's smile faded. "They're down the hall from one another, of course."

"I wish them to be adjoining."

"The room adjoining your wife's is very small."

"I'll make do, whatever it is."

Ross bowed stiffly. "Very well." He turned to the butler. "Escort Mr. and Mrs. Hurst to the yellow suite. Mr. Hurst will take the smaller of the rooms."

Robert ignored his almost challenging tone and nodded. "Excellent." He walked over to Moira and offered his arm. "My dear, shall we?"

"Yes, of course." She took his arm and smiled at Ross. "Until dinner, then."

He brightened immediately. "Yes! We shall serve at seven, but if you'd like a tour of the castle I would be happy to meet you at five." He sent a reluctant glance at Robert. "And you as well, of course, Mr. Hurst."

Robert yawned delicately. "I daresay I will still be napping, but Mrs. Hurst is free to do as she wishes. She enjoys old houses. I'm more interested in the quality of your port."

"Very good. I trust that neither of you will be disappointed."

"I should hope not." Robert gestured to the butler. "Lead the way."

They were quickly led up the stairs. After they'd reached the landing, he leaned close to Moira. "This might be easier than we thought."

She gave him a tense smile. "I hope so."

They turned down several more halls, and climbed two more sets of stairs before the butler paused outside a set of wide double doors. "Mrs. Hurst, this is your room." He opened the doors and they passed through. It was a huge chamber; over a dozen large beds could have made their homes here without crowding. The lone bed was set upon a platform at one end of the room, the pale blue and yellow silk draperies fluttering in the small wind stirred by the roar of a truly humongous fireplace edged with white marble. Four pairs of wide windows overlooked a small faux balcony and allowed light to spill over several clusters of gilt-edged furniture. "My," Robert said, lifting his monocle. "This is certainly impressive. I think more and more of our host." He turned to the butler. "And my bedchamber?"

The butler bowed and nodded to the doorway. "Your room is next door."

"I don't see an adjoining door."

The butler bowed again. "There isn't one, sir.

However, the hallway doors are adjacent to one another."

Robert strolled to the wide windows, opened one, and looked outside. They were several stories up. A wide stone ledge ran the length of the castle wall, punctuated by large, snarling gargoyles. Judging by the closeness of the windowsills lining the ledge, every room had at least one window.

"The wind is brutal at this height." Robert closed the window with a snap and turned to the butler. "I will see my room now."

"Yes, sir. *Madame*, your luggage will be brought up once it arrives. A maid will arrive shortly in case you need anything until then."

"Thank you," Moira said.

The butler bowed and crossed to the door. He held it open and stood to one side, staring stoically ahead.

Robert bowed to Moira. "I shall give you a few hours to rest. I know you must be tired."

She smiled. "I am. We've traveled a long distance over the last week."

"Yes, we have." He looked at her narrowly, noting the faint circles under her eyes. "Our luggage is still a good two or three hours behind us. You should use that time to rest." Aware that the servant watched, he said in a cool tone, "You don't wish to look haggard. That will never do."

Her eyes sparkled, but she kept in character and merely said in a repressed tone, "We should take advantage of Lord Ross's offer for a tour of the castle. It was quite kind of him."

"I've already seen that ghastly entryway. I don't think I could stomach more of the same."

"I thought the entryway was beautiful."

Aware that the servant could hear every word, Robert replied in a bored tone, "You would. Do as you will. It will be drafty. You might want to wear your pelisse."

She murmured, "Of course."

"I shall return to collect you at dinnertime." He left the room and followed the butler.

His bedchamber was tiny compared to Moira's, though no less luxurious. He suspected it was actually a maid's quarters, though a generous one.

He opened his windows, which overlooked the courtyard below. The wind whipped his hair and the curtains on either side of him when he leaned out. He was high enough that no noises drifted up from the courtyard.

He leaned out farther over the ledge to look down the long, winding road. In the distance he could already see two heavily loaded coaches. *Buffon has made excellent time, as usual.* Robert had no wish to trust his cravats to Ross's laundress.

Satisfied, he closed the window to wait on his servant.

CHAPTER 16

Diary entry by Michael Hurst from today.

One. More. Day. When will this ever end? I've been in this godforsaken place for almost six months and every day seems to last longer than the one before. William has supposedly arrived to free me, yet the sulfi cannot be bothered to meet with him. I attempted to ask that the matter be expedited but was rudely silenced by the sulfi, who seemed insulted by my desire to leave his house, even though I was brought here unconscious and trussed up like a wild boar, and have been held under lock and key and musket ever since.

Miss Smythe-Haughton has advised patience and has gone to speak with the sulfi herself, which is a complete waste of time. Still, at least she is no longer underfoot while I'm pacing my bedchamber from end to end. If I am not released soon, I will be forced to escape, musket-bearing guards or not.

Several hours later, Robert tilted his head to one side and stared at his reflection in the mirror, his gaze narrowing as he examined the intricate folds of his cravat. After a long, silent moment, he nodded. "It will do."

Behind him, Buffon clasped his hands and gave a relieved sigh. "*Oui*! Very good, *monsieur*. I feared the starch would not be to your liking."

"It's well enough." He deftly placed a sapphire pin in his cravat. "I am ready for dinner and there's still thirty minutes to spare. I'll wear my robe until it's time to put on my dinner coat, so it won't wrinkle."

"Very good, *monsieur*." Buffon went to the wardrobe and removed a brilliant red silk robe.

He lovingly carried it to Robert, who eyed it with disbelief. "Where's my blue robe?"

Buffon appeared pained. "*Monsieur*, will you at least try the new robe? It is very fashionable and—"

"The blue robe. *Now.*"

Buffon's lips thinned, but he went to the large wardrobe and, with a great show, lovingly hung the red silk robe inside. He yanked out a blue robe from the bottom of the wardrobe, muttering under his breath in French.

"That robe is *not* a rag."

Buffon sniffed but held out the robe.

Robert slipped it on. "When you are done pouting, I have a task for you."

Buffon had turned to put away the cravats that had not been used, but he paused, his dark gaze locking on Robert. *"Oui?"*

"It may not be pleasant."

"Your tasks rarely are, *monsieur*. But you are here on a mission, which is why you are now pretending to be married to *madame*."

Robert tied the belt on his robe, hiding a grimace. Telling his servants he was pretending to be married had seemed easier than trying to explain the true circumstances. For some reason, though, hearing his own words rankled. "It's a very important mission; lives are at stake." *One in particular.*

The valet draped the cravats over his arm and stood as if at attention. "What do you need of Buffon?"

"Information. Rumor has it that Ross has a secret chamber somewhere inside this castle."

"Intriguing!"

"That item I purchased from Ross, the one I told you about?"

"*Oui.* The onyx box."

"Yes. It appears Ross has decided to switch it for a copy."

Buffon gave a visible start. "*Mon Dieu!* Does he not know who you are?"

"Ah, Buffon, not everyone holds me in such high regard as you."

"I know what makes a gentleman," Buffon said loftily. "This Ross is not a gentleman, but a barbarian. And no wonder, for he lives here in this wretched countryside, far from civilization. I daresay he does not even wear a cravat!"

"He wears one, but he mangles the knot. Regardless of your opinion of Ross's neckwear, I need to find this secret chamber so I can retrieve the original box. It's possible that the servants may know where to look, and that is where you come in."

"Of course, *monsieur*. I shall take great pleasure in discovering where this chamber may be."

"Excellent. I don't know the size of it; it may be quite small."

"Do not worry; wherever it is, Buffon will find

it." The valet put his hand over his heart and said in a voice replete with feeling, "Even if I have to seduce a dozen chambermaids, I will discover the secret."

"I'm moved by the sacrifices you make for me."

"I *am* very loyal, am I not? Fortunately, I do not mind seducing the chambermaids. I have done so for you before, and I will do it again."

"Considering the number of maids here, I daresay you can find at least one who is attractive. But if you cannot find any unfreckled chambermaids, feel free to glean your information from a casual conversation with a footman."

"I beg your pardon, but I do not speak with footmen. The butler, perhaps. The housekeeper, *oui,* for I shall need her assistance when I perform some of my duties for your wardrobe. And I *may* speak with Ross's valet, *if* he is polite—though I daresay he is a fool, for his master cannot tie a cravat." Buffon bowed. "I shall begin my investigation immediately. Before I leave, shall I assist you into your coat?"

"No, thank you. I can do it myself."

Buffon gave a haughty sniff. "Very well, *monsieur.*" He crossed the room with a stately tread and left, closing the door softly behind him.

If there was a secret anything in this castle, Buffon would find it. Robert had learned long ago that servants knew far more of their master's business than their master knew of theirs.

Robert found his monocle on the dresser and slipped it into his pocket. Then he removed his robe and put on his coat, adjusting his lace cuffs before he stepped out into the hallway.

Instantly, twelve footmen straightened to attention.

"Goodness, but there are a lot of you." Robert paused by the tallest footman and examined the man from head to foot through his monocle. "Is the entire castle so well staffed?"

"No, sir. Just this wing."

"How convenient for us all." Robert walked on to Moira's door and knocked softly.

A very short, very portly maid with short brown curls clustered about her face answered the door. She curtsied and when Robert informed her that he was Mr. Hurst, she opened the door wider.

Moira called out, "Fiona, thank you. You may go."

The maid curtsied again and left, closing the door behind her.

"Well?" Moira asked. "What do you think?" She twirled before him, radiant in a gown of bronze silk, the skirt resplendent with a heavy cream lace overlay. The color made her skin look even whiter and her eyes luminous.

The gown appeared very simple, the bodice cut at a decorous level, the sleeves puffed at her shoulders. But the second she walked, the cream overgown parted and the bronze silk was left in full view to cling lovingly to her long, slender legs.

Robert nodded. "That will do very well."

"Good." Moira picked up a small cream-colored reticule and slipped it over her wrist.

"How was your personal tour of the castle?"

"Interesting. We didn't have time to walk through all of it, but I have a fairly clear idea of how the main wing is laid out. I'll draw up a map after dinner."

"And our host? Did he behave?"

"Barely." Moira's eyes twinkled. "Whenever I felt uneasy, I mentioned your skill with dueling pistols."

Robert caught her arm and pulled her to him, looking into her upturned face. "Moira, you're not to put yourself in harm's way. Do you understand?"

"I was never in harm's way. And if I ever found myself there, I'd use my pistol."

"I'm certain that you're deadly with the blasted

thing, but still . . . for Rowena's sake, please be careful."

Moira nodded.

Robert released her, his chest oddly tight. "By the way, we're blessed with an inordinate number of footmen standing in the hallway."

"How many?" she asked curiously.

"Twelve."

"Good God, are we at Versailles?"

"You'd think so. I wonder if they're here to serve . . . or guard."

Moira's brow lowered. "That will make searching the castle much more difficult."

"I shall think of something."

She sent him a crooked smile. "I'm sure you will. Are you ready to spend a few hours insulting Sir Lachlan?"

"Are you ready to spend a few hours shamelessly flattering him?"

"Indeed I am."

"Then we are both ready." He opened the door. "After you, Mrs. Hurst."

"Thank you, Mr. Hurst." She swept past him into the hallway.

The next morning, Robert flipped back his curtain, the sun pouring in as he surveyed the courtyard far below. Except for two horses held at wait by grooms, it was empty.

The evening had gone smoothly. Ross had been charmed by Moira, annoyed by Robert, and increasingly curious about their marital relationship. This morning, Moira had gone to breakfast with Ross while Robert stayed in his room, ostensibly too languid to face the sunrise.

If things were going according to plan, Moira was on her way to an energetic ride with her host, leaving the way clear for Robert. *Except for those damn footmen. I shall have to do something about that.*

The grooms below brought the horses to the front steps as the huge doors opened and Moira came out, her gloved hand upon Ross's arm. Ross's deep voice echoed through the yard, Moira's head bent toward him as she listened.

Her habit was a masterly creation; though buttoned to the neck and showing not an inch of skin beyond her face, it molded to every curve. Ross was much closer to her than politeness dictated, his hand placed over hers in a possessive manner. A flare of red-hot jealousy caught Robert, and his hands clutched the windowsill until his knuckles were white.

How ridiculous. She was doing exactly what she

was supposed to be, and doing it well, too. Ross was quickly becoming enslaved.

So why am I so angry? Robert could think of only one reason: he was beginning to have feelings for Moira. *Damn it. That will not do.*

Buffon's knock sounded on the door as Moira and Ross mounted their steeds and trotted out of the courtyard. Robert turned from the window and called for the valet to enter.

Buffon carried a breakfast tray, a small note tucked on one corner. "You have dressed! If you'd told me you wished to do so, I would have come immediately and—"

"I didn't want anyone to know I'm awake."

"Ah. More intrigue, eh?" Buffon set down the tray and picked up the small note. "From *madame*."

Robert opened the note.

Robert,

This morning went as planned. I told Ross you never rise before noon, and he took great delight in disparaging "lazy city ways." He has quite a distaste for Edinburgh and especially London. Inside is a sketch of the castle from last night's tour.

My maid let slip that Sir Lachlan is very fond of his study and spends much of his time there. It may be a good place to begin, if you can find a way to get around the footmen. There must be a hundred of them throughout the castle. On our tour, we were never out of sight of at least two.

Now we're off on a ride. I expect we'll return at noon or later, if I can arrange it. Best of luck in your hunt.

Moira

Robert glanced at the map, noting the location of the study, and then slipped it into his pocket. "Buffon, have you found out anything of use yet?"

"*Oui, monsieur.* I discovered that Ross brags of his collections to all of his visitors, and often brings out special items to win praise. He is a bit of a braggart."

That could be useful. "Good. What else have you discovered?"

"Not much more, although I have made inroads in cultivating various personages below stairs, including"—Buffon made a face—"Ross's valet. He might know something, which is why I make the sacrifice."

Buffon picked up the wrinkled blue robe from the end of the bed and, holding it between thumb and forefinger, carried it to the wardrobe and dropped it inside.

"Thank you, Buffon. Now I need to find my way to Ross's study, but there is a problem. I don't wish the footmen to know I'm wandering about. Do you think you could create a diversion, to draw them from the hallway?"

"It would have to be a big diversion, but *oui,* I could do it. I think for this, I will need fire."

Robert raised his brows.

"Nothing less would draw them all. I will use just a small flame, but much smoke." Buffon picked up a napkin from the tray and dipped a corner of it into the washbasin. "Shall I begin my diversion now?"

"Yes. I may only have two hours before *madame* and Ross return."

"Very good, *monsieur.* Then I shall endeavor to start a second fire in a different corner around that time."

"That would do very well."

Buffon bowed and left. A few minutes passed, then one of the footmen gave out a sharp yell. Footsteps thudded, followed by more yells.

Robert peeked out the doorway as the faint scent of smoke wafted in. The hall was clear except for two footmen who hovered at the end, looking uncertain if they should follow their brethren.

"Bless you, Buffon," Robert murmured as he slipped out of his room and hurried to the opposite end of the hallway.

CHAPTER 17

A letter from Mary Hurst to her brother Robert as he became an agent selling antiquities for their brother Michael.

Michael told me he was well pleased with how you are handling all of his sales, and that you've made him more money than he thought possible. He attributes it to your unique salesmanship. He said he knew there was something good to come of your dandified ways, even if it was to lure your victims (clients) into a false sense of security before you pounced on them with a steep price.

After Michael mentioned that, it dawned on me that you've been playing that part your whole life. He's right; it has served you well.

*I*t took Robert almost half an hour to reach the study without being seen. Footmen were everywhere. If he was caught sneaking about, Ross would increase the number of his men, and it would be impossible to look for anything. It was almost impossible now.

Robert slipped between two large tapestries adorning a wall and consulted his map. One more long hallway and he'd be at the study door. He tucked the map back into his pocket and peeked around the corner just in time to catch sight of two footmen. They were young and obviously bored, for they wandered down the hall without any air of purpose or urgency.

He pressed back against the wall, obscured from sight by a display of shields on one wall, and listened as their footsteps moved away from him and toward the very far end of the hall.

Keep going.

Fortunately, they took his silent advice and the

footsteps faded. Robert looked around the corner again and saw their shadows fading away down the conjoining hallway.

Now's my chance.

He made a quick dash to the huge study door. Luckily it was unlocked; he wouldn't have to stop to pick it. He slipped inside, closed the door, and pressed his ear to the cool oak panel to ascertain if anyone had seen him and put up an alarm.

All was blissfully silent. But then, he heard the footmen's voices growing closer and closer. Another set of footsteps joined the first two, and Robert heard the butler's impatient voice. "I came to make certain you've not strayed from your posts."

"Och, we've been 'ere the whole time, sir," said the footman. "As ye requested."

The butler gave a disgusted sigh. "You were in the South Wing when I arrived, so I know that's not true."

"No' fer long. Me and MacPhearson just wished fer a bit o' fresh air, and the windows were open to the sun so we—"

"Take your post and *do not move.* Understood?"

"Yes, sir!"

Now I'm stuck here, and I'll have to find a way out when I am done.

Robert walked to the center of the room, examining it in a sweeping glance. It was very large, with a fireplace at each end, a very high ceiling, a wheeled ladder to reach the highest shelves with ease, and several cozy furniture clusters that suggested one might find the settee of one's dreams if one kept searching. At one end of the room several small statues and ancient figurines were displayed on a neat row of shelves. Adjacent to the shelves was a large oak desk, resplendent with carving.

It was the most obvious place to hide something, and he wasn't convinced of Ross's ability to think like a thief. That would take some intelligence beyond the norm, and thus far, Ross hadn't exhibited such.

Robert sat down at the desk and examined every drawer, every nook and cranny, finding no sign that it held anything of value. *Too bad. I was hoping this would be simple.*

He leaned back in the chair and surveyed the room again. The wall shelves were filled with an impressive assortment of books. He rose and scanned a few titles of the closest. Ross kept a decent collection of research tomes about ancient Greek civilizations, but they were unused-looking. *I'd wager my last groat Ross hasn't read any of these.*

He went to the largest, most ornate shelves, which were deeper and held larger books, many of them ancient maps held in binders. It was difficult not to succumb to temptation and get lost in examining them, but Ross and Moira would only be gone another hour, two at the most.

Is that blasted secret chamber here? It certainly looks like the sort of room to have one. The shelves seemed the best place to begin. Could one be hiding a secret doorway?

He felt along the edges, noting any dip or impression along the way. He moved from bottom to top, using the wheeled ladder to reach the higher shelves. On and on he searched, finding nothing.

Frowning, he examined where the final set of shelves met the wall beside two windows. The shelves were flushly mounted, bolted solidly against the wall. *Not the shelves, then. Where else? The exposed walls near the windows? A door could be hidden there.*

He couldn't knock along the panels, listening for a hollow spot, due to the footmen in the hallway. So he rolled some thick blotter paper from the desk into a heavy tube, lit it, then held it to the bottom of the baseboards, looking for a waver in the flame to show there was an opening. He had no fear that the smell of smoke might alert the footman because, thanks to Buffon, the entire castle now carried the scent.

Twenty minutes and another rolled tube of blotter paper later, he blew out the flame and sighed. *It has to be here.* The shelves and walls weren't the answer . . . what about the floor? A trapdoor could be concealed beneath the polished wood.

He went to one corner and slowly examined each plank, each opening. After he'd walked the exposed portions, he began to work on the clusterings of furniture, all placed on thick rugs. He rolled up first one corner, and then the other, running his hand over the smooth wooden planks. Still, nothing.

Frustrated, he stepped back and surveyed the room again. *Where could that blasted thing be? Am I missing something?*

The sound of activity outside made him cross to the window and flick back the edge of the curtain. Footmen were scurrying down the front steps, and when a shout went up, Robert followed the direction the men all turned. Moira trotted her bay around the final curve of the drive, patting the horse's neck. She was alone, having apparently outdistanced Sir Lachlan.

"He couldn't catch you, could he?" Robert

murmured, smiling as Moira pulled her magnificent steed to a halt at the bottom of the stairs. Her red hair drew the eye as did her sapphire blue habit, but she would have commanded attention in sackcloth and ashes. She had presence, that indefinable something that made the eye follow her every move.

Most women had to rely upon artifice or displaying themselves improperly, or drawing attention by adorning themselves with baubles. Moira needed no augmentation. She was a rare woman; one who carried her beauty rather than wearing it.

Ross came galloping around the bend in the drive, his mount foam flecked as he struggled to catch up.

Robert's smile disappeared. There was no excuse to use a horse in such a way.

Ross paid the horse no heed. He was off his mount as soon as he drew it to an abrupt halt. He then tossed the reins to the nearest footman and pushed two more out of the way so that he, and he alone, was there to help Moira down from her mount.

Robert saw Moira's cool gaze travel past Ross to his horse, which now stood with its head down, foam running down its neck and dripping from its mouth. Her lips pressed into a straight line before she murmured something to Ross that made him flush a fiery red.

He bowed stiffly, then snapped an order to a footman, who immediately went to talk to one of the waiting grooms. Within moments, the heated horse was being walked up and down the drive, a blanket over his heaving shoulders.

Robert regarded Moira curiously. It was risky to reprimand their host at this early stage, yet that hadn't stopped her.

She was a woman of great emotion. Robert thought of the pain he'd seen in her eyes when she'd talked about Rowena, and to his surprise, his own throat tightened. He'd reassured Moira for the past few days that Aniston would keep the child safe—physically safe. What Robert hadn't shared was his fear of the damage being done to the child by being locked away, and the traumatic experience of being separated from her mother for so long. Since Rowena had only one parent, the separation from her mother would be that much more traumatic.

I should have been allowed to be a part of Rowena's life, damn it. I should have been told about— He swallowed back the thought. *I can't think about that right now. I need to find that damned box.*

Still, Robert found himself looking out of the window. Ross reached up to assist Moira from her mount. She unhooked her knee from the pommel and said something that made him laugh as she jumped from the horse's back, Ross's hands firmly about her waist as he assisted her to the ground.

Robert scowled when Ross didn't immediately release her, bending forward to whisper something in her ear. Moira blushed adorably before turning and dashing up the front steps, her skirts fluttering behind her. With a bemused grin, Ross hurried after her, and they disappeared.

Robert realized his hand was fisted about the heavy silk curtain. He released it, disgusted by Ross and irritated by his own reactions. *She is doing as she is supposed to do, nothing more. I need to stop this ridiculous possessiveness.*

There was something about Ross that infuriated Robert. *Perhaps it's his overanxious air, as if he's desperate to prove himself. That might explain why he takes such delight in collecting other men's wives as trophies.*

Robert stepped back from the window and glanced at the clock. Buffon had promised a diversion, but not for another twenty minutes. And there was no getting past the footmen without some help.

He looked back outside. There was a ledge here, similar to the one outside his bedchamber, but there were too many men in the courtyard to escape that way.

He'd have to leave through the hallway as soon as Buffon produced the promised distraction. Robert just had to wait and—

Moira's voice sounded from the hallway, laughing merrily at something, and Robert grimaced. *Damn it, they are coming here!*

Sir Lachlan patted Moira's hand. "I look forward to sharing some of my treasures with a true appreciator of art."

"Egypt is so romantic."

He laughed indulgently. "It's certainly profitable." He allowed a footman to open the study door and gestured for her to precede him. "After you, my dear."

Just before Moira stepped forward, a movement danced at the corner of her eye and she saw Buffon darting across the end of the hallway.

Ross must have seen the surprise on her face, for he turned to follow her gaze.

If Buffon is nearby, then— She glanced at the open study door and then forced a laugh. "Don't mock me, but . . ." She pointed to a suit of armor that stood guard by the door. "For a moment, I thought I saw it move. One of your ghosts, perhaps?"

Ross laughed. "Not that I'm aware of. We have no ghosts who fancy suits of armor."

"It must have been a trick of the light."

"It had to be, since—" He frowned and wrinkled his nose. He turned to one of the footmen. "I smell smoke!"

The man stiffened and answered immediately, his Scots burr pronounced. "I'm sorry, sir. There was a slight fire in the upstairs hallway shortly after you and Mrs. Hurst left. Actually, there were *two* fires, both small and quickly extinguished."

"Who started them?"

"I dinna know, sir, for I've been here since, but I'll run and see what's been discovered."

"Do that and report back."

The man gave a short bow and raced off.

"Goodness," Moira murmured.

Ross turned back to her, his face an unhealthy red. "I can assure you *that* wasn't caused by ghosts, either." He took her elbow. "Now, where were we?"

She smiled and covered his hand with her own. "You, my lord, were about to show me something from Egypt."

His expression softened and he squeezed her fingers. "Ah, yes!"

They entered the study and Moira's gaze instantly swept the room. There was no sign of Robert.

Is he hiding in the curtains?

Her gaze swept across the floor to the curtains. There was no way a person could hide behind them without their feet showing.

Robert would find a better place.

She smiled up at Ross. "Do you mind if I open some curtains? It's a bit dark in here."

"Of course. I shall help."

"Thank you." She crossed the room, waiting until Ross's back was turned so she could look for Robert. She bent over to peek under a settee, but saw nothing. Scurrying, she went to another large grouping of furniture and looked under a fringed chaise. She'd just straightened when Ross turned.

She dropped into the chaise. "What a lovely ride! I can't thank you enough for taking the time to show me your beautiful mountains."

He beamed as he crossed to her. "They are lovely, aren't they? Although not as lovely as my companion."

She pressed a hand to her cheek and said in a

chiding tone, "Oh, Sir Lachlan!" *Perhaps Robert escaped and we just missed him. He could have—* Then she saw the edge of his shoe under the huge oak desk, in the direct line of sight of anyone sitting down.

She hopped up, surprising Ross. "So? Where are these treasures of yours?" she asked.

"A few of them are on display here." He waved a hand toward the shelves at the far end of the room.

She gave them a cursory glance, not daring to move away from the desk. "I see. Those are . . . nice. But do you have some that *aren't* on display?"

"Of course. There's not room here for all of them."

"Where do you keep those?"

"Somewhere safe," he replied in a tone suggesting it was too complicated for a mere female to understand.

She'd love to smack that patronizing look off his face. She walked to where Ross now stood beside the shelves he'd pointed out, making certain she was between him and the desk. "Your collection must be worth a fortune. Is that why you have guards set up outside?"

"Guards? No, no, Mrs. Hurst, you mistake. They're merely footmen."

"But there are so many."

"I dislike surprises. They make sure there aren't any." He chuckled, then captured her hand and pressed a fervent kiss to it. "No need to worry your pretty head over it, m'dear. Some things are better left to the men."

The words grated on Moira's nerves. She'd never counted on a man in her entire life and was glad of it.

Some of her irritation must have shown on her face, for Ross's thick brows lowered and he said in a rather uncertain voice, "Is-is something wrong? You seem—"

"I'm fine, thank you. I was just wondering about your artifacts. Tell me about them."

He launched into a rather thin explanation that made it obvious he knew only minimal information.

While he spoke, she moved to the desk and leaned against it, spreading her skirts a bit to cover the edge of Robert's shoe. Then she stepped on it lightly.

From where he hid, Robert grimaced and pulled in his foot. *Damn it, I thought I was well hidden.*

As soon as he moved, Moira whisked away from the desk.

Robert tilted his head so that he could see her standing by a large black marble sculpture of a jackal. Ross's back was now to Robert, too. *Clever girl.*

Moira touched the statue's wolflike head. "Ah, Anubis."

"Who?"

"Anubis is the god the jackal represents. He was the god of death. Where did you find this piece?"

"I have many sources for my collection. I buy. I sell. Sometimes I keep something special."

Yes, something you think has extra value.

There were many men who collected artifacts for the sheer pleasure of owning a piece of history. They were very careful with the objects, and many items would be lost or destroyed if not for them. Robert disliked it when men collected artifacts solely for their monetary value, without regard to their historical worth. Their possession of such valuable treasures was like hanging a diamond necklace on a donkey.

Robert watched as Moira sent Ross a look from under her lashes. It was an intentionally sensual look, and yet she made it somehow seem innocent. "I would love to see your private collection. *If* there are Egyptian items in it."

"There are a few. Since you know so much about artifacts, what can you tell me about that one?" Ross pointed to the next statue on the shelf.

"The Madonna? Fifteenth century, I'd think. Perhaps Spain."

"How can you tell?"

"The style, the smoothness of the stone—even the base tells you something about the piece. Hurst is an avid collector, and I've picked up information here and there."

"I've no doubt you're vastly superior in judging such artifacts." His tone indulged her.

"Not compared to Hurst. When it comes to collections, Robert is an expert though it's a love of mine, too. Some women love jewels, some houses, some gowns." Robert saw her elegant shrug. "I prefer antiquities."

"Perhaps that is the reason you married Hurst. I haven't been able to see what the attraction could be. He's not the sort of man I'd think a woman like you would enjoy."

"He has his uses, as do all husbands. But one should never expect too much from a husband. They can't answer *every* need."

"My dear," Ross murmured.

The reprobate must have made a move toward Moira, for she spun away and Robert saw only her riding boots as she strode across the room toward the far fireplace, Ross following like a well-trained pup.

The little minx already has him under her spell, Robert thought, amused and annoyed.

He moved so he could watch Moira approach the fire. Something about her carriage sent the unmistakable message that while she was interested in a conversation with Ross, she by no means wished to be touched . . . yet.

Robert couldn't decide what exactly sent that message. It was a combination of her upright carriage, her expression, and the manner in which she tilted her chin. She was masterful. *No wonder I fell for her all those years ago.*

He suddenly wondered if she'd played the same tricks on him—but of course she had. He'd been no more important than Ross.

Except . . . Robert had made it through her defenses and to her bed. Which raised a new, far more interesting question: why had she made an exception for him?

Robert saw Ross's hand curl into a frustrated fist as he faced the invisible wall Moira had erected about herself.

"Ross," Moira almost purred the name.

The hand relaxed.

"This piece my husband purchased from you, the onyx box. What does it look like?"

"It's rather plain, though it is inscribed with some interesting runes." He shrugged. "I can't imagine it is worth much."

"That is the problem with Hurst. He never pursues the *really* fascinating pieces. Just last week someone approached him about a jade funeral mask. *Jade*. And he would have nothing to do with it."

"Perhaps it was a fake. There are many of those about."

"I'm certain that it wasn't. Besides, the man had to know who he was dealing with. Robert would have called the man out, had he suspected such a thing."

Robert heard the interest in Ross's voice as he said in far-too-casual a tone, "Oh, really?"

"Oh, yes. Robert considers people who deal in fakes the lowest form of humanity, and he is quick to exact revenge, regardless of the embarrassment it might cause."

There was a definite pause before Ross said, "That's very conscientious of him."

"You may have noticed that Hurst is a bit . . . particular about things."

"That had dawned on me," Ross said drily.

"To him, a person who deals in fakes is like a badly tied cravat. It's just bad form. And nothing matters more to Hurst."

Ross made a disgusted noise. "There is little that matters to Hurst. That form should be one of them is—" He stopped, apparently too disgusted to continue.

Moira sighed. "Well, we all have our shortcomings. I fear I often crave excitement. I also possess a bit of a temper, and am impulsive. I'm no angel."

Robert almost chuckled at Moira's consummate ability to present herself as the perfect woman to seduce, while throwing up roadblocks to that seduction that were as large as a crypt door.

"Ross, if you don't mind, I should return to my room now. I would like—"

A shout arose in the hallway, and cries of "fire" sent Ross running to the door. In the hallway footmen ran every which way, a low curl of smoke drifting between their legs.

Ross grabbed the closest footman. "What in the hell is going on?"

"Och, sir, we've two *more* fires on our hands."

"Two?"

"Aye!" The footman gulped, obviously unhappy to be the one to have to report distressing news. "A tapestry in the main galley burst into flames at almost the same time a rug in the front hall began to smolder."

"Damn it, that can't be an accident!"

"Ye wouldn't think it, sir. But it appears some-one put a candle too close to the tapestry and for-got to snuff it this mornin'."

"And the fire in the front hall?"

"It was caused by a hot coal from the bucket the sweeps carried after cleanin' the fireplace."

God bless Buffon. Right on time, too.

"Damn it! I hope that wasn't one of the Danish tapestries; they cost me a bloody fortune." Ross turned to Moira. "I'm sorry for the inconvenience, but I must go; I shall have a footman escort you back to your room."

"Thank you, but I believe I can find my own way."

Ross took her hand and pressed a hasty kiss upon her fingers. "I hope we may ride again soon."

She dropped into a curtsy. "As do I, my lord."

With obvious reluctance, he released Moira's hand and disappeared down the now-deserted hallway, calling for his butler.

Robert immediately climbed out from under the desk, then smoothed his coat before joining her. "I'll walk you to the steps leading to our bed-chambers, but then I plan on using Buffon's distur-bance to search a few more rooms."

"I assumed this was his doing. I caught a glimpse of him at the end of the hallway when I first arrived. That's how I knew you were hiding in there."

Robert pulled her hand through his arm and strolled into the hallway, through the running servants who paid them no heed. "Thank you for hiding my shoe. I had no idea it was in sight."

"I take it you didn't find anything."

"Not a damn thing. Wherever the secret chamber is, it's not in that room."

"So what do we do now?"

"You will return to your room, for you're far too noticeable wearing that habit."

"And you?"

"As I said, I shall wander about a bit more and see what I can discover. If anyone sees me, I'll tell them the noise awoke me and I had to come see the madness for myself. Did you learn anything from our illustrious host?"

"Beyond what you heard in the library? Not really. Riding isn't conducive to conversation."

"Perhaps you can lure him into revealing more at dinner." He turned the corner, where a large tapestry smoldered on a wall, footmen with buckets standing around. A large puddle of water pooled upon the floor, and he carefully led Moira around it and on to the stairs.

As they climbed the stairs, Moira said, "Robert,

it might be useful if you have a headache this evening."

"And excuse myself early?"

"Yes. If I can convince Ross that I *must* see his
secret collection, and that I would find that *very*
exciting, I think he's fool enough to show it to me."

"Why wait until dinner?"

"Because I think he will be more foolish after
some port."

"Ah. I will see to it that he imbibes more than
his usual amount."

"Good. Few men can refuse a true challenge."

"Moira, I don't like you spending too much
time alone with Ross, so pray be cautious. He's not
a nice man."

"Ah, but I'm not a nice woman." Moira patted
her skirt. "And I have my pistol."

"You have it with you now?"

"I had a band made for the holster so I can
strap it to my thigh."

That made for an interesting image. "Very well.
I'll leave you alone with Ross after dinner, but only
for an hour. I will be awaiting your return in your
bedchamber."

"Hopefully I will have something significant
to tell you." She smiled at him, and he was struck
anew by the directness of her expression. *She trusts*

me. The thought unexpectedly made his chest tighten in an odd way.

She paused by the steps that led to their bed-chambers. "If all goes well this evening, I should have the necessary information to find the onyx box."

He bowed. "Until later, madam."

Chapter 18

A letter from Captain William Hurst to his sister Mary, sent today from Egypt.

Mary,

I hope this finds you well. I write to tell you that I have at last secured our brother's freedom! Michael is resting comfortably upon my ship. He appears healthy, although he claims to have gained weight from too much rich food.

All is not well, though, as the sulfi who held Michael prisoner appears to have become enamored of Michael's assistant, Miss Smythe-Haughton. Michael refuses to leave without her, even though I pointed out the dangers. The box we gave the sulfi is not the original one, and it is only a matter of time before the deception is discovered.

If we see no progress in freeing Miss Smythe-Haughton within the next day or two, I shall forcibly bring William home. Personally, I don't believe his assistant needs saving. From what William has told me about that redoubtable female, we should be more worried about the sulfi.

*B*ecause of the ruckus caused by Buffon's carefully lit fires, Robert was able to wander freely about the castle for the next hour and a half until calmer heads prevailed and it was noted that none of the footmen were at their stations. Slowly, the hallways filled up once more with liveried men and Robert was forced to call off his search.

Later, while getting ready for dinner, he admitted to himself he was getting frustrated. That damned hiding place had to be in this castle and it had to be large enough to hold a number of artifacts . . . but where? He studied the map to no avail; the castle was too large to simply guess at a location. They needed more clues.

Soon, Buffon arrived, fresh cravats carefully folded over one arm. "Good evening, *monsieur*. I've ordered a bath. I thought you might need one after climbing under furniture all day and rolling about on the floor."

"It was amazingly dust free."

"I am not surprised. Sir Ross has far more servants than he needs. The number of chambermaids is astounding and many of them have nothing to do but talk, talk, talk."

"Have you discovered any information yet?"

"I'm very close, *monsieur*. *Very* close."

"I hope you discover something, for I'm at a loss. I've searched the obvious areas, with the exception of Ross's bedchamber. That will be my next goal, though it will be quite difficult." Robert sent a sharp glance at Buffon. "I shall reward you handsomely if you find any information leading to discovering that damned box. I'm certain Ross will try to pass a fake to us this evening."

"If that barbarian is so bold as to attempt to cheat *you, monsieur* . . . Pah! The blood boils at the thought."

"Yes, it does." Robert's blood boiled even more, thinking of Moira's flirtation with the man. One way or another, it was time for this game to end. "By the way, you did an excellent job of providing distractions today."

A pleased smile crossed Buffon's face. "*Oui, monsieur*. I am quite good at distractions. It is my *forte*."

"I shall have to increase your pay if you continue being so indispensible."

"It is my job, *monsieur*. It is what Buffon does."

It was difficult to stay discouraged in the face of Buffon's confidence. The bath arrived shortly, and Robert washed and dressed for dinner, with the exception of his coat. After a brief tussle with Buffon over which robe he would wear, Robert sent the valet on his way and settled by the fireplace.

He wasn't comfortable with the way Ross looked at Moira. It wasn't a look one gave a woman one wished to conquer, but something more primal.

Robert didn't like it. In fact, he hated it with a passion. *Damn it, I need to regain my perspective. I'm here to get that damned box, and that's all.*

Still, he should remind Moira once again to be cautious around Ross. He was a very large, very powerful man. A mere pistol might not be enough.

Robert rose and turned the key in his lock, then he crossed to the window and pushed back the curtains. The wind had picked up as night had fallen, and gusts danced along the stone façade. It was pitch-black outside, although the courtyard far below was pooled in yellow, flickering light.

Robert pulled the collar of his robe a bit higher and opened the window, then stepped out onto the wide ledge. The wind tugged at his trousers and the folds of his robe. Placing his hands to either side of him, he edged along the ledge toward Moira's room. Halfway there, the edge of his foot hit something. He paused to look down. The pale light from his window outlined one of the stone gargoyles, the little creature hunched in place, his face frozen in a mocking sneer.

Robert stepped over the creature and continued to Moira's window. There, he peered through the crack in the curtain where he could plainly see a fat maid carrying Moira's riding habit. With a deep curtsy, the woman said something in a low voice and then left.

As the door closed behind the maid, Robert pushed the window open and shoved back the curtains.

Moira whirled to face him. She was dressed in a gown of periwinkle blue decorated with knots of ribbons in dark blue and pale green. She pressed a hand to her chest. "Good God, you scared me."

"I apologize. I wished to see you without our movements being reported."

She ran to the door and turned the key in the lock. "How on earth did you get here?"

"By the ledge."

"Good heavens!"

"I've walked a far narrower one before, and for far less reason."

She laughed softly and came to him. "Why am I not surprised?" Her gaze took in his robe, and she touched one of the *very* slightly frayed cuffs. "I never thought to see you in anything so tattered."

"It's not tattered. My sister Triona bought this robe for me, and it's very comfortable." He took a seat by the fire and beckoned her over. "Buffon is coming back to assist me into my coat before dinner. I didn't want it to wrinkle."

Moira took the seat opposite his. "I'm glad you came to visit. In talking to my maid I've discovered a few interesting tidbits, though nothing that will assist us in our search, I fear."

"Oh?"

"I asked if our host had ever been married, and I was informed that Ross was too busy to take a wife, though many of his neighbors had tried to fix his interest with their daughters. He rarely travels, spending time with his horses and his collections. He goes very few places and does very few things—he is a strange man."

Robert considered this. "He is very strange, seducing every female who crosses his threshold. He certainly made sure your accommodations outshine mine. Perhaps, in his mind, he has been seducing you since you first arrived."

"Are your accommodations so poor?"

"Compared to your suite, my bedchamber is little more than a closet."

"That explains the quality robe, then."

His gaze narrowed. "Let's not bring my robe into this conversation."

Moira fought a gurgle of laughter. "I suppose I could grow used to it."

"Good—for I've every intention of seeing you wear it at some point." His eyes darkened, and she grew breathless.

There was such a pull between them, a tug of like meeting like. She'd felt it from the first time she'd met him. She'd known he hadn't believed she was a Russian princess, but to her surprise he hadn't called her out. Later, it became apparent that he'd approached her merely because he'd been instructed to, but at the time, she'd foolishly allowed herself to think he'd been just as intrigued with her as she'd been with him.

The tug of camaraderie was still every bit as strong as that first meeting.

He was aware of it, too. It showed in the possessive way he looked at her. He caught her gaze now and gave her a dark smile. "Perhaps you'd be more comfortable here." He patted his knee.

If I sit on his lap, I may want to stay forever. "No, thank you. I have more room here."

"That was the point."

It was so tempting. She tingled just from remembering their tryst at the inn. *I need to stop remembering that morning. I'll just miss him all the more once this is done.*

The thought caught her unprepared. The bald truth was that she *would* miss him—far more than she wished. "Robert, perhaps . . . perhaps we should keep this relationship professional."

"Why? We haven't done so yet."

"We will be more effective."

"I disagree. I think a full partnership is in order. After all, we are already parents. We share that much, at least." Robert regretted the words as soon as they left his mouth. All humor fled from her face and she winced as if struck.

Damn it, I am ten million times a fool. "Moira, I'm sorry. I shouldn't have spoken so lightly of Rowena. I wasn't thinking." He leaned forward and took her hands. "We will be partners however it is easiest for you. And we will never cease our efforts until we have her back."

She managed a faint smile and gently withdrew her hands. "Thank you. That helps." She brushed back a lock of hair that had fallen from its pin to caress her cheek. "The nights are the hardest. I wake up thinking about her, and it is impossible to go back to sleep."

"Would it help to talk about her? Or would that make it worse?"

"I don't know. I haven't had anyone to talk with."

He leaned back in his chair. "I am curious about our daughter. I've never thought of myself as a parent."

She gave him a twisted smile. "I never thought of myself as a mother until I was one, so I know what you mean. But now I can't imagine my life without her."

He nodded, noting how her eyes shone. "Is she a very quiet child?"

Her expression brightened. "Oh, no! She is so curious, always asking questions and—" Moira laughed. "She would drive me mad asking more and more questions, until sometimes I was ready to snap at her."

He grinned. "Neither of us are shy or retiring."

"Oh, but she's not merely articulate. She loves a good argument, too, and adores horses more than—" Moira's voice broke, as tears gathered.

"Oh, Moira. Don't." Robert pulled her onto his lap and tucked her against him, resting his chin on her head, wrapping his arms about her as she wept softly into the shoulder of his robe, clutching the collar.

"Easy, sweetheart," he whispered against her

silken hair. Over and over he murmured reassurances, promising they'd get Rowena back, that all would be well. Silently, he added that he would make certain George Aniston paid and paid for the pain he'd put them through.

He let her weep, running a soothing hand over her shoulders and back. Eventually her tears began to dry, and she finally subsided into a quiet sniffle.

She reached into her pocket and withdrew a handkerchief to wipe her tears. "I'm sorry. I think I'm fine with everything, and then this happens."

"I shouldn't have asked about her. I have the most damnable curiosity."

"As does she." Moira's smile twisted. "It's all right, Robert. Really. It's good for me to talk about her. I just didn't have anyone to speak to before, and I'm not used to it."

"You don't trust many people, do you?"

"Not where Rowena is concerned."

He placed a finger under her chin and lifted her face to his. Her thick lashes were spiked by her tears. "If you decide that this is too much for you, just say the word and I'll send you home. It may take me a day or two longer to get that box, but then I'll join you and—"

"No! This is my fight, too." Her jaw was set, her full mouth set.

She pushed herself away and tried to rise but Robert refused to let her go. "I rather like having you in my lap. I have very thin blood, you know. You keep me warm."

Her lips quirked. "You do not have thin blood."

"Fine, then. I'm a spoiled sophisticate who cannot hold a conversation with a beautiful woman unless I have my hands on her."

She burst out laughing and relaxed against him. "You're spoiled; that much is true."

He grinned, glad to see the humor back in her eyes. "Now that we're both comfortable, we should discuss this evening. I'm having qualms. Ross seems unstable. I worry that he might step over the line when I'm not there to protect you."

She shrugged. "I have my pistol."

"That's not enough. I think we should cease attempting to woo Ross, and instead give Buffon time to work his magic. Someone in this castle has to know where that chamber is."

"No, we must press every advantage we can. I know I can convince Ross to show me his collection if I just have a little more time."

She looked so earnest that he could not refuse her. He rested his forehead against hers. "You're set on this, are you?"

"Yes." She glanced at the clock on the mantel.

"You should return to your room and finish getting ready." She placed her hands on his chest to sit upright, but he kept his arms about her.

It was so pleasant, snug by the fire in her room, her warm curves fitted against his lap. A moment of complete peace before they began their performance.

He'd never relished peace before, and if anyone had asked, he would have sworn that he would find it boring. But sitting here, with Moira wrapped in his arms, was anything but boring.

"Robert, my maid will return before long."

"I know." He sighed and released her.

She slipped her arms about his neck and gave him a quick, fierce hug.

He blinked in surprise but wrapped his arms back about her.

They stayed like that for a long moment, her face buried in his neck. But his body was awake now, and he had to fight the urge to press against her, to slip his hand beneath the blue silk and touch the warmth of her creamy skin, to—

Moira gave a heavy sigh, then rose from his lap. She caught sight of herself in one of the large gilt mirrors and chuckled. "I'll have to fix my hair again."

Robert stood, too, glad that his robe covered

his response to her. He went to the window and opened it, the swirl of wind hitting him and cooling his senses.

"I don't like you using the ledge."

"Don't worry. The old oak beside Wythburn Vicarage was more dangerous. It was conveniently located outside my window. When my father thought I was studying the *Iliad,* I was actually riding across the moors."

He stepped onto the ledge. "Shut the windows behind me, but do not latch them. I may need to return sometime."

She came to stand by the large window and smiled up at him, looking absurdly young in her gown and piled-up hair. "Yes, sir. Is there anything else I should do for you?"

He smiled. "Nothing that we would want to finish in the few minutes we have left before our servants return. It is time to focus on our mission. Here's to our success." He winked and left.

CHAPTER 19

Michael Hurst's diary, dated today

I am going to slowly throttle Miss Smythe-Haughton until she begs for mercy... right after I rescue her.

*D*inner was finally over. Robert leaned back and lifted his monocle to observe the cherry tart that had been placed before him. He crinkled his nose and pushed the dish away. "Ross, thank you for an *interesting* dinner."

"It was quite good, wasn't it?" Moira said.

"It was *interesting*," Robert repeated. He eyed his host, who sat at the head of the table. "I don't wish to be rude, but the time has come to take possession of the box I purchased from you."

Robert had done his part during dinner, slyly suggesting that Scotsmen couldn't hold their drink, which had caused their host to imbibe what Moira suspected was much, much more port than he normally drank.

"We shall get to that presently." Ross held up his empty glass. "Oh ho, *another* measure gone. And you, Mr. Hurst? Is *your* glass empty?"

"No, I fear not." Robert examined Ross's flushed face. "When may I have the box?"

Ross frowned. "You're insistent, sir."

"I've already paid for it, and I must return to London before this treacherous damp air gives me a lung infection."

Moira hid her chuckle behind a cough.

Ross took a deep drink. "I shall give it to you in the morning."

"Why not now, pray tell? Unless . . . you *do* have it, do you not?"

"Of course I have it," Ross returned testily. "I just don't wish to run all the way upstairs and fetch it."

Moira said sweetly, "If it will help, I would be glad to ask one of the footmen to fetch it for you."

"No, no. No one is allowed in my—" Ross blinked, realizing he was in the process of saying something he shouldn't.

Moira leaned forward. "Or if you wish, I could get it for you—"

"No! No one is allowed there except me."

"Allowed where?" Robert asked smoothly.

"Allowed in—" Ross's gaze narrowed. "No one except me is allowed near my collection." He paused, then said in a more measured tone, though his words were slightly slurred, "Mr. Hurst, I didn't mean to withhold your purchase from you. I was merely enjoying the presence of you and your lovely wife and thought you were doing the same."

"I suppose we both needed the rest," Robert returned in a sulky tone. "Your castle is certainly comfortable, I'll give you that."

"Thank you," Ross said in a stiff tone that indicated he'd rather punch Robert than smile. "I will have your artifact ready by breakfast. I trust you are satisfied with that."

"Perfectly." Robert sighed. "Moira, I think I will retire. I have quite the headache; I vow this damp country air is poisonous."

"You should have Buffon fetch you some lavender water from my chamber. If you rub it on your temples, it might ease your headache."

"I shall do that." Robert stood, pausing when Moira stayed in her seat. "Aren't you coming, my love?"

"No, I thought I might stay here, with Sir Lachlan. I'm not a bit tired."

Robert shrugged. "Very well. Just don't be up too late. We'll be leaving in the morning, and if you don't get enough rest it makes horrid circles under your eyes." He bowed. "Good night, Ross. Good night, Moira."

Moira's heart fluttered a bit as Robert left. *This is my big chance.* She smiled at her host. "I hope you don't mind if I stay a bit longer?"

"Of course not. You may stay as long as you wish."

"Thank you. You are such a gracious host."

He captured her hand and placed a kiss on her wrist. "And you, *madame*, are a lovely guest."

She looked demurely away but left her hand in his possession. "Thank you. W-we should talk about something else, please."

"Anything you want, my dear, but first, if you'll give me a second..." He stood, tottering unsteadily for a moment, then walked to the wide doors and shut them.

She frowned. "Lord Ross, what are you doing?"

Ross turned and leaned against the door, his hands behind him. "There. Isn't that better?"

"Lord Ross, I—"

"One kiss, Moira. Just one, and I shall let you leave."

She *was* supposed to encourage him a little. Under normal circumstances she would have done so without thinking, but she couldn't help but imagine that Robert would not be pleased.

A ridiculous thought; why should she care what Robert thought? She tamped down her qualms. "I *might* kiss you ... if you'll show me your collection."

His gaze narrowed. "Why do you want to see that? You keep bringing it up and I wonder—"

"*I* keep bringing it up? Oh, no, my lord, *you* keep

bringing it up and I take that as a challenge. Why, this evening over dinner you flatly said that no one—*no one*—was allowed in the room where you house your treasure. If that's not a challenge, then I don't know what is!"

He laughed. "I suppose it was, of a sort, though not to you."

"Oh, to Robert, then? He can be quite rude." She gestured about the room. "But he's not here, is he?"

Ross's eyes gleamed and his breathing seemed to come harsher. "No, he's not. There's no one here but you and me. Come, Moira, one kiss—"

"Not without seeing your treasure room."

He scowled, looking like a child deprived of a candy. "I can't do that."

"Then I can't kiss you," she said primly. "I want to see these artifacts you've told me about. Hurst says you may have the biggest collection on earth."

Ross looked mollified. "It's tolerable. The room is almost the size of this."

Finally, some details. She clasped her hands together and said in a breathless voice, "And it's *filled* with antiquities?"

"To the top." He tottered back to the table, pausing to steady himself by holding on to the back of a chair. When he reached her, he took her hand

and patted it. "One kiss and I shall show you my treasures."

"Tonight?"

"Why not?" He stroked her hand. "You are *completely* charming, which is why I *must* kiss you. Something to remember you by, since you and Hurst will be gone as soon as I give him that damned box."

The man was an imbecile. He was as subtle as a bullet, which made it hard to pretend the innocence he found so attractive. *Better to get this over with.* "If you want a kiss, then we should do it quickly, before the servants come to clear the table." *And before I change my mind.* She was not looking forward to this at all.

"You're an eager little thing, aren't you?" He took her hands in his and pulled her close.

Moira tilted her face to his and lifted her lips. To her shock, he grabbed her with both hands and yanked her against him, then kissed her hard, his thick tongue pressing between her lips.

She struggled, turning her face to one side. "Sir Lachlan, *no!*"

He laughed, his hands busy as he shoved aside the neckline of her gown so roughly that he ripped it. The sound seemed to excite him for he began to feverishly press against her, pinching her breast.

Suddenly Moira knew why Ross had been in two duels: he was planning on taking her right then and there.

Moira crammed her arms between them and managed to get one hand flat on his chest to give herself some room. She kept moving her head so he couldn't capture her mouth. "Stop it!" Moira used her most authoritative voice, her words ringing clearly and sharply.

His expression turned ugly and he tightened his hold, grinding his hips to hers. "You little tease!"

He held her so tightly that she couldn't bring her heel down on his instep, so she kicked him in the shin as hard as she could.

He grunted, his hold slackening as she twisted free. The second she had room, she tugged her pistol from her pocket, pressing the tip firmly against his chest.

Ross's eyes widened and he froze. "You— That's— What do you—" His mouth opened and closed as she cocked the pistol.

"It's time for you to retire for the evening."

An ugly red flush rose across his neck and cheeks. "You wanted me to kiss you! You practically begged me!"

"No, I agreed to kiss you *once*. And I did *not* invite you to assault me."

"I didn't assault you." His lips thinned when she lifted her brows.

She stepped back, keeping the pistol aimed steadily on his chest. "You touched me and ripped my gown and tried to—"

"Fine!" He eyed her and her pistol with disfavor. "I suppose you'll tell your husband about this."

Of course she was going to tell Robert though she dreaded his reaction. *We'll find that secret chamber without Ross's help.* "Open the doors. In the morning, once Hurst and I have that box, we will leave."

"What if I refuse?"

"Then I will shoot you and leave Hurst to deal with the mess. He's very good at cleaning up unpleasant situations."

"Your husband couldn't butter his own bread, much less deal with any kind of situation. But fine—I'll open the doors. And you, my little tease, can go to hell!" Muttering under his breath, he walked to the doors and threw them open. "There!" he said in a sharp tone. "Now be gone!"

Moira backed out, slipping her pistol away as soon as the footmen standing outside the doors came into sight. Ignoring their surprised looks, she hurried up the steps toward her room.

She paused outside of Robert's room and

pressed her ear to the door, but could hear nothing. *He is probably already asleep.*

Her hands shaking, she went to her own room and locked the door behind her. Then she dragged a chair over and pushed it under the knob. Once that was done, she scrubbed her mouth with the back of her hand, catching sight of herself in the gilded mirror over the fireplace. Her hair was falling down, her beautiful gown ripped at one shoulder, her face flushed, her eyes shiny with fear. She'd thought Ross a fool, not capable of violence, yet— She rubbed her lips again, trying to get rid of the memory. Robert had been right; Ross was the worst sort of man and she had been a fool to think she could handle him so easily.

Out in the hallway, she heard a voice. Her heart leapt in her throat. Had Ross followed her? Her heart beat wildly and her gaze found the window Robert had climbed in before. She wished with all her heart that he was with her now. She would feel safer.

There are no princes ready to ride up on a white horse. If I want to talk to Robert, I will have to go to him. She kicked off her slippers, jammed her feet into some sensible boots, and scooped up her cloak.

She blew out all of the lamps, plunging the bedchamber into darkness. Her heart pounding, she opened the window; then with a deep breath she climbed onto the windowsill and stepped out onto the ledge. The icy wind clutched at her, swirling her cloak and stealing all of her warmth. Moira took a hesitant step.

Was that a sliver of light through his curtains? She took another step, releasing her hold on her own window as she did so.

Robert had claimed that the ledge wasn't narrow, but it certainly seemed so, especially in the dark. Well, she'd just have to take her chances. It was fortunate that the rough-hewn stone would provide decent handholds.

She edged along, one foot after another, and soon she was halfway there. One step. Another one. Another—her foot hit something hard, and for a horrible instant she teetered before regaining her balance.

Panting, she looked down to find a gargoyle sneering up at her at the edge of the ledge. Gritting her teeth, she stepped over it. Her heart pounded in her ears. She was so far up, and there was nothing to break her fall if she slipped.

God, what had she been thinking? This was crazy! The gravity of her situation held her immobile, her feet seemingly locked into place.

The wind whipped up the castle face and sent

her robe and skirts swirling, cold air rippling up her bared legs. *Damn it, Moira, move!*

She took a deep breath, and began to edge toward Robert's window again. One step. Another. Yet another. She sang along in her mind. One step. Another. Yet another. Finally, she found herself right where she wished to be.

She reached down to tap on the glass, then realized she could hear *two* masculine voices inside the room.

She pressed against the cold stone wall. *What do I do now?*

CHAPTER 20

A letter from Triona Hurst MacLean to her sister Lady Caitlyn Hurst MacLean, a month ago.

Hugh wishes to go to Edinburgh and then to London in the near future, which I would enjoy above all things. Pray see if you and Alexander and the children can come, as well. It will give us the opportunity to find out what is going on with those brothers of ours. They are too close with their information, sharing nothing unless you drag it out of them.

Something is going on; I can feel it. As Mam always says, "Gut is always right."

A soft knock announced Buffon's entrance, and Robert looked up from Moira's map. "I've marked where I've searched and where you've gone, but the castle's so large it would take two weeks to search it thoroughly. I want to leave in the morning, but—" He sighed. "Damn it. Where can that chamber be?"

"It would be delightful to have that information, wouldn't it, *monsieur*?" Buffon smiled.

Robert did, too. "You know something."

Buffon looked pleased. *"Oui."*

"Out with it, then!"

"There is a room in the West Wing, a part of the castle rarely used, that Ross will not allow the maids to dust. He has been known to spend hours there by himself and when he returns he is much invigorated."

"It must be there, then."

"I think so, *monsieur*. May I see your map?"

Robert held it out.

The valet studied it and then pointed a thin finger to one of the lower reaches of the castle. "It is here, *monsieur*."

Robert picked up his pen and marked the spot. "I shall slip out later tonight. Can you create another diversion?"

"As you wish, *monsieur*. Hmm. Perhaps a ghost is in order."

"Good. It's interesting that Ross doesn't trust the servants."

"*Non*. It appears Sir Ross leads a lonely life, as he deserves."

"Indeed. I shall sleep for a few hours and get up at three. Can you do your haunting at that time?"

"But of course." Buffon arched a brow. "But first, there is the matter of compensation. You indicated that I would be rewarded."

"Of course. Fifty pounds? A hundred?"

"Your robe, *monsieur*."

Robert blinked. "What?"

"*Oui*. The blue one. It pains me to see you wear it."

Robert sighed.

Buffon waited.

"Very well. Take the damn robe. I shall have Triona make me another."

"Thank you, *monsieur*! Until then, you will wear the red silk one?"

"Yes, yes."

Buffon beamed and wasted no time in removing it from the wardrobe. "Here, *monsieur*." He held it out.

Robert sighed but slipped it on. As he did so, a noise sounded at the window. Robert frowned at the closed curtains.

Buffon tilted his head. "Did you hear—"

"The wind, yes. You may go, Buffon. I will be ready at three."

"Very good, *monsieur*." With a stately nod and a satisfied look at the red robe, Buffon left, holding the blue robe before him like a moldy rag.

Robert hurried to the windows. One glance out told him all he needed to know; seconds later, he was pulling Moira inside.

She was shivering, her skin as cold as river stones. "What the hell are you doing?" he hissed as he set her upon her feet, wrapping his arms about her to warm her.

Moira had never been so glad to see anyone in her life, even though Robert was pale with fury. "Y-you climbed across the ledge," she pointed out through chattering teeth.

"Not in long skirts and slippers with smooth soles. Damn it, do you never think?"

"Y-yes, and I n-n-needed to visit you. Furthermore, these"—she showed him her sensible boots—"are not s-slippers."

He cursed, swept her up, and carried her to his bed. "Take off those boots."

She tried, but her fingers were too cold to undo the laces. He muttered a curse and did it for her, yanking them off and tossing them into the corner.

Robert supposed he should be grateful she'd at least worn good shoes, but he was too furious at the chance she'd taken. Her skirts could easily have wrapped around her legs, and he had an instant vision of her terrified expression as she plunged off the edge and into the—*She could have died, damn it! Died and left me*—

His heart aching in an unfamiliar way, his throat tight, he closed the window and tugged the curtains into place.

Her gaze locked on his red silk robe. "That's very . . . bright."

"Yes, it is. My blue one is gone."

"Oh." She looked about his room. "This is very cozy."

"It's a bit larger than a water closet, which our host is well aware of."

At the mention of Ross, her expression closed.

Robert's anger tightened further. "What happened? Did that ass—"

"No. But I'm glad I had my pistol."

Robert's hands fisted at his sides as fury raced through his blood. "*Damn* him! I'll—" He was almost at the door when she caught up to him, grabbing his arm with both hands.

"*No*, Robert! We have to do what's best for Rowena."

In her eyes, he saw that she was barely holding on to her own composure.

He took a deep breath and then reached for her, holding her close against his heart. He pressed his cheek against her hair, willing away the bloodlust that held him in its grip.

"I want to kill that man," he snapped, every fiber of his being screaming for justice.

"As do I," she said, her voice soft and soothing. "But we can't. We have one goal here and that's to rescue my d—" She took a breath. "—*our* daughter."

Despite his anger, he had to laugh at the reluctance in her tone. Robert lifted her face toward his. "Come, Moira. Was that so very difficult to say?"

She smiled at his teasing tone. "It will take some getting used to."

"I can see that. Well, I've made a decision, and this incident with Ross has made me even more committed to it."

"What's that?"

Robert straightened. "Box or no, we leave in the morning."

She paled. "But—"

"I think I know where that damned box is, and I shall attempt to get it tonight. But if I fail, we leave anyway. I will take care of Rowena, I promise. I will make Aniston give her up, and she will be safe with you once more."

Her shoulders sagged and she said in a broken whisper, "I wish I could believe that."

He sighed. She still didn't trust him, which was disheartening. It was odd, for in every relationship he'd ever had, he was the one unwilling to trust, to care, to commit. And yet here he was, yearning for—damn it, what *did* he yearn for? Well, there would be time enough to think about that once he and Moira were gone from this cursed place. "In the morning I will have Leeds and Stewart ready with the coach. You will wait with them. As soon as I get the artifact, we go. I'm done playing Ross's game."

She hesitated, then nodded. "Very well. We will try it your way."

Robert's gaze traced the curve of her cheek to the delicate line of her throat, and down to the swell of her breasts. His fingers itched at the thought of cupping them through the fabric, teasing them until—

"Robert, kiss me." Her gaze locked with his. "I don't want to think any more."

He kissed her with all his pent-up emotion and passion, bunching her gown in his hands. In seconds, he had her undressed and in bed. Her skin looked peach-warm in the lamplight that caressed her curves, which beckoned to him irresistably.

She smiled tantalizingly. "Well? Are you just going to look?"

What man could resist her? He swiftly undressed. Her gaze immediately went to his erect cock, fanning his own desire.

He got into the small bed, eager to touch her. He cupped one breast and flicked his thumb over the nipple. It hardened immediately and Moira gasped, her lashes fluttering. God, he loved it when he made her look like that.

Then her warm hand encircled his cock, and Robert caught his breath at the eruption of sensations that rippled through him, teasing and tantalizing.

Before he could say anything, Moira released him, pushed him to the mattress, and straddled him. His cock was firmly pressed against her backside as she grinned down at him, her hair streaming over her shoulders. "It's time you stopped ordering me about." She raised up on her knees, and then slid down onto him.

Robert grabbed the mattress edges with both hands, trying to keep control. "Moira, don't—" he choked out.

Moira lifted up until she was poised over his cock again. "Well?" she whispered. "Shall I?"

He couldn't resist her. He grasped her waist and answered her with a firm downward tug.

She engulfed him in a tight, velvet grip that sent his senses spiraling out of control. She rode him again and again, teasing him to madness. Just as he was on the edge of no return, she stopped, her head tilted back, her glorious red hair streaming about her, an expression of pure ecstasy on her face.

Robert lifted his hips, and she gasped, rocking back on her heels, her hands flat on his stomach. Robert wished he could take this moment and hold it forever.

He held her waist and slowly lifted her, then slid her back down, and she moaned. They found a steady rhythm, their breathing growing more erratic, the pressure building until Moira gasped out his name and threw herself forward to rock hard back and forth. Suddenly, she stilled and gasped his name as she gave way to the wave of pleasure that engulfed her.

Robert immediately followed, erupting with deep tremors that he thought would never stop.

Moira collapsed against him, and they clung to each other, breathing heavily, their hearts pounding together. She felt so good in his arms, so peaceful and right. He was almost afraid to move.

There had been too few of these moments in his life, when he'd felt completely at peace, and he wanted to hold on to it for as long as he could. He rolled to his side and held her against him as he ran his fingers over her silky skin, luxuriating in the warmth that radiated from her. The moment stretched, the silence warm and comforting.

Finally, he lifted up on one elbow and smiled down at her. "Well?"

Moira opened her eyes. He was so smugly satisfied that she had to chuckle. "Well, Mr. Hurst, that was very invigorating."

"It was." He brushed her hair from her forehead. "But that's not what I meant."

"Oh? What did you mean?"

He threaded his fingers through her hair and fanned it out. "I meant how right it is that we still have this."

"Oh. Yes, it is." She tried to keep her attention on his face, though it was difficult with his bare chest. He was the most beautiful man she'd ever seen, all lean and elegant sinew. His muscular body showed the effects of many hours of boxing, fencing, and riding.

She traced her fingers over his chest, noting how warm his skin was. It was as if he was heated by an internal fire, and she snuggled deeper against him.

He raised his brows, still smiling. "Making yourself comfortable?"

"Mm hmm." She breathed in the scent of his skin. How she loved the feel of him in her bed, hard muscles and angles, the feel of strong legs entwined with hers. It had been so long since she'd felt this pleasure. "We should rest a bit and then try it again." She opened one eye and flashed him a sleepy, satisfied grin. "If you're up to it, of course."

He shook his head in wonder. "I've never met a woman who was so comfortable with her life and decisions and yet determined to be on her own."

She wondered at that, for there was no denying

his masculine appeal. Good God, how could anyone resist those blue eyes, that black hair, that flat stomach? She ran her hand over his muscular chest. "Perhaps that's your fault."

His brows shot up. "My *fault*?"

"Women want to feel cherished, not possessed. Being with you is very . . . intense. It's difficult not to be overwhelmed."

His lips curved into a pleased smile. "Overwhelmed, eh?"

"Don't take that as a compliment."

"Too late." He bent and pressed his lips to her ear and then whispered, his breath warm against her ear, "I heard your moans, *ma chère*. 'Overwhelmed' is a good thing."

She chuckled, suddenly sleepy from the trials of the day and especially her exertions with Robert. "With you, 'overwhelmed' can be a very, very good thing." She pressed her lips to his cheek, noting how his blue eyes were lit with the fire he usually hid beneath his French cuffs and laces.

Robert continued to run his fingers through her hair, spreading it across her shoulders. "I've always had a weakness for your beautiful hair."

And I've always had a weakness for you. Moira smiled sleepily. "I'll want to sleep here. I locked the door to my room."

He kissed her nose and pulled the blankets up. "Sleep, Moira." Then he tucked her close, her back to his chest. "I'll keep watch while you do."

Moira smiled and drifted off to sleep with Robert curled around her, his arm over her waist, his leg across hers.

CHAPTER 21

Letter from Robert Hurst to his brother Michael, who was being held by a sulfi in a foreign land.

William is on his way with the required ransom to win your freedom. The onyx box is a lovely artifact and reminds me of the times we used Mother's empty jewelry box as our treasure chest when we played at being pirates.

I remember being very angry when one of you attempted to "steal" the treasure chest from me; even then I didn't like it when something was taken from me . . .

S ir Lachlan awoke with a start in his firelit room, panting hard in the grip of a nightmare where the delicious Moira Hurst turned from a sweet temptress into a pistol-wielding goddess of fury.

Ross pressed a hand to where his heart hammered against his chest, wishing his head didn't pound so as well. He'd drunk far too much port, egged on by that fool Hurst.

Ross was done with them both. In the morning, Moira and that fop of a husband would be gone, fake box in hand. Who would be smirking then?

Well before the Hursts were awake, he'd leave for his hunting just in case Moira had been right about her husband's ability to spot a fake. Ross had no patience with fusses, and—

A faint noise tickled his ears, Frowning, he lifted up on one elbow as the ice-cold end of a pistol pressed against his forehead.

Startled, Ross found himself staring at Robert Hurst. The man was sitting in a chair that had been pulled beside the bed. Gone was the fanciful fop who'd irritated Ross since arriving; in the fop's place was a man who knew how to hold a pistol steadily.

"Good morning, Ross," Hurst said, his usual bored tone replaced by a deep intensity that made Ross's stomach tighten uneasily. "Having a bad dream?"

Ross cleared his throat. "What are you doing here?"

"I came to tell you good-bye. Oh, and don't worry about the onyx box. I fetched it myself."

Ross's gaze fell on the box sitting in plain sight on Hurst's knee. It wasn't the fake one, either. *Damn it!* "How did you find that?"

Hurst's eyes gleamed in the firelight. "When I buy something, I expect to get it. And when I don't, then I make certain I do."

It suddenly dawned on Ross that this stern, powerful man had been hiding his true self all along. "You play a deep game, Hurst."

"Not as deep as you. Move your left foot."

"What?"

"You heard me." Hurst stood, his pistol never wavering.

Ross moved his left foot and touched something hard. "What's that?"

"The matching pistol to this one. Do you recognize these pistols? They're quite beautiful."

Ross pushed himself upright. "They're my dueling pistols. So you're stealing them, too."

"No, *I'm* not the thief here," Hurst said insultingly.

"You can't prove a damn thing, and you know it."

"I don't need to. Pick up that pistol. It's loaded with one bullet. Just like this one."

A coldness settled in Ross's head, making his headache all the worse. "Pick . . . pick up the pistol?"

"Yes. Pick it up and rise."

Ross looked at how Hurst stood, his body relaxed, the pistol unwavering. *This man has killed before.*

Hands damp, Ross asked, "And if I don't?"

"Then sit there and die in your bed. *No one* touches my wife without her permission." Hurst's voice was so icy that Ross had to fight a shiver. There was power in that voice, and a deadly cold determination to exact revenge.

Pale with fear, Ross tried to clear his throat. "Hurst, please. I didn't—"

"Careful, Ross." The soft voice almost purred. "I'm in a foul mood and another lie will make it worse." The pistol cocked loudly. "You don't want that, do you?"

"N-No."

"Good. Well, Ross—will you pick up the pistol, or be killed in cold blood in your bed?" Hurst smiled coldly. "The choice is yours."

Ross tried to swallow but couldn't. He wished with all of his heart that he'd never met the Hursts. But it was too late for that.

"*Madame?*"

Fighting her way up from a deep sleep, Moira opened her eyes to find Buffon standing beside the bed. The Frenchman was fully dressed, one of her gowns over his arm.

She blinked rapidly. Where was she? And why was Buffon— Ah, yes. She was in Robert's room.

Rubbing sleep from her eyes, she began to sit up, then realized she was naked. "Oh—!" She clutched the sheets to her, her face and neck ablaze.

Buffon had already turned his back and was facing the door, standing as if at attention. "There is fresh water on the washstand. The chemise and gown I've placed upon the chair are from your trunk. *Monsieur* asked that you dress quickly, for we must go before the footmen return."

She frowned. "Where is Robert?"

"I am not certain, *madame*. I was only told to fetch you. I shall step outside while you dress."

"Yes, but I'll need pins for my hair and—"

Buffon held up a card of pins, then set it on the chair.

Moira looked at the card. "How did you get into my room?"

"Monsieur climbed the ledge and unlocked the door."

"Oh!"

"Pray get dressed quickly. We are to leave soon." With that, the valet stepped outside, closing the door softly behind him.

Moira quickly washed by the firelight, then put on the chemise and gown. When she was done she twisted her hair into a knot, then slid her feet back into her boots.

When she finished, she opened the door. "I'm ready."

Buffon entered again. "Excellent, *madame*. Your cloak is. hanging in the wardrobe. Mr. Hurst is meeting us in the courtyard soon; the coach is ready with your trunks packed and loaded."

She collected the cloak and pulled it around her.

"We must be very quiet and avoid any servants," Buffon warned.

He opened the door and they slipped into the hallway, then through the castle. To Moira's surprise, the entire place appeared to be deserted.

As they walked across the dark courtyard, Moira whispered to Buffon, "What happened to the footmen?"

"The ghost of Balnagown Castle left four kegs of whiskey in the servants' quarters. Very large kegs."

"How do they know a ghost left it?"

"He wrote a note saying it was to reward them for their excellent service."

"They can't have believed that."

"*Non, madame.* But when one is faced with wonderfully aged casks of whiskey, one does not question where they come from. One simply enjoys."

Her lips quirked. "That was very clever of you."

"Thank you."

Moira's booted feet clicked on the mist-covered cobblestones; the scent of spring heather tickled her nose. Ahead was the coach, the horses' breath puffy white in the night air.

A muffled pistol shot cracked across the silence, the sound obviously coming from inside the thick castle walls. Moira stopped and sent a wild gaze at Buffon, who continued walking toward the coach.

"It is nothing to worry about, *madame.*"

"But I heard—"

Another shot rang out.

Buffon took her elbow and gently tugged her on. "Ah, two shots. That is good."

"Why?"

"Because it means that both participants in the duel got off a shot. It is only fair."

She came to an abrupt halt, the blood leaving her face. "*Duel?*"

"*Oui. Monsieur* could not allow Ross's insult to your honor." Buffon glanced at the castle, the light showing respect on his face. "He has a Frenchman's soul, that one."

"Buffon, he could be dead or—"

"*Monsieur?* Pardon, but no." He pulled her with him, saying in a calm voice, "There is no better shot, no better fighter, no better fencer. I daresay he would wield a battle ax equally well. Efficiently, with deadly force."

Ahead Stewart stood by the open coach door, looking toward the castle. "Och, it looks as if someone kicked over an anthill."

Indeed, havoc had broken loose. People were scurrying here and there, excited voices raised.

Moira pressed a hand to her chest. *Robert, please don't be hurt. Don't be—*

Robert appeared from a dark corner of the

courtyard and strode toward them, tall and powerful, his black cape swirling about him. The mist seemed to part before him.

Moira closed her eyes and said a quick prayer of thanks.

"Stewart, get us off this mountain as fast as you can."

"Ye know I'm good fer tha', sir! Buffon, ye can ride with me." The groom and Buffon disappeared on top of the coach.

Robert opened the door and assisted Moira inside, climbed in behind her, and banged the flat of his hand on the ceiling. Instantly, they lurched forward. They'd just reached the edge of the courtyard when the front door to the castle opened, spilling golden light across the black cobblestones.

Moira saw Ross standing in his white night rail, the left arm of his shirt covered in blood. His other arm held a long musket. He lifted the musket to his shoulder and aimed it at the coach.

Instantly, Robert scooped Moira from her seat and held her in his lap, curving his body over hers. A huge boom rang off the castle walls and echoed in the courtyard.

The coach turned a corner, and it was dark, except for the moonlight and the lanterns that hung from the coach front.

Moira said, "I think the danger is over now. You can release me."

Robert laughed softly, his breath warm against her ear. "There was never any danger. That man couldn't hit the side of a barn."

"So why are you holding me?" The scent of his starched cravat tickled her nose.

"Ross's parting shot was wonderfully dramatic, wasn't it?"

She snuggled deeply against Robert. "You shot him, didn't you?"

"We had a duel. Unfortunately, he lacked the honor to wait for the ten paces."

"He shot *early*?"

"Yes, but his bullet hit the wall beside my left ear."

"That blackguard!"

"Exactly. Then it was my turn. Because I knew it would please you, I didn't kill him. Instead, I gave him the chance to select which limb he wanted my bullet in."

Moira had to smile. "That was very good of you. Astoundingly so, considering he tried to trick you with a false artifact, too."

"I thought so."

She suspected that Robert wasn't completely honest about how close of a call he'd just faced.

"You took a foolish risk for nothing. If my honor was impugned, it was my job to satisfy it, not yours."

"As long as our marriage stands, I will protect you."

As long as our marriage stands. That implied it was temporary, which made her chest ache, as if her heart were struggling to beat. *Don't be ridiculous. As soon as Rowena is free, Robert will ask for an annulment and I will see that he gets it.* Still, her eyes stung, and she had to blink back tears.

Robert reached into his cloak and withdrew a velvet bag, which he placed on her knee.

She opened it, her fingers trembling. "The onyx box."

"The real one. I found it, along with the fake, in Ross's secret chamber."

"How on earth did you find it?"

"Buffon charmed the location from a besotted chambermaid. Now we are ready to take on Aniston."

Moira looked down at the box. Was Robert right? After all these months, would she finally win Rowena back?

Unaware of how her heart was racing, Robert added, "It will take us a week to get back to Edinburgh, then Rowena will be free and you and I can—"

Moira threw her arms around him and kissed him passionately. Surprised, he kissed her back with equal enthusiasm.

A soft thud broke them apart.

"What was that?" Robert asked, voice husky.

"The onyx box fell. Perhaps we should put it somewhere safe?"

"An excellent idea." He retrieved the box and put it under the seat across from them, then he settled Moira back in his lap. "We should talk about what will happen after we rescue—"

She placed a hand on his cheek and smiled. "Hurst, has anyone ever told you that you talk too much?"

And all of his words fled, chased away by a red-headed vixen with eyes the color of a Scottish glen.

CHAPTER 22

A letter from Lady Caitlyn Hurst MacLean to her sister Triona Hurst MacLean.

You would think, since we wed brothers, that we would not be forced into secret stratagems to spend some time together, but thus it is. Pray inform Hugh that the Earl of Tunbridge has been forced to sell all of his horses because the new Countess Tunbridge has decided he spends too much time in the stables. Hugh has always coveted Tunbridge's gray matched set, and he will instantly wish to go to Edinburgh for the sale.

Meanwhile, I shall inform Alexander that the countess is also selling many of the furnishings in their various houses, because they once belonged to her mother-in-law. Alexander cannot refuse a good estate sale.

By the way, when we get to town, the Countess Tunbridge wishes us to go to tea with her. You'll like her very much; she is ever so charming.

It took a week and a day to reach Edinburgh. The closer they got, the more anxious Moira became. Robert did what he could to while away the time—he told stories, played cards, made up silly games, shared court gossip that made her chuckle. But mostly he drew Moira into telling him stories about her life with Rowena.

He learned a lot, seeing Moira in a new light. It astounded him that a woman who could trick the entire polite world into thinking her a Russian princess had the gentleness of spirit to be a devoted mother. But her love for Rowena showed in every sentence as she told of the dolls and flower chains, the colds and bruises, and the laughter and sadness of a normal childhood. Moira obviously loved her cottage in the country, and Robert wondered if Hurst House was the right sort of place for a child. Or for Moira.

He no longer wondered if he wished them in his life—the events of the last three weeks had erased those doubts. Others now tumbled through his mind. Would Moira want to be a part of his life? Would Rowena accept him? He had no idea how to be a good father or husband. What if he couldn't do it well enough? Would they all be miserable?

There was only one area he was sure about, and he held Moira close every night while she slept. And most mornings he awakened her with a kiss that didn't stop there.

As they drew closer to Edinburgh, Moira fought her own fears. She no longer worried that Robert might whisk Rowena away. He would never take a child from her mother; she knew that now. But would he wish to be part of Rowena's life after they had her safe? Did she *want* him to be part of Rowena's life?

Including Robert in their life would change everything. For months, Moira had longed for things to return to the way they had been; now she didn't know what she wanted. Robert was a complex man; she couldn't ask him to stay within the safe little world she'd built. Even if he agreed to, out of a sense of responsibility or because he'd come to care for Rowena, he would eventually tire of the smallness of the community—the very thing that Moira had come to love. It simply couldn't be.

Parting from him would be difficult, for she had

seen another side of the most fascinating man she'd ever met. And despite their desperate dance to keep their attraction contained, she'd fallen deeply in love all over again.

She stole a glance at him as he looked at the cards in his hand, deciding which to play. Today was the final day of their journey; they were only six hours from Edinburgh.

Robert caught her gaze and placed his cards on the seat. "Moira, we must talk."

Her heart gave a lurch as she set her cards down as well. "Of course."

"We will see Aniston tomorrow." Then he said firmly, "Rather, *I* will see him."

She frowned. "No. I must be there."

"It's not safe for you. We don't know what he's capable of. We underestimated Ross, and you almost paid the price for it. That will not happen again."

"Robert, this is my battle. I will tell him he cannot have the onyx box until he gives up Rowena. I've never had any leverage before and it will make all the difference."

"He won't agree to it."

She set her jaw. "He has to, or the box will be gone."

"And what if he calls your bluff? He knows you

will never trade against Rowena's freedom. Meanwhile, he has every reason to think I don't care about her."

"He'll know that's not true when you appear instead of me. Otherwise, you wouldn't bother." She picked up her cards. "I am going to see Aniston, not you, and that's that."

He looked thoughtful. "You're right. Fine. Then we'll go together, as partners."

At one time, she would have agreed to that wholeheartedly. But the more she allowed Robert into her life now, the harder it would be to keep him out later. Besides, he didn't know Aniston as she did. It would be easier—and safer—to do this on her own.

But Robert wouldn't take "no" easily, so she merely said, "All right." She nodded toward his cards. "It's your turn."

He smiled and selected a card from his hand. "Tomorrow we deal with Aniston and Rowena will be freed."

She smiled in return though she couldn't disagree more. This was her fight, and no one else's.

In the dim predawn light, Moira tugged her overcoat about her shoulders, adjusted the lace at her cuffs, and then regarded herself in the mirror.

Looking back at her was a slender man of average height, dressed in the French manner. Lace spilled from her wrists and adorned her cravat behind a thick-cut emerald that was as large as it was fake.

She tugged the dark wig more firmly into place and placed a curly-brimmed hat upon her head, wincing as a hairpin dug into her scalp. "Thank God I'll only have to wear this for a short while," she told herself, deepening her voice and adding a French accent.

She posed before the mirror, one hand lightly resting on an ornate sword that wouldn't have been amiss on a stage. From the way she stood to the haughty expression on her lightly powdered face, she was no longer Moira MacAllister, but a high-born French émigré with more money than manners. The disguise served several purposes. For one, it would allow her to escape the notice of anyone at the inn, including Stewart and Leeds. For another, she could travel to Aniston's abode without interference. And lastly, she might be able to surprise Aniston and give herself more of an edge in their coming meeting.

"You, *monsieur*," she told her reflection, "have much to accomplish today." But before she could face Aniston, she had to procure a horse from the landlord. She tugged on a pair of gloves to hide her feminine hands. It was time for the game to begin.

Moira turned from the mirror, the overcoat swinging out as she moved, the pockets both weighted. Inside one pocket rested the long velvet bag holding the onyx box and a small but very full coin purse, while in the other was her pistol.

She paused to replace the false bottom in her trunk and locked it tight before pushing it under the bed. Then, straightening her shoulders, she opened the door and stepped into the empty hallway. She was glad Robert had chosen an inn on the outskirts of Edinburgh; there were far fewer people to contend with.

Better yet, French émigrés weren't frequent visitors at such inns, so anyone she met would likely have only a vague, theater-induced concept of a Frenchman, which was perfect for her cause. The secret of a good disguise was to be exactly what people expected. That way, no one gave you a second glance.

As she went down the hall, her gaze lingered on the door to Robert's bedchamber. When she'd slipped out of the room earlier he'd been asleep, his hair falling over his brow, his stern mouth softened.

Last night had been their final hours together. She'd spent it the way she'd hoped—passionately. With each kiss, each caress, each sigh, and—after he'd fallen asleep in her arms—with each tear, she'd been telling him good-bye.

The memory tightened her throat as she walked down the stairs. A faint light gleamed from the back hall, indicating that the innkeeper and servants were beginning to stir.

Moira peeked out the front window and, seeing no servants in the inn yard, she opened the front door and then slammed it shut, turning around so that it appeared that she'd just entered.

She instantly heard footsteps from the back hall, followed by the glow of an approaching lantern. Moira quickly arranged her face into a haughty expression.

The innkeeper looked surprised to find a well-dressed gentleman in his foyer so early in the morning, but his shrewd gaze noted the lace cuffs and the emerald pin in her cravat. "Och, sir!" He offered an eager bow. "Sorry no one was here t' greet ye, but I wasna expectin' anyone as 'tis early yet."

"*Oui.* I need a horse, and I need it now."

The innkeeper rubbed his nose. "I can assist ye in that. O' course, it'll cost ye a bit, fer I've no' so many nags as to easily afford to lose one."

Moira pulled a few large coins from the stuffed purse in her pocket. "Just tell me the amount."

The innkeeper's eyes gleamed. "Tha' should do it."

Moira dropped the coins into his outstretched hand.

"I'll have a mount saddled right away. She's older, but she'll get ye where ye need t' go." The innkeeper went to the door and opened it, then looked back at her. "Pardon me, sir, but how did ye get to be here if ye've no mount?"

"I was riding to Edinburgh to visit the Earl of Stratham when a damned thief attacked me." Moira allowed a sneer to touch her mouth. "That was his last mistake."

"'Tis a shame how the brigands run amuck. The crown should do somethin' aboot them."

"This one won't trouble anyone again." Her hand rested upon the hilt of her sword and she permitted herself a faint, superior smile. "In the commotion, my horse ran off. A farmer gave me a ride to your inn. And now I must get to Edinburgh."

"I'll have a horse saddled fer ye right away."

"I shall wait by the fire in the common room." She sauntered into the room as if it were her God-given right, and a second later she heard the door close behind the innkeeper.

So far, so good.

The big room was lit by a single lantern, a low fire crackling in the grate and doing little to banish the early morning chill. She stood before the fire, leaning against the mantel and watching the flames crackle. Soon she'd have Rowena back. Yet she was leaving the man she loved forever.

It didn't seem fair that the two people she most cared about would never share her life at the same time, but it was better for them all not to have to deal with the complications that could cause. But then life had never been fair, and it was silly to wish otherwise.

The front door opened and closed and the sound of booted footsteps came down the hall. Good—the horse was ready.

Stewart stood in the doorway, a heavy overcoat making his small frame appear as wide as he was tall. His eyes widened as he took in Moira.

She pressed her lips into a thin line and said in her best French accent, "What do you want?"

Stewart seemed frozen, gawking as if she were a giraffe.

She scowled. "You've come to tell me the horse is ready, no?"

Stewart shook his head slowly. "The master had it right, mistress; ye're right good with disguises. A bloody genius."

Moira's heart sank. "Damn it," she snapped. "Where's Hurst?"

"Gone," the servant said almost apologetically.

"When?"

Stewart pursed his lips and glanced out at the sky. "An hour ago, mayhap more."

She closed her eyes. *He must have left our bedchamber the second I slipped out to change clothes, damn him!* She felt betrayed, even though that was ridiculous when she'd been the first to leave. "He knew I was leaving, then."

"Aye, mistress. He put me an' Leeds to watching the cattle, and said that as soon as someone came askin' fer a horse, 'twould be ye and that ye'd be disguised. Which ye are," Stewart added, admiration in his voice. "If ye'd walked past me in the inn yard, I'd have ne'er taken another look."

Moira scowled and yanked off her hat and wig, stuffing it into her pocket. "Damn it, I must have a horse! It is urgent that I get to town."

"He tol' us about Mr. Aniston and how that horrible man has yer daughter. But Mr. Hurst said ye was to stay here and not to go runnin' into a hornet's nest where ye could get killed."

"Like hell! That's *my* daughter. I'm going, and—"

Leeds stepped around the corner, looking embarrassed, a rope coiled in his hands.

Moira stiffened. "What are you going to do with that?"

The servant sighed. "Mr. Hurst said we might have to tie ye up to keep ye here."

"He did, did he?" Moira fisted her hands. "That—that—*ass*!"

"Aye," Stewart said apologeticly. "Sit yerself down, mistress. We canno' allow ye to go."

Moira looked at the chair but made no move toward it. "No."

The two men approached, Leeds moving to her left, and Stewart to her right.

Moira watched them narrowly, her fury incinerating the fear that beat through her veins. *Damn you, Robert Hurst!* Her gaze narrowed on her opponents. *Damn you to hell.*

CHAPTER 23

Michael Hurst's diary entry as he set sail for England on his brother's ship.

With William's help I finally rescued Miss Smythe-Haughton from the amorous clutches of the sulfi, and we are now under way. I won't burden this epistle with the details; suffice it to say that the sulfi met his just deserts, and Miss Smythe-Haughton is about to receive the most severe talking-to. Which will doubtless be met with her amusement.

It is more and more obvious that her parents must have been exceptionally lax in her upbringing, for she will not listen to a word I say.

*R*obert halted his horse in front of a small town house on the end of Regent Terrace. The town houses, part of Edinburgh's famed New Town, gleamed like seashells lined up in the morning sun. Robert climbed off his horse and walked it to a man across the street.

"Mr. Hurst?" The man's voice had a strong cockney accent.

"Yes. You must be Mr. Norris."

The man tipped his hat. Short and stout, with powerful shoulders and a thick neck, he had the build of a boxer. "Indeed, sir. I be Norris."

Robert looked at the house across from them. "This one, I presume?"

"Aye, sir. As ye requested a month ago, we've been watchin' George Aniston, and here's where he's landed."

"And the child?"

"That was a mite trickier. We found no evidence of a child until last night."

"What did you discover?"

Mr. Norris grinned, revealing several missing teeth, and laid a finger beside his nose. "We found the tell, guv'nor. Laundry."

"Laundry? Ah, you mean for the child."

"Aye. I pretended to be lookin' fer me lost dog, and struck up a conversation with the maid as she was hanging the laundry in the back. In the bottom o' the basket was a night rail, several gowns, things as a small girl might wear."

Robert nodded and wondered if Moira had already sent word to Aniston that she wished to meet him. It was difficult to tell what Moira had or hadn't done.

She hadn't trusted him enough to include him. That stung, but Robert accepted it. It would take a lot to completely gain Moira's trust. And while he'd made significant inroads over the last three weeks, it would take several months, if not years, before she completely let down her guard. She'd had it up too long, and the price of this was too dear for her to simply turn it over to him.

But he was the best person to deal with Aniston. Moira's emotional attachment to Rowena made them both more vulnerable, and now was not the time for vulnerability of any kind.

He turned to the Bow Street Runner. "Tell me

everything you've found out. Aniston's habits, the number of men in his employ, and where you think he might be keeping the child."

Mr. Norris began to rattle off an impressive amount of information, reaching into his coat pocket for a map of the house with Aniston's bedchamber and all entrances clearly marked. "There are twenty-two servants in all, three of them naught but ruffians, and a harsh lookin' woman who acts as a nurse. Those, he keeps with the child."

I can handle three. "Where does he keep her?"

"The attic rooms, sir." Mr. Norris's stubby finger poked the map. "This set of steps leads to the attic. I'm sure she's there, fer there were no lamps lit in that part of the house before, and now they're ablaze."

"Good." Robert examined the map, then folded and tucked it away. "Thank you for the information."

"Indeed, sir. The little girl . . . she looked scared. I've a daughter of me own." The man's clear eyes met Robert's. "Ye wouldn't be wishin' fer some help, would ye? I've not had a good brawl in a month and I'm due fer one."

"I could use a diversion. Something to set the place in an uproar and draw attention to the lower floors."

The man smiled. "I can do that."

"Good. I'll be ready at the back of the house when it occurs."

"Very good, sir. I'll give ye ten minutes and then begin."

"One more thing. My wife is quite anxious to assist in saving our daughter. She might arrive before I've completed my task. She'll be carrying a weapon, perhaps two. And don't be surprised if she's dressed as a man."

Mr. Norris blinked. "Pardon, guv'nor?"

"My wife is a bit of a gypsy. It's difficult to tell what she might or might not do."

Mr. Norris let out a long, silent whistle. "Very well, guv'nor. We'll be on the lookout."

"Thank you." With that, Robert crossed the street.

Moments later, he was at the rear of the house. The servants were just beginning to stir, the kitchen door opened as the undercooks prepared the morning fires.

He slipped inside while two sleepy-looking men collected wood from the stack by the back door. Robert hurried through the kitchen to a back hallway, sliding into a pantry when footsteps approached.

He'd just exited the pantry and found the back

stairs when he heard Mr. Norris yelling like a drunken coalman, shouting that he'd been cheated and wanted his dibs for the coal already delivered, or he'd call the constable. Footsteps raced toward the front of the house as the servants attempted to silence the overwrought coal vendor whose loud voice might rouse their master.

Robert slipped up two flights of stairs, taking refuge in a linen closet when heavy footsteps tromped down from the attic. When the footsteps passed by, he peered out and saw two big men disappear down the steps. *So Aniston's thugs think they are needed. Mr. Norris might meet with some trouble.* But somehow, Robert thought the Runner would do just fine.

Robert hurried up the stairs. At the very top was a landing with three doors. He listened at each, deciding the middle one held the most promise.

He silently checked the knob and, finding it locked, backed up a few steps and then slammed his shoulder into the door. It broke, and he staggered into the room, where he found himself facing the third large brute.

With a roar, the man bunched his huge fist and swung in Robert's direction. Robert ducked and, using the man's momentum, shoved him into the wall, where his head hit with a spectacular thud.

In a perfect world, the maneuver would have ended with the giant senseless on the floor. Instead, after shaking his head like a wet dog, the man whirled to face Robert, ready for another bout.

But Robert had his pistol out and ready before the man could swing again. "Don't even consider it. I'm quite capable of shooting you through the eye."

The man growled. "What do ye want?"

"My daughter." Robert pulled a small bag out of his coat pocket and tossed it to the man.

The guard caught the bag without thinking and eyed it suspiciously.

"That's twenty guineas. More than you make in a year from Mr. Aniston, I'm sure."

The man tugged open the bag and poured the coins into his hand.

"You are here because you've been paid to be here. Now you've been paid *not* to be here. You can either stay and face a bullet, or you can leave with twenty guineas in your pocket and pretend you never saw this place. I don't care which you choose, but be quick about it. I've things to do."

The man stared at the coins before he raised a bemused gaze to Robert. "And the lass is yer daughter?"

"My only daughter."

The man poured the money back into the pouch and stuffed it into his pocket, then he lumbered to the door. "I never liked Aniston, no ways."

"Where is she?"

The man jerked his head to another door by the small coal heater. "She's in there with her nurse, a mean woman. She's no' so good to the lass."

Robert's jaw tightened. "Thank you."

The man nodded and left.

Robert opened the door the giant had indicated. A hard-faced woman stood before the small fireplace. She looked sour even before she spat out, "I heard ye speakin' in t'other room and I know ye came fer the lass."

"Where is she?"

A hard line formed on either side of the woman's mouth. "I'll have me own coins afore I tell ye tha'."

Robert had several more pouches of coins in his pockets, but said, "Get out."

Her lips thinned. "I'll scream, I will, and raise the household."

"They're already raised. I fully expect to see the entire group before I'm done, so scream away."

A desperate look entered her eyes. "If ye're the father, ye should know the mither promised me coins fer keepin' the lass in good health and fer not hittin' her—though she sorely needs it sometimes."

Robert's hand was so tight on his pistol that it shook, his fingers almost white. He lowered the pistol and snapped, "I've warned you. Get. Out."

"I want the coin she promised me or I'm not leavin,' and not tellin' ye where the child is, either!"

Robert grasped her thin arm and dragged her from the room, out to the landing, and to the top of the steps.

"I want me money!"

"And I want *you* to suffer for every moment of fear you gave that child—but neither of us is going to get what we want." He pointed to the steps.

After a moment, she hunched her shoulders and marched down the stairs.

Robert hurried back to the room. A small bed was in one corner, the sheets awry, as if someone had hurriedly left them. A series of trunks lined one wall.

He softly called, "Rowena?"

No answer was returned. The din outside had quieted, so his time was short. "Rowena, I've come from your mother. She's waiting for you. We have to hur—"

One of the trunks opened and a small, tousled head peeked over the edge. Robert found himself looking down into a small face framed by a wealth of curly dark hair. For an instant he couldn't think, feel, or breathe—he could only stare. *Good God, she looks exactly like me.*

The little girl returned his gaze solemnly. She was dressed in a ragged gown of dark blue that matched her eyes, and he knew without hesitation that she was his.

She gulped and he caught panic in her gaze. "Where is my mother?"

Robert found his voice. "She will be along soon, but we must hurry."

Rowena nodded. "You must be my father, then."

Robert caught his breath. "How . . . why do you say that?"

"Mother said that if we ever needed you, you would come." Large blue eyes looked directly into his, so honest they almost pained him. "What took you so long?"

Robert's heart tightened and he said in a choked voice, "Many problems, but I have come. And I will save you, no matter what."

In that instant Robert faced a powerful truth: she was his daughter, and he never wanted to be without her again.

He lifted her from the trunk and set her on her feet. Rowena slipped her small hand into his. "Are we going home now?"

We. She accepts me without question. Robert's eyes stung with tears, and he had to clear his throat. "Yes. We will be going home today."

"With my mother?"

"Yes." After he'd stomped George Aniston into dust for what he'd done to his child.

Robert stooped down so that he was on a level with his daughter. "We have to make a run for it and it could get difficult. There might be some fighting."

"I can fight, too. Will we be fighting the bad man who's mean to Mama?"

"We might."

She sent him such a ferocious look that he wanted to swoop her into a hug.

"I feel the same way about him. We must go now, and I need you to stay behind me. Can you do that?"

Rowena nodded. "I'll need my shoes." She pointed to her boots that lay discarded in a corner.

He fetched them and then helped her put them on.

And that was how Moira found them when she slipped into the room a few moments later.

Robert was down on one knee in front of Rowena. Their heads were very close together, and her throat tightened at seeing how much alike they looked. To see Rowena so trustingly close to Robert, both of them engaged deeply in conversation, made Moira's heart ache in a new way.

Robert had claimed that by not informing him of Rowena's existence, she had stolen something from him. Seeing them together, a dawning look of delight on Rowena's small face, Moira realized he was right.

Robert solemnly held out his hand. Her big eyes fixed upon him, Rowena spat into her hand and then slapped it into Robert's.

He chuckled, released her hand to spit into his own, and reclasped her hand. "It's a bargain," he said.

Moira started forward, and they both turned toward her.

"Mama!" The word broke Moira's heart, and she sank to her knees to catch her daughter to her. With a sob, she buried her face in the girl's silken hair. "Oh Rowena, I'm *so* happy to see you. Are you well?" Moira held her daughter from her to examine her dear face.

Tears streamed down Rowena's face, but she nodded, her lips quivering slightly. "I'm fine. Mr. Robert told me—"

"My, my," said a silky voice. "Such a tender scene. I hesitate to interrupt."

Moira was on her feet in an instant, clutching Rowena to her as she turned to face George Aniston.

He stood in the doorway, a dueling pistol in his hand. She had no doubt that the trigger was made to discharge at the faintest squeeze of his finger.

She started to push Rowena behind her, but Aniston's chilly voice ordered, "Don't move."

Moira froze, her heart thudding sickly.

Behind her Robert cursed, drawing Aniston's attention. "I almost forgot about you, Hurst. Put down your pistol if you wish to keep these two alive."

Robert dropped his pistol to the floor.

Aniston curled his lip at Moira's attire. "I fear that Hurst's ruinous company has destroyed your sense of fashion. Even I wouldn't wear a such a profusion of lace." His gaze returned to Robert. "Now join your lovely lady so I can keep an eye on you both."

"No."

Aniston's jaw tightened. "Don't tempt me, Hurst."

"If you waste your bullet on me, you'll have Moira to deal with. *If* you hit me, which I doubt will happen. Moira, did you know that Aniston was once in a duel? He lost, of course. He shot so wide of his opponent that he nicked a bystander who was ten paces to the side."

Aniston's face was bloodred. "I did that on purpose. It was a matter of honor—"

"Before the duel, you made a big show of paying an undertaker to prepare to carry off your opponent's body—so don't pretend you didn't mean to kill him. You're just fortunate that he was a horrid shot himself."

Robert chuckled, as if he didn't see the mounting fury in Aniston's thin face. "It was most amusing, Moira. The fat squire hit Aniston, but not where he intended. He shot off one of Aniston's toes. The biggest one, I believe, wasn't it?"

Moira noticed that Aniston's gun hand was shaking slightly; his body was stiff with outrage.

Yet Robert continued on. "I daresay you have to order specially made shoes, don't you? Most cripples do—"

"*Stop it!*" Aniston started forward, the gun pinned on Robert.

Moira realized then that as he'd been speaking, Robert had moved away from her and Rowena. He was now almost at the window.

As Aniston went forward he was moving away from the door, and soon she and Rowena could make a dash for it. Moira grasped Rowena's hand

and caught a flicker of a glance from Robert. *So this is his plan. But what would happen then?*

"Where is the onyx box?" Aniston asked.

"It's gone," Robert said. "I sent it to London this morning."

Aniston's jaw tightened. "I want that box."

Robert shrugged.

Moira could hear Aniston's teeth grinding. "Damn you!"

"Yes, quite." Robert yawned and sat on the edge of the bed. "Early morning rescues are so tiring."

"Don't try anything," Aniston snapped. "I don't trust you, Hurst. Put your hands in your pockets and keep them there."

Robert rolled his eyes but did as he was told. "Happy now?"

Aniston smiled. "I've finally gotten the better of you. The great Robert Hurst, brought low by me. I will relish telling the tale in White's."

"I'm afraid you won't be able to do that—because I've already won."

Aniston laughed. "Oh, really? How—"

A shot rang out, and Moira screamed and shoved Rowena behind her.

Aniston's gun fired even as he looked down at his chest where a thin trickle of blood marred his shirt. He turned an amazed look at Robert.

One pocket of Robert's coat was smoking slightly. He stood, leaning lightly against the window frame as he pulled his pistol out. "Never underestimate a Hurst."

His face set and white, Aniston took a step toward Robert, but Moira stepped forward, her own pistol at the ready. *"Don't."*

Aniston sent her a startled glance, his hand still gripped over his wound as blood steadily soaked his side. As it dripped through his wide-spread fingers, he looked down and turned even paler, visibly sagging.

Then, with a moan, Aniston crumpled to the ground.

Robert patted the pocket of his greatcoat where a wisp of smoke still rose. But it was the smaller hole at his shoulder that caught Moira's attention. "No!" She rushed forward as he swayed.

The small circle began to turn red, blood seeping into the heavy wool. "We'd better leave," he said in an odd voice.

Moira hurried to support him, wedging her shoulder under his good one. "Rowena, hold the door for Mr. Hur—" She stopped and looked up at Robert. "For your father."

Robert's expression softened. "Thank you."

They made their way downstairs with difficulty,

for Robert was quickly weakening, blood now dripping upon the steps.

Moira feared they would be stopped by the servants. Instead, as they were halfway down the stairs, they met a burly, square-looking man followed by several others.

With one quick look, he summed up the situation. "Lor' love ye, guvnor! Got yerself knocked to the nines, did ye?"

"Somewhat," Robert agreed. "Who are these men?"

"I brought them wit' me to be certain no one interfered wit' our business. 'Tis a good thing, too, fer it took us all to round up Aniston's mob. They've been taken to gaol fer the time bein' and won't be a bother."

Robert managed a smile. "Very clever of you, Mr. Norris. I shall be sure to write a letter of thanks to the Bow Street Runners for sending their best in rescuing my daughter."

Mr. Norris pinkened. "I'm glad t' see ye got her back." He jerked a thumb toward Moira. "I'm glad ye tol' me that the mistress might be wearin' a disguise, fer I almost mistook her for one o' Mr. Aniston's men. Is Aniston still upstairs?"

"Yes, he is injured. Perhaps fatally."

Mr. Norris nodded his head toward the stairs.

"Griswald, Smith, go and see to Mr. Aniston. If he's still alive, he's not t' escape, no matter how ye have t' see t' it."

Two of the bigger men went past them on up the stairs, their heavy feet clomping upon the treads.

Mr. Norris turned to Moira and he said politely, "And now, mistress, if ye'll stand back, we'll help Mr. Hurst to his carriage. I know a good doctor."

Moira carried Rowena downstairs, her heart filled with so many emotions that she couldn't untangle them, but so worried about Robert that she couldn't even cry.

And when they were in the carriages, on their way to the doctor, Moira began to pray.

EPILOGUE

Michael Hurst in a letter to his brother Robert, that same day.

I've just met William's wife, and I hear that our sister Mary has also managed to wed. While I do not begrudge them their happiness, it seems that I might have been rescued faster had you not all been busy making love matches.

I hope that I never catch that malady, which steals away common sense and replaces it with fluff.

$\mathcal{M}$oira stood looking out the window. A warm summer wind swirled across the stone drive and made the grass ripple around the pond. It was an idyllic setting and fit Robert's majestic house. Yet despite the day's warmth, Moira couldn't shake the feeling that the cold hand of fate hovered over them all—especially Robert, whose injuries were even more dangerous than they'd first realized.

Moira said another prayer of thanks for Mr. Norris and his quick actions. The rough man had indeed known an excellent physician, who was with Robert even now, a week later.

Moira rubbed her arms and started to turn from the window, when the sight of a carriage racing up the drive made her stop. As the horses clattered to the front door, a small hand slipped into Moira's.

She smiled down at Rowena. "You're up from your nap."

"I didn't really sleep. I kept thinking about . . ." Rowena glanced at the ceiling, her brow knit.

Moira nodded. "I know. Me, too." She knelt beside her daughter. "But he's very strong, and the doctor is with him."

"He will be fine," Rowena said, her gaze unafraid. "He told me so, so he will be. I just don't want him to hurt."

"Yes, but . . . He had a very bad fever, and the doctor says—"

"He will be fine," the child said quietly. She put her small hand on Moira's cheek. "He never breaks his promises. He told me so."

Moira nodded helplessly, unable to fight a deep, icy cold fear. The doctor had been so grave, so serious. Moira was thankful for Buffon, who not only continually ran up and down the stairs seeing to Robert's comfort, but also found the time to keep her informed of every development, good and bad.

It said something about Robert that his servants were so obviously fond of their master. They tiptoed about, whispering in concerned tones, and made certain the house was in perfect order for when he finally emerged from the sickroom.

Moira hugged Rowena and looked about the comfortable sitting room. She'd been amazed to discover that Robert owned a house near

Edinburgh, so close to her cottage. And such a house, too. *You are always a surprise, Robert. In so many ways.*

Rowena's gaze was on the drive, where the carriage had stopped. "Who is that?"

Moira looked to see a small, plump woman exit the carriage, assisted by a tall, distinguished man. "That's your father's sister, Mary, and her husband, Angus."

Rowena watched the woman hurry up the steps, her husband's broad strides easily keeping pace. "Do you think my father will be glad to see her?"

Moira rather doubted it. If there was one thing Robert detested, it was being fussed over.

Moments later, the couple were escorted into the sitting room. "My dear!" Mary came to take Moira's hands. "I came as soon as I could. How is he?"

"The doctor said the situation is grave. He's with Robert now."

"I shall go up and see—"

"His valet won't allow anyone in his room. Robert snaps whenever anyone tries to bypass Buffon. The doctor said it was dangerous to let Robert be upset, so it is best to stay away."

Mary turned. "Did you hear that?"

Her husband nodded. "Some people don't wish to be disturbed when they feel ill, Mary."

"But *someone* must make certain he is well. He could be dying, and—"

"No," Rowena said firmly.

Mary pressed a hand to her chest. "Goodness, you startled me! I didn't see you there." Mary blinked. "Oh my. You look just like—"

"Her father," Moira interjected.

"Oh. Yes. Of course." Mary cleared her throat. "I can see I've rushed in and made a muddle of this."

"Excuse me," came Buffon's voice from the doorway.

All eyes turned to him, and he bowed. "Mr. Hurst would like to see his wife."

"*Wife?*"

Moira suppressed a wince. "That would be me."

Mary plopped her fists onto her hips. "Robert never tells me a thing!"

Her husband took her elbow. "Come, my love, let's meet our new niece. Her mother will be busy for a while." Though obviously reluctant, Mary allowed Angus to take her to sit down near Rowena, where they began to talk.

Moira followed Buffon to Robert's door, where Doctor MacPherson met her.

"He's better?"

The doctor beamed tiredly. "Yes. Last night I wouldn't have given you a farthing for his chances. But he made a turn in the middle of the night when the fever broke. He's not out of the woods yet, but he has a good chance now."

Moira bit her lip to keep from weeping. "Thank you."

"I'll leave him in Buffon's hands. The man is a capable nurse."

Buffon bowed, then opened the door. "*Madame?*"

Moira expected to find the curtains drawn and the room dark. Instead, sunlight streamed through the room, casting a bar of warmth across the large bed.

Robert sat propped up by pillows in his red silk robe, his face cleanly shaved, his hair neat.

But he still had a deep pallor and faint circles under his eyes.

"Buffon wouldn't allow me to have guests until I was presentable." His faintly caustic voice filled her with joy.

"Bless Buffon, for I don't know if I'd recognize you without a cravat."

"He has been impossibly bossy since my illness—which is to say, he is exactly as he was before." Robert patted the bed. "Come and sit with me. We have much to say to one another."

She walked over, feeling oddly shy yet overwhelmed with the need to touch him. She perched on the edge of the bed. "This is certainly a large bed."

"Yes, ten people could sleep in it and never touch. Unless two of them were us, of course."

"Unfortunately, you tend to steal the covers," she said primly, aching to throw her arms around him and hold him tightly.

"And you snore—very softly, but still." His lips twitched. "I'd say we're even."

It was pure luxury to be able to banter with him, even this little bit.

"Where's Rowena?"

"In the sitting room, talking to your sister Mary and her husband."

"Oh no. If she's here, my other two sisters cannot be far away."

"It wouldn't surprise me if they all come before dinnertime."

"You'll have to inform the housekeeper to open some rooms and have something on hand for dinner."

"Me? Robert, I'm just a guest and—"

"No." His hand closed over hers. "And that's

what I wish to talk to you about. Moira, I don't want to be left out of your and Rowena's lives."

Her heart twisted. "You love her. I saw that when I found you together in the nursery at Aniston's."

"Yes. When I saw her and knew she was mine, my heart—" He shook his head. "I never knew what it meant to be a parent. I will never look at my own the same again."

"It's an eye-opening moment, isn't it?"

"One that you faced alone. That will never happen again. Moira, I love you. I think I always have. Even when I knew you were lying about who you were, I couldn't stay away from you. And now that I've met our daughter, I can't go back to being alone."

He took her hand and pulled her closer. "I bought this house thinking I might find a place where I belonged. But it's nothing but empty stone walls without you and Rowena inside it."

Tears stung her eyes. "But . . . it's not always fun and exciting being a parent. Sometimes it's difficult."

"Then we'll face the difficulties together."

"And if you get bored?"

His lips quirked. "I don't see that being a problem. But if it happens, I suppose you'll just have to entertain me here in my boudoir." His eyes twinkling wickedly, he kissed her fingers one by one.

"And if Rowena gets ill or—"

"—we run out of funds, or our family demands to move in with us, or any of the million things that could happen, then you and I will face them together."

He put his hand on her cheek. "I love you, Moira MacAllister Hurst. I refuse to live without you. If you say no, I will ask again. And if you leave Hurst House, I will follow you once I'm able."

Moira's heart melted. "You really mean it."

"With every breath I take. And I could die at any moment, so you'd better say yes now, while you can."

"Yes, Robert Hurst. Yes, yes, *yes*—"

The rest of her yeses were lost in a kiss. One of the million or so she planned on sharing with him over the happy, blissful years to come.

Turn the page for a sneak peek
at the next delightful
Hurst Amulet novel
from *New York Times* bestselling author
Karen Hawkins

Coming soon from Pocket Books

Michael Hurst ignored the stir of excitement that flowed through the ballroom at his entrance. "Damn fools," he muttered, tugging on his neckcloth.

His sister Mary sent him an exasperated glance. "Leave that alone."

"It's choking me."

"It's fashionable and you must look presentable. This ballroom is full of potential investors for your expeditions."

Potential headaches was what they were. "I'm here, aren't I?" he asked irritably. "Where's that damned refreshment table? If I'm going to face these monkeys, I'll need a drink."

"Lady Bellforth usually sets the refreshment table by the library doors."

He nodded and stepped forward. As if in answer, fans and lashes fluttered as if hoping to trap him in a gossamer hold. "For the love of Ra," he said through gritted teeth, "don't they have anything better to do than stare?"

"You're famous," Mary said calmly. "Get used to it."

"I don't wish to be famous."

"But you are, so you'll just have to live with it. Just smile and nod, and we'll navigate through this crowd in no time at all."

He scowled instead, noticing with glee that several of the flowery fans stopped fluttering.

"Michael, you can't—"

He placed his hand firmly under Mary's elbow and led her into the crowd, scowling at first one hopeful-looking miss and then another. They blushed and then sagged as if he'd stabbed their empty little hearts.

Mary made an impatient noise. "We'll never get another sponsor if you keep this up. These women are the daughters and sisters of wealthy men who could benefit your endeavors greatly."

"They are cotton-headed misses and I refuse to pander to them." One of them boldly winked at him. "Good God, what happened to female modesty while I was in the wilds of Egypt?"

"More to the point, what happened to gentlemanly manners?"

"I left those worthless skills on the shores of the Nile," he retorted. "Good riddance, too."

"Your time away has turned you into a barbarian."

"I won't dignify that with an answer." Just as

they were within a few feet of their destination, a young woman stepped into his path, almost thrust into place by the girls who circled behind her.

Tall, with a large nose and auburn curls decorated with pearl pins and cascading over one shoulder, she appeared all of seventeen. "Mr. Hurst! How nice to see you again." She dipped a grand curtsy, her smirk letting him know that she expected a greeting of welcome.

Michael lifted a brow, but said nothing.

Her cheeks bloomed red, her lips pressed in irritation, though she hid it almost immediately behind a forced smile. "I'm Miss Lydia Latham. We met at Lady MacLean's soiree."

Michael stared as Miss Latham held out her hand expectantly.

Mary jabbed her elbow into his side.

With a grimace, Michael took the girl's hand, holding it the minimal time required by politeness.

Miss Latham beamed. "I *knew* you'd remember me! We spoke at length about the Rosetta stone."

"Did we?" he asked in a bored tone.

"Oh, yes! I've read every word you've ever written."

"I doubt that, unless, of course, you've managed to sneak into my bedchamber and procure my diaries. I'm fairly sure no one but me has read those."

Miss Latham's face turned several shades pinker and she tittered nervously. "Oh, no! I would never sneak into a man's bedchamber."

"More's the pit—"

"What my brother means to say," Mary said hurriedly, "is that *The Morning Post* serial is but a small portion of his writings. He's the author of many scientific treatises on artifacts and ruins that he's unearthed, and—"

"And my diaries," he interjected smoothly.

One of the other girls clasped her hands together and said in a soulful tone, "I've never known a *man* to keep a diary."

"And just how many men do you know?" Michael asked, irritated to be placed upon a pedestal for the most mundane of things.

Mary glared at him as if she were fighting the urge to smack his head, as she had when they were children. "No one will invite you anywhere if you continue like this," she hissed.

"Nonsense. They are too silly to know any better."

As if to prove his point, a girl with brown hair and a protruding chin said brazenly, as if every word were a challenge that he wouldn't be able to resist, "Mr. Hurst, I daresay our petty little parties bore you to death."

"Yes, they do."

Not realizing he found the ball boring because of inane comments like hers, she sent her companions a triumphant glance over her shoulder. "Of course! This must seem so dull after your adventures on the Nile. Especially after wrestling crocodiles, and—"

"I beg your pardon," Michael interrupted. "Did you say 'wrestling' and 'crocodiles'?"

The girl blinked. "W-why, yes. You wrote that you were forced to do so last January, during mating season when they're at their most fierce."

Michael crossed his arms and glared at his sister. "Mary?"

She blushed, a bit of desperation in her tone as she said, "I daresay you'll remember it quite clearly once you've had some refreshment." Mary curtsied to the small group. "I hope you'll excuse us, but my poor brother needs some nourishment. If you don't mind, we'll make our way to the refreshment table." Without waiting for a reply, she grabbed his arm and burrowed through the crowd.

At the table she quickly took two glasses and a small plate with a tiny piece of stale cake on it. With an air of determination, she found an alcove safely hidden from prying eyes.

Mary let out a huge sigh as she sat upon the small settee provided for those fatigued from dancing.

"A crocodile?" Michael asked. "You've been wielding your pen far too artfully in my serial for *The Morning Post*."

"You asked me to write the serial for you," she pointed out.

"Yes, because I didn't have the time to do it. Not because I wished someone to fabricate ridiculous stories. When I first arrived in town, I thought people were beginning to warm to true scientific discovery. Now I see that they were merely amazed at the preposterous tales you've told about my expeditions."

"People *are* interested in your research. Just last week, Lord Harken-Styles said he wishes to invest even more in your adventures."

"Lord Harken-Styles waylaid me in White's last night and asked if he could see the arrowhead from the savage who shot me through the neck."

"Oh."

"Yes. His lordship seemed to be under the delusion that not only had I been shot through the neck with an arrow, but that I was such a sapskull as to wear the arrowhead around my neck as a good luck talisman."

Her lips twitched. "I thought that was a very romantic touch."

"And thoroughly untruthful," he replied sternly. "Are there any other surprise adventures that I should know about? A duel over a foreign princess in the desert? A missing limb? An extra toe?"

She giggled. "It is all your fault, you know. You are such a horrid correspondent that I was forced to make up things."

A commotion suddenly roiled across the ballroom.

"What is it?" Mary asked, who could see very little since she was sitting.

"I don't know. Everyone has turned toward the door and— Ah! Jane has arrived."

Jane Smythe-Haughton had been his assistant for almost four years now, and he almost couldn't remember his life before she'd swept in and begun arranging his expeditions. Things were infinitely better with her around. His meals were more to his liking, his clothes where they should be, his pen nibs sharpened just so, and his scientific equipment always at the ready. She was extraordinarily efficient and, except for a very few times, he rarely had to think about her at all—exactly as he liked it.

Mary lifted her brows archly. "So you call her Jane, do you?"

"Of course I call her Jane," he said impatiently, disliking the interested note in his sister's voice. "My tongue would be weary if I had to say Miss Smythe-Haughton every time I needed a fresh pair of socks or couldn't find one of my notebooks."

He could see Jane standing on her tiptoes by the door now, looking about the room for him.

He lifted his arm and let out a shrill whistle.

Everyone looked startled except Jane, who began to make her way through the sea of people, her large hat making her look like a wide, yellow lily pad swimming across a pond of reeds.

Michael frowned as he saw that his sister was holding her hand over her eyes. "What's wrong? Do you have a headache?"

Mary dropped her hand. "Michael, you cannot whistle for the poor girl as if she were a dog!"

"I didn't. When I whistle for a dog, I do it like this—" He whistled two short whistles. "When I whistle for Jane, I do it like—"

"*Don't!* Once was enough." Mary shook her head.

"I quite misjudged your relationship with Miss Smythe-Haughton. We all have."

"You thought I was romantically involved with *Jane*?"

"You write about her in almost every letter you send," Mary answered in a defensive tone.

"Probably to complain. She can be a bit demanding. When you meet her, you'll understand."

"Oh. Is she plain?"

"She's—" He hesitated. Jane *was* plain—rather wren-like, all small and brown and quick. But she always seemed bigger than her size, more visible than other women. "Jane is . . . just Jane."

Mary put aside her glass and stood, peering at the crowds. "Ah, there she must be, for the crowd is parting and—Good God!"

Why did she sound so alarmed? "What?"

"She's wearing a *hat*," Mary said in a choked voice.

"Yes."

"For a *ball*?"

Michael glanced at the hat, a wide yellow confection. It was large, though surely not any larger than those he'd seen paraded about Hyde Park this afternoon. It also seemed to have quite a few feathers. Very big feathers. So large that when Jane turned her head, the feathers slapped some silly bumpkin in a ridiculous orange waistcoat. "I like that hat."

Mary muttered under her breath.

Michael looked about the room at the other women and noted that no one else was wearing a hat.

He shrugged. "Jane should have left her hat with a footman in the vestibule."

"I should have known that Miss Smythe-Haughton was so unconventional, seeing as she's been shepherding you through the wilds of Africa for the last four years."

"And doing it very well. She organizes our travel arrangements and makes certain the men and I are fed, and writes up our schedules and catalogues the finds, and all of that sort of thing."

"Someone needs to take her to a good *modiste*. That gown and that hat—" Mary shuddered.

Michael could not have cared less. Jane was Jane, and he was perfectly comfortable with that staying as it was.

Jane paused by the silly bumpkin and was speaking to him, probably apologizing.

The man no longer appeared upset. In fact, he was regarding Jane with sudden interest.

Michael frowned. Women never paid Jane heed, but men frequently did, though she never seemed to notice. When he and Jane had been abroad, he'd decided it was because she was often the only white woman present.

Here there was no such excuse, yet—he looked about the room and scowled as he noted several sets of male eyes firmly locked upon her, many with pronounced interest.

What the hell?

For the first time since he'd hired her, Michael

looked at Jane critically, trying to see her with fresh eyes. She wasn't a beauty, though she wasn't ugly, either. She was a small woman, with a slender figure. She had brown hair, brown eyes and, because of her years spent in hotter climes, brown skin. Her face could only be described as piquant with its high cheekbones, straight nose, and stubborn little chin. In fact, everything about her was small—except her thickly lashed brown eyes and her wide, mobile mouth.

Those two items seemed overlarge for her face, yet oddly enough they balanced one another.

He rubbed his chin, finding the mystery intriguing.

Perhaps it was her mouth that attracted such attention . . . something about it made her appear sensual. Now that he thought about it, the sulfi who'd held him prisoner had been most vocal in his admiration for the no-nonsense Miss Smythe-Haughton and her lush mouth. The man had been a positive idiot about it, even writing a poem. "A *poem*," Michael muttered.

"Pardon?" Mary asked.

"Nothing."

"Michael . . . is she wearing *boots*?" Mary's voice held a strangled tone. "You can't allow her to dress like that when she's in town!"

"What does it matter how she dresses? No one is funding *her*." He was a little envious of Jane's freedom, truth be told.

Mary gave a puff of indignation. "Because she will be laughed at. Surely you don't want that!"

His jaw tightened. "I *dare* anyone to laugh at her."

Jane wasn't like other women, who had to don silly finery to prove their worth. She already *had* worth, making his life go as smoothly as possible.

Jane laughingly left her new conquest, who sent a longing glance after her. *Fool.* Jane would never be interested in such a useless man. Jane never showed the least interest in *any* man, which Michael found quite satisfying. He paid her far too much to be forced to deal with female whims.

She finally reached them and he said "Jane, this is my sister Mary, the Countess of Erroll. Mary, this is Jane, Miss Smythe-Haughton."

Jane instantly dipped a curtsy that even the biggest stickler couldn't fault. As she rose, she held out her hand and smiled warmly. "Lady Erroll, I finally meet you! Michael has spoken of you frequently."

Mary looked pleased. "He's mentioned you quite a number of times, too."

"Probably to complain about something, but I never take it to heart." Jane chuckled. "You know how Mr. Hurst can be."

Michael watched as Mary melted before that friendly chuckle and the genuine note in Jane's voice. Mary was in the hands of a master. That was one of Jane's gifts: no matter where they were, in the wilds of Africa or a sulfi's palace or even the treacherous ballrooms of London, she knew just what to say and how to say it.

It was partly that ability to understand and blend into whatever society she was in, that made their expeditions so profitable. Where another explorer might be greeted with distrust, after a few deft words and gestures from Jane, Michael and his party were almost always welcomed. They remained that way, too, with Jane there to soothe over the inevitable awkward moments.

He watched as she worked her magic now. In just a few moments they were talking animatedly about marriages and children and other frivolous topics that Michael knew Jane cared nothing for.

She must have read his thoughts, for though she continued to chat with his sister, Jane sent him a laughing look beneath her lashes. He answered it with faintly raised brows and a mocking smile. He liked how she controlled a room without seeming to. It made his life so much easier.

After several more moments of female chatter, Michael yawned.

Jane halted in mid-sentence. "Mr. Hurst, do you wish to leave?"

"He can't leave," Mary exclaimed. "He hasn't spoken to a single potential sponsor yet."

"I'm not going to, either," he said. "This damned neckcloth is too tight and I wish to go home."

Jane tsked. "Mr. Hurst, you must speak to at least *one* potential sponsor. If you don't, you will have wasted the time you have spent wearing such an atrocious neckcloth and will just have to don it again."

He'd been yanking at the damned thing again, but now stopped. "Atrocious?"

"Oh, yes. Especially now that you've been tugging on it."

"Oh, look!" Mary gestured to the crowd. "There's Devonshire! He expressly asked to meet you. The duke is one of the wealthiest men in the kingdom."

"He might support more than one expedition," Jane said, looking thoughtful.

"So?"

"So if you speak nicely to him, he might be the *only* sponsor you'll need for the next year or two, and you can get out of that neckcloth for a long, long time."

"Fine," he growled. "Let's get this over with. Which asinine fop is he? Please tell me he's not the man in puce who and— Bloody hell, are those diamonds on his shoe buckles?"

"He may be a fop, but he's very interested in sponsoring the great Michael Hurst," Mary said. "He told me that he's an avid follower of the newspaper serial."

Michael sighed. "Which means he thinks I wrestle crocodiles by the dozen."

Jane burst into laughter.

Michael eyed her sourly, even more unhappy when Mary grinned. "Blast you both! I wish these fools would just mail me a checque and leave me the hell alone."

"So do I," Jane said in a soothing tone. She deftly

smoothed his lapels and tucked a corner of his cravat back into his coat front. "But fools that they are, they seem to wish to speak to you first. If they knew you better they'd never wish for such a thing, for you're by far the rudest man I've ever met."

"Thank you," he snapped.

"You're welcome. Unfortunately, that's what happens when you allow a nice person to write your newspaper serial—now the world thinks *you're* nice. It's a burden, but one that you must bear."

"If I have to speak to that fool, you do, too."

"No, I don't. I've realized that though I'm wearing my best gown and my favorite hat, I'm woefully underdressed. So I must leave before I undermine your efforts."

Michael was about to answer with a strong "Nonsense!" when Mary nodded. "Miss Smythe-Haughton, since you're leaving, I'll be glad to escort my brother to meet with the duke."

"A perfect plan." Jane's eyes shimmered with mockery. "You're such a fortunate man."

"And you're such a pain in the rear."

Mary looked shocked. "Michael!"

Jane just twinkled up at him. "Mr. Hurst, I won't work for you if you cannot pay me, so you'd best find a sponsor soon. For if I don't work for you, then who will make certain your favorite pillow is there when you climb into your tent at night?"

"I don't have a favorite pillow."

"You do; you just don't know it. You also like your

meals on time, your notebooks stowed in a particular order, and clean socks at every stage of the journey. If you wish those things to continue, then you'd best set about earning my very respectable wage." She turned to Mary and held out her hand. "Lady Erroll, it was lovely finally meeting you."

Mary clasped Jane's hand warmly. "It's lovely finally meeting you, as well. I can see that Michael is in good hands when he's on expedition."

"Thank you, I do my best. Good-bye."

She turned and went back into the crowd, her large hat wreaking havoc as she made her way to the door.

Michael grinned until he noticed that the bumpkin who'd so eagerly spoken to Jane was pressing through the crush, trying to reach her. But Jane was too swift and she managed to slip out of the room, her yellow hat disappearing from sight.

Michael turned to his sister. "Now, where's this duke of yours? I'll be damned if I wash my own socks on my next expedition."

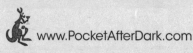

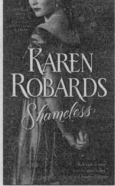
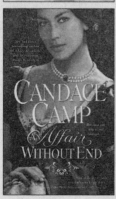
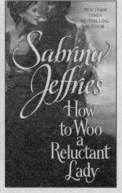

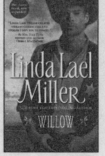